I0638853

Cruise

A Rory Mack Steele Novel, Volume 10

Eugene Lloyd MacRae

Published by CreateSpace, 2015.

CRUISE

First edition. June 22, 2015.

ISBN: 978-1927767139

Written by Eugene Lloyd MacRae.

Chapter 1

"I WANT HIM DEAD. And I want him dead now!"

Igor Koreshevko looked at his boss for a moment. He had worked for him as he rose to power and had always acted as the devil's advocate in the relationship. "Are you sure you want to do that?" he asked softly.

But Alexei Vinokurov hardly heard the question as he paced back across the room. "He thinks he can threaten me. He thinks he can limit me." His arms gestured wildly as he yelled, "Does he really think he can ruin everything I have worked for?"

"Maybe there's another way–"

Alexei Vinokurov whirled around, spit flying from his mouth, "I don't want it done another way. This has gone beyond politics. He took it to a personal level, not me. I want him dead!"

Koreshevko nodded, "You know he is leaving on a working vacation for a few weeks. He'll be in–"

"Then go and kill him there," Vinokurov demanded.

Koreshevko raised an eyebrow, "Alexei, you know the problems that could create with the Americans. That could harm everything–"

Vinokurov raged, "Then cover it up. Create a conspiracy. Cast the blame on someone else. I don't care how you do it. I just want the President dead and I want him dead now! Do you hear me? I want the President *dead*."

Chapter 2

DAY 1

Port of Miami

RORY MACK STEELE strode up the gangway to the giant cruise ship. The Caribbean StarLiner was the newest, largest and most opulent ship in the world. Calypso music played through speakers around the ship, setting a happy mood. The scent of salt water was rich and enticing and held promise of the adventure to come. This was Rory's first vacation in years and he had plans to relax in the sun, a Scotch-on-the-rocks in his hand. Although, maybe that wouldn't happen. He couldn't help but notice the bevy of beautiful women boarding the cruise ship along with him. And there were dozens more in eye-pleasing bikinis, lining the railings on the upper decks as they waved goodbye to loved ones along the dock. Maybe relaxing wasn't the word. Maybe this would be more about enjoying himself in any number of ways.

Rory passed through the entry portal and a security guard directed him to the line of passengers on the left. Another stout member of the crew took his boarding documents from his hand and looked them over. "Welcome aboard, Mr. Steele," he said as he handed the papers back to Rory. "You're cabin is on Deck 9, which is the Vista Deck. You're presently on deck 3, which is the Lobby deck. Just walk directly ahead and then turn left in the lobby area. That will lead you to the elevators and the central stairway. Your luggage will be delivered to your cabin later, sir."

Rory began following the noisy crowd towards the lobby but decided he wanted to get a bird's eye view from the railing first, like the others. He approached a porter, "Excuse me, when I was coming up the gangplank, I saw people lining the railings up higher. How do I get up there?"

The porter pointed to the right and spoke in a thick Filipino accent, "Those stairs will take you one deck up, that's the Empress deck, sir. There are also stairs on the outside deck that will take you to the higher decks."

"Thank you."

"And you came up the *gangway*, sir," the porter said with a smile. "Pirates make you walk a gangplank...which I hope won't happen while you are with us."

Rory acknowledged the correction with an embarrassed smile. Slinging the strap for his carry-on over his shoulder, Rory took the stairs two at a time, turned left and pushed open a brass and teak door and stepped outside onto the wide outer deck.

A beautiful brunette was pulling a yellow dress over her head. A moment later, all that remained between modesty and her birthday suit was a tiny, yellow bikini. She flashed Rory a smile as she rolled the flimsy dress into a tight ball and turned to stand against the railing beside a shapely redhead in a black bikini.

You just had to love the world of advertising, thought Rory. Especially when it was practiced by bright-eyed young ladies on a Caribbean cruise. He moved to an empty spot on the railing between a blonde and another redhead.

Rory could now see a number of people on the dock far below. But he was disappointed to see most of them were coming from the building where he had left his luggage to be transported onto the ship. Only a scattering of people were waving up at the ship. And most of the view overlooked industrial-looking gray and white buildings and warehouses. Not exactly the 1930s romantic feel he had expected from watching all those old movies as a kid. A porter was walking by. "Excuse me," Rory asked him, "how long before we...set sail?"

The porter smiled and spoke in a heavy Spanish accent, "We get underway in one hour, sir."

"Oh. Okay" Rory said as he nodded his thanks.

Most of the young women around him started moving towards the rear of the cruise ship. He heard talk of finding the on-deck pool and taking a dip. Rory admired the shapely bodies as they moved away and contemplating following along. *No, plenty of time for that later.* He really wanted to watch the view as the cruise ship moved away from port. But he had some time, so the next best thing was to put his carry-on in his cabin, find a cool, double, Scotch on the rocks and return to the railing. He headed inside through the brass and teak door and checked his documentation for his cabin number on Deck 9. He also found he had a mini-guide to the various decks and he began to work his way to the main staircase through the crowds of fellow passengers. He always avoided elevators whenever possible. It had nothing to with health. He always felt the elevator was going to drop like a stone for some treason. Stairs didn't do that. Well...they shouldn't.

The decor on the ship was amazing. Rich woods, fancy carpeting, and brass fittings left him with the feeling he was in an upscale hotel. An upscale, floating hotel.

Rory found the central lobby area. It was an amazing, spacious atrium that soared two decks high. Threading his way through the noisy, excited passengers, who were equally amazed at their surroundings, he finally reached the opulent, wide central stairway. He worked his way up six decks, threading his way through passengers heading down. Once he reached deck six, another kind Filipino porter checked his documentation and directed him to the passageway that led to his cabin.

Fitting his keycard into the lock, Rory went inside and stopped dead in his tracks. Amazing! That was the only word that came to mind as he dropped his carry-on to the floor as the door closed behind him.

Chapter 3

HIS SISTER SKYE had set this trip up for him and she had definitely surprised him. He had expected a small, cramped cabin. This was far from that. It was an elegant, luxurious penthouse suite. At 1,300 square feet, it was far more spacious then he had expected. A fine dining table, decorated with crystal and with chairs for eight surrounding it, was on the right. On the left was a small kitchenette area. Straight ahead sat a white, baby grand piano, on the edge of an entertaining area that consisted of a royal-blue sofa with white pillows, four plush royal-blue chairs, and a massive, flat screen television. On the far side of the cabin was a glass wall with royal-blue sheers that let the light in. The central opening in the curtains gave an unobstructed view to the outside. He checked a door past the kitchenette and Rory found himself in a large bedroom decorated in royal-blue and white. It was connected to a large bathroom and a smaller en-suite.

Returning to the entertainment area, Rory found glass doors that led to a personal, 400 square foot balcony complete with a whirlpool and wicker lounge seating. Stepping outside, Rory found himself overlooking the docks again, but from a much greater height. He concluded *this* would a much better place to watch as the cruise ship headed out to sea. Only one other thing would make it better. Stepping back inside he headed over to the minibar he had spotted in the small kitchenette area.

An announcement sounded over the ship: it was time for those not sailing to leave. It was nearing time to cast off.

His sister Skye had been at work behind the scenes again. In the minibar, Rory found his favorite drink. A bottle of Talisker Scotch whiskey from the distillery on the Isle of Skye, where their ancestors had come from two centuries ago. He grabbed the bottle...popped some ice in a glass...and returned to the balcony where he happily waved for a time to everyone on the docks below, who were now waving up to their loved ones on board. Then melancholy set in. He was probably the only one on board who didn't have a partner to share this with. Rory was a Private Investigator with Highland Investigative Services, a family business started by his Uncle Murdock MacLeod in New York. Rory joined the company, opening a branch office in Toronto after a ten-year stint in the Canadian Army, the last six years serving with the Canadian Special Operations Regiment. The army and the dangerous missions he constantly volunteered for had been used to help him forget after his teenage bride, Kitty Black, had died from cancer less than six months after their wedding. But it never worked. Still didn't. Rory had found it difficult to forgive himself for not being able to save her. One army shrink said it haunted him. Another said it drove him. Both agreed it created a need to help others, despite personal danger. Rory wasn't sure about the haunted part, or if it was self-inflicted punishment or penance, but it gave his life purpose. *But it hasn't given me another Kitty.*

Rory pushed the bad thoughts from his mind and settled back in a wicker chair, sipping his drink and determined to enjoy the whole cruise experience. *Maybe I'll meet someone nice. Or at least find some enjoyable company.*

It was amazing how deftly the huge cruise ship maneuvered away from the docks and slowly began its journey away from the Port of Miami. The scenery passed by slowly, with beautiful high rise buildings, surrounded by a low skirt of lush palm trees, all standing out against a backdrop of blue sky and white clouds. The power of the massive engines pulsed faintly through the deck as the massive vessel slowly began to pick up speed, heading eagerly towards the sea.

Seasickness had never been a problem for Rory and the gentle rocking of the giant cruise ship was relaxing. He closed his eyes as the promise of an enjoyable sea voyage arrived on the scent of salt water.

A FEW HOURS LATER, Rory left his stateroom wearing a tuxedo, heading for the formal dinner taking place in the main dining room on Deck 4, the Empress deck. He found the opulent stairway filled with men and women dressed in similar formal attire. The women were especially glamorous, dressed elegantly from head to toe and glittering with jewelry.

Rory took his time as the glittery crowd flowed out onto the amazing gold and marble atrium on the second deck. He just had to stop at the railing and drink in the atmosphere. The entire towering space ran from one deck lower to one deck higher and was filled with voices buzzing in excitement. He knew his sister Skye had chosen this cruise liner because of his love for old movies and the romance of a sea cruise. Now it was up to him to add the romantic part. He admired the beautiful women around him for a few moments, wondering which ones were single...and looking for romance.

A beautiful brunette winked at him as she passed by and gave him a coy smile.

Rory left the railing and followed after her. But a moment later he lost her in the large crowd headed for the double doorway that led to the formal dining room. A porter at the doorway checked his dinner seating assignment and then turned to call another porter over and said something to him in Filipino.

The porter gave Rory a quick nod, "This way, sir."

Rory followed behind, listening to the chatter of excitement at each table he passed in the enormous, formal dining room. He looked around the room and saw tables loaded with assorted dishes and the smells were mouthwatering. The only problem was, he couldn't see the beautiful brunette anywhere.

"Here you are sir," the said porter as he pulled out a chair at a long table.

Rory thanked the man and sat down. He was surprised to see a sign designating this as The Captain's Table. Skye's work again, he thought.

"Well, hello there," a husky voice said beside him.

Rory turned his head to the right and found himself looking into a sparkling pair of hazel eyes. The woman attached to them was a sultry, dark-haired beauty with a golden tan.

"My name is Tanya Beno," she said as she held her right hand out to him. Her voice had the traces of a Hungarian accent.

Rory looked into her eyes as he shook her hand, "Rory Mack Steele." He was surprised by the suggestion of strength he could sense in her grip.

Her red lips formed into a mischievous smile, "Is there a Mrs. Steele?"

"No. Do you want to audition for the job?" he replied.

"The audition we can arrange," Tanya said with a saucy wink. "The rest I'll pass on for now."

Before he could reply, Rory heard another feminine voice.

"Are you a Canadian?"

Rory turned his head. Sitting in the chair to his left was a platinum-blonde with beautiful, deep-blue eyes. Her smile gave Rory the sense she was the sweet and innocent type. "Yes," Rory confirmed.

"I knew it," enthused the young woman. "My grandmother was Canadian. She lived in Niagara-on-the-Lake. Have you ever been there? My brother Landry and I used to go up there every summer."

Rory smiled at her eagerness, "Yes, I've been there. It's a beautiful place."

"Sorry. My manners, I'm Jaimee Morrissette," the beautiful young woman said as she held out her hand.

Rory took her hand, "Rory Mack Steele—"

The conversation was interrupted by a voice at the head of the table, to the left of Jaimee Morrissette. "Good evening, ladies and gentlemen, my name is Captain Tor Amundson. I'm very glad you could dine with me this evening." Amundson was a tall, regal looking man with white hair and the expected full white beard of a sailor. His white uniform was filled with gold buttons and gold trim.

Rory pegged the Captain's accent as Norwegian and he noted the man genuinely was enjoying the opportunity to interact with the ship's passengers.

Captain Amundson motioned to one of the waiters standing nearby, "You can begin please, Jomari."

Jomari was a middle-aged man with a swarthy complexion, dark hair and an infectious smile. He nodded to the Captain and gestured to the other staff members to begin serving the guests around the table. Each waiter wore white gloves and they started the dinner by offering each one at the table either a 1982 Chateau Haut Brion Pessac-Lognan red wine, which Rory remembered as being worth something like $600 a bottle, or a white wine which he didn't recognize. But he assumed it was equally expensive.

Chapter 4

DURING THE DINNER, Rory learned the names of the others nearby around the Captain's table

To the Captain's left was a beautiful woman with ebony skin and long, shiny black hair who introduced herself as Raychel Butler. Raychel was the eldest daughter of a couple in the state of Ohio who had won a $200 million Powerball lottery two years ago. Raychel wasn't the one who brought it up. One of the men at the table had recognized her from the television coverage on the family after the lottery win.

Next to her, and directly across from Rory, was a well built, middle-aged man by the name of Salman Valid, "My friends call me Sal," he said. Rory detected a slight Russian accent. From the conversation through the dinner, Rory concluded Valid had been a well-to-do businessman in Europe who had moved to America some years ago to pursue further opportunities. His physical movements gave Rory the impression Valid had spent a lot of time in the gym, probably engaged in some martial arts activities.

Next to him was an American woman in her mid-thirties by the name of Cassiopeia Lopez. Rory had the immediate impression she was a sophisticated beauty with a brain. And that proved true over the evening as Rory found out she was the youngest law professor at Yale Law School. At one point, as Rory addressed her as Cassiopeia, she said "Call me Cassie. And call me anytime." Her dark eyes twinkled with suggestion.

The man seated next to her, Blake Smallridge, had an English accent. He constantly talked about the various gambling establishments he had frequented on the Continent and in the United States. He had a slick, easy manner about him and Rory couldn't tell if he was a wealthy playboy or a con artist.

Next to Smallridge was Loretta Black. Jaimee whispered to him that she was a famous television star. Rory vaguely thought she looked like someone he had watched briefly on a television sitcom, but he wasn't entirely sure. He preferred watching old television shows and movies. But one thing *was* certain. Loretta Black was a shapely, world-class, platinum-blonde beauty with a great set of white teeth. *I wonder how much those teeth cost her?*

Next to her was a sandy-haired Dutchman by the name of Adriaan Kosters. His company in Europe had sent him to head up the American division of a high tech company. Kosters constantly flashed his Rolex watch and talked about the upscale Bavaria Vision 42 sailboat he had just placed in the waters off Nantucket. Rory wasn't impressed.

AFTER THE DINNER, EVERYONE around the table posed for a picture with Captain Tor Amundson. Rory found himself sandwiched between Jaimee Morrissette and Tanya Beno. He felt the side of each woman's breast deliberately pressing against him as the photographer moved them all closer together.

Tanya Beno's hand slid across Rory's lower back and she pulled herself closer against him. She looked up into his silver-blue eyes and winked. She was quite aware of what she was pushing against him.

Jaimee lightly tugged on his elbow on the other side, trying to get his attention away from Tanya.

Rory looked at her and smiled.

Jaimee snuggled against him with her upper body, raising an eyebrow to emphasize what she was also mashing against his body.

Rory gave her a wink.

"Alright everybody," the photographer said, "say cheese."

Everybody responded appropriately by laughing and then saying 'cheese'.

Rory's smile grew a little bigger when he felt Tanya's hand slid down and squeeze his butt cheek on her side.

AFTER THE PICTURE WAS taken, the Captain asked everyone to join him at back at the table for a moment. "First," Captain Amundson said, "everyone at this table is invited to a tour of the bridge at 0:800 hours tomorrow morning."

Claps and cheers greeted the invitation.

"So don't stay up too late or you'll miss it," Amundson teased them.

Good-natured laughter erupted around the table.

Amundson then nodded at a group of porters who moved quickly to the table and handed each person a clear, round holder containing a stack of poker chips. "Compliments of the cruise line," the Captain said. "The casino is one deck higher, on the Promenade deck. Shall we go try our luck?"

THE CONVERSATION WAS noisy and animated as they all moved with the crowd flowing up the main stairs to the next deck and into the Promenade area. It reminded Rory of a large mall with colorful high-end shops. Jaimee Morrissette and Tanya Beno stayed close to Rory as they all neared the entrance to the casino. He was surprised when Loretta Black, the television star, cut across his path and gave him a wink. He suddenly had the impression the attention he was getting was less about him and more about which one of them was more attractive and sexy. He felt a little deflated.

Jaimee Morrissette suddenly pulled the stack of chips from Rory's hand and passed them over to Tanya Beno, "Here, why don't you go play with yourself?"

Tanya had a total look of surprise on her face as she now held two stacks of poker chips. She watched in amazement as Jaimee brazenly pulled Rory away from their little group.

Rory found himself pulled into a loud retro-disco. A light ball in the ceiling splashed shafts of colors spinning around the room. People were bumping, grinding and dancing to a heavy calypso beat.

"Too noisy," Jaimee yelled. She pulled Rory back out the doorway and through the crowds before she pulled him through another doorway. It was a glitzy ballroom and couples were gliding around the room to waltz music, holding each other closely.

Jaimee pulled Rory onto the dance floor, "My mother always said the old dances were much more romantic."

"You mind if I lead?" Rory asked amiably after a moment.

Jaimee giggled, "My mother always said I was more tomboy than girly. Do you think I'm a tomboy?" She fluttered her eyelashes.

Rory shook his head, "No, you're a long way from a tomboy."

Jaimee Morrissette pulled herself a little closer and looked up into Rory's silver-blue eyes, "What do you do, Rory? Are you an international playboy? Should I be concerned about being seduced?" Her blue eyes had a mischievous look in them.

Rory couldn't help but smile, "My family owns Highlander Investigative Services. I work out of the Canadian office in Toronto and I'm a private investigator–"

"Really! That sounds exciting. Chasing criminals, getting the girl...."

"More like helping you to find your cat," Rory said.

"That's it?"

Rory gave a little shrug, "Most of it is boring work. Helping a company find out who is stealing the paper clips...tracking down relatives for estates...divorce work... that kind of thing."

Jaimee nodded, then her blue eyes took on that mischievous look again, "What about getting the girl or the seduction part–?"

"Excuse me!" The voice was more than a little angry.

It was Tanya Beno.

Rory felt Jaimee pulled from his arms.

Tanya crossed her arms in anger and stood firm, looking directly at Jaimee Morrissette. "What exactly do you think you're doing?" she demanded in a loud voice. "Rory and I were having a perfectly good time–"

"Oh really!" Jaimee shot back as she crossed her arms and stood nose to nose with Tanya. "It looked more like he was being bored to death!"

Rory felt retreat was a great option right now. Moving discreetly through the crowd of people, who were now onlookers and not dancers, Rory found his way across the dance floor and left the ballroom. Attracting women had never been a problem. *But why does trouble seem to come with it?*

Out in the atrium area, Rory found the crowd a lot thinner. It appeared most people had found their way into the disco, the ballroom or the casino. Not seeing any unattached woman to talk too, he decided to call it a night. Making his way to the wide, opulent stairway, Rory made his way back up to his penthouse suite on the Vista deck.

Once inside, he popped some ice in a glass, retrieved his bottle of Talisker Scotch whiskey from the minibar and headed for the balcony. As he slid the glass door open, a knock sounded on the penthouse suite door. Rory wondered what trouble had followed him upstairs. Reluctantly, he set the glass down on the table and walked back across to the door, still holding the bottle of scotch. He didn't bother looking through the peephole. He simply pulled the door open, "Yes?"

Standing there was the blonde and beautiful television star, Loretta Black. She pouted and waved a bottle of expensive Tequila, "Awww, I guess you don't need this silly little bottle that I brought with me."

Chapter 5

DAY 2

Straits of Florida

Heading: Cozumel, Mexico

RORY HAD A LATE BREAKFAST delivered to his suite, then headed for the bridge. He didn't want to miss the tour of the bridge offered at the Captain's table last night. He hustled his way past a bevy of beautiful young ladies, eager to catch his eye, but he was equally eager not to get sidetracked. The bridge was on Deck 8 and he wound his way towards the bow of the ship to finally reach his destination.

One of last night's table mates, Sal Valid, was talking to Captain Tor Amundson in the passageway just outside the entrance to the bridge.

"Ah, Mr. Steele if I remember correctly?" Amundson asked him as he approached.

"Yes. Good memory, Captain Amundson," Rory said as he shook his hand. Even at 6'-2" tall, Rory still had to look up at the Captain.

Amundson was about to say something when a crew member stepped outside the bridge and approached him, whispering something in his ear. The Captain nodded and then turned to

Rory and Sal, "Gentlemen, if you'll excuse me, I have a matter to take care off. Please proceed to the bridge and the crew will be happy to answer any of your questions. I'll be back shortly."

"Of course," Rory said.

The Captain and the crew member left in a hurry.

"Wonder what that was all about?' Valid said as he watched the two men disappear down the passageway.

Rory wondered the same thing as he followed Valid into the bridge. He saw Blake Smallridge, Adriaan Kosters, Raychel Butler, Cassiopeia Lopez and several other members from last night's dinner had already started their tour, talking with a number of ship's officers in white uniforms. The bridge area was far more spacious than Rory had imagined it would be. It was filled with a wide array of equipment, large flat tables and several swivel chairs set into the decking. The view over the ocean ahead of the cruise ship was breathtaking. Rory could swear he could see dolphins leaping out of the water, leading the charge across the sea.

A heavy-set man approached and held his hand out, "Good day sir, I'm Magnuson. I serve as First Officer and Officer of The Watch. That means I'm responsible for all navigation and watch duties. Please look around and if you have any questions...."

"Icelandic?" Rory asked him.

"Pardon? Oh...yes sir," Magnuson replied, a delighted look on his face. "You have a good ear for accents. Many would say Swedish or Norwegian –"

"I went out with an Icelandic girl once," Rory commented. "Never forgot that accent..."

"Just once? Too much for you, so no second date, right?" Magnuson said with a very serious look on his face. Then he winked.

Rory had to smile. He liked this man.

Valid wandered away towards one of the large flat table,

Rory looked down through the glass at the wide deck below and noticed a large green circle at the very front of the ship's bow. It was a landing area for a helicopter! He shook his head in amazement, "This is one huge ship."

Magnuson nodded, "The Caribbean StarLiner is the largest vessel I've served on to date. 230,000 gross tons, 1200 foot long, 215 foot across at the beam, 2,800 staterooms with a capacity of 6,000 passengers. We boast a state of the art integrated bridge system, multifunction workstations, enhanced conning display and enough redundancy to ensure we're never without a way to guide the ship."

"Four football fields long," Rory muttered to himself.

"We have state of the art diesel-electric propulsion as well," Magnuson added as he stood with his hands behind his back, looking around the bridge with obvious pride.

"Diesel-electric? I've never heard of that," Rory said.

"The diesel engines themselves don't drive the propeller shafts directly, as you normally find in a cruise ship," Magnuson explained. "The diesel engines are connected instead to enormous generators to produce electricity, which is then used to drive the propellers. It's a very efficient system right through the entire range of speeds we need –"

They were interrupted by Sal Valid who suddenly appeared beside them again, "Isn't this all amazing, Rory. I always pictured the crew up here driving a large wooden wheel like you see in those pirate movies." He pantomimed the action.

Jaimee Morrissette and Tanya Beno entered the bridge. They were together... talking...and laughing.

Rory thought about taking out his eyeballs and checking to see if they were working. Last night they were fighting and this morning –

And right behind them was Loretta Black, Rory's late-night visitor. She waved at Rory.

Rory stood very, very still, fascinated by what he was seeing.

The three women walked together across the bridge, pointing out interesting things to each other and giggling.

He shook his head. He started wondering about the incident he had witnessed last night and why they were such good friends this morning...then he decided to forget about it. Not worth it. Just enjoy what was good...and forget about the confusing parts.

He realized someone was talking to him. It was Sal, standing beside him and expecting an answer to a question he must have asked. "Pardon?"

"I said, are you interested?"

Rory blinked, "Interested? In...?"

Sal shook his head and smiled. Then he gestured towards Captain Amundson.

Rory had missed the Captain coming back onto the bridge. He was now standing in the middle of the bridge, talking to Magnuson and several of the other officers.

"When I saw the Captain return," Valid said, "I told him I was very interested in hearing more about the diesel-electric engines one of the officers was telling me about. The Captain has offered us a personal, behind the scenes tour of the two lower decks, including the engine room. Are you interested?"

"Oh. Yeah, that would be great."

"Great, that makes four of us," Sal grinned as he clapped his hands.

Chapter 6

CAPTAIN AMUNDSON led Rory, Sal, Blake Smallridge and Adriaan Kosters out to the elevator and they rode down to the lowest deck of the ship.

"The front half of the ship down here serves as the hold, the cargo storage area," Amundson said as they emerged from the elevator. "We bring provisions and other items through the loading doors one deck up and use large freight elevators to bring them down here where we store them."

"It must take a lot of provisions to take care of everyone on board," Kosters said.

"Very much so," the Captain said as he led them down a passageway towards the stern of the ship. "In an average week, we go through 25,000 pounds of beef, 25,000 pounds of vegetables, nearly the same thing in fresh fruit and–"

"We're on a two-week cruise!" Adriaan Kosters exclaimed. "You must have extremely large refrigeration units to carry enough for the two weeks?"

"We take on additional provisions when we land at various ports during those two weeks," Amundson explained. "While the passengers enjoy a port visit, crew members are working hard to re-stock the shelves, so to speak."

"Ahhh," Kosters said, now understanding.

"Considering what we all drank at the meal, I can only imagine your bill for alcohol," Blake Smallridge said.

The Captain laughed and nodded, "Each week our passengers go through 3,500 bottles of assorted wines, nearly 300 bottles of vodka, 350 bottles of whiskey, 10,000 cans of beer –"

"And you restock that as well?" Kosters asked him.

"At every port," the Captain confirmed.

"Mr. Kosters was suddenly afraid you would run out of rum," Smallridge interjected.

"I'll personally make sure that doesn't happen," the Captain told him.

Kosters laughed.

The Captain opened a large, watertight door. "Mind your step," the Captain said, gesturing down at the lower frame of the door where they had to step over.

Each passenger stepped through as the Captain held the door open.

"This is the air-conditioning compartment for the ship," Amundson said as he shut the door behind everyone. "As you can see, this is a watertight compartment that runs two stories high."

"Amazing," Smallridge said as he looked up through the catwalks above them.

"There is a second watertight compartment off to our right that is a complete back-up to this one. It's used if this one stops operating for some reason," the Captain explained as he led them down a steel grate walkway.

"So you have a backup system. That's something I never knew," Kosters said as he looked around in amazement.

The Captain explained the various pieces of the air-conditioning system as they did a brief tour around the compartment. Then he led them through another watertight door, holding it open as everyone entered the next compartment.

"And this is the water filtration compartment. This one is three decks high," explained Amundson as he shut the door behind them.

"It's also a waterproof compartment set off from the rest?" Valid asked him.

"Yes, it is," Amundson said.

Kosters whistled as he looked up through the catwalks, "And you have a backup for this as well?"

"Legislation is pushing modern cruise ships to have complete backup systems for all essential equipment on board," the Captain told him.

"I guess you're a long way from a garage when you're at sea," Rory commented.

"Exactly," the Captain agreed with a smile. "And all the compartments are watertight for safety reasons. If there is a fire or the hull is completely penetrated, the problem can be completely isolated."

They were approaching a double door at the end of the passageway. The left side opened and two crew members, dressed in dark shirts and pants, emerged. They acknowledged the Captain and kept the door open for the visitors to pass through.

A distant rumble reached Rory's ears as he stepped through the doorway to join Amundson and the other passengers in the next compartment. The Captain was already twenty feet away with Valid following close behind. Rory could smell industrial oil, grease and the faint scent of diesel fuel.

"We are in the engine section," Amundson said back over his shoulder. "It runs three decks high," he said as he jerked a thumb upward.

Kosters stopped dead in front of Rory, bent over backward and looked up, "Three decks! Amazing."

"And there's a second engine room as well?" Rory asked the Captain as he came to a quick stop to avoid running into the Dutchman.

"Yes," the Captain proudly said. "We want to make sure we're not dead in the water for days waiting for rescue."

Kosters shook his head in amazement as he started walking again.

Rory followed behind, looking down to see they were now walking on a steel grate just wide enough for one person. Blue pipe railings lined both sides of the tight walkway. The bulkhead walls of the compartment were painted the same blue color as the railings. Roy couldn't help feeling small and insignificant as various pieces of equipment towered over him on either side of the walkway. The engine compartment was immense.

The Captain stopped and began explaining some of the equipment that surrounded them. After a few minutes of discussion, he led them further along the steel grating to an area that had green pipe railings and green bulkhead walls. On either side of the walkway were large pipes going in and out of large steel boxes, also painted green and lined with valves and gauges. The Captain turned right along the walkway, went down three stairs and then turned left. He walked a few feet and turned left again into an area that was painted yellow. The walkway became very wide and they were now walking on steel plating. The throbbing sounds were getting louder and increased in intensity as the Cap-

tain led them past a line of tall, metal boxes that looked like electrical panels.

Rory could see large open areas off to the sides that were
filled with more pipes and electrical panels.

The Captain turned a corner and the throbbing sound became intense.

Rory realized the towering, gray steel wall on his right was
actually the side of an engine. He was surprised by its enormous
size. And even more surprising was the fact there were three
equally large engines up ahead.

Captain Amundson turned and began to talk to them in a
loud voice. "This cruise ship is actually moved by means of a
diesel-electrical propulsion system. These are the diesel engines,"
said Amundson as he patted his hand against the gray, steel wall.

Smallridge bent over backward to look up at the engine.
"These are enormous."

The Captain nodded with a smile, "They can use up to 400
tons of fuel daily, depending on how fast we're traveling. Fuel
is another item we need to replenish when we visit a port." The
Captain moved to the end of the diesel engine and pointed,
"Take a look down there."

Everyone crowded around the Captain to look down at an
enormous, steel shaft that was turning rapidly in a blur.

Kosters leaned over the green railing and watched the rapidly
spinning shaft, "So this drives the propeller?"

"Actually no," the Captain replied.

Kosters was puzzled, "No? What *does* it do?"

The Captain motioned for everyone to follow him. He led
the entourage further down the walkway to stand beside the first
in a line of tall, steel boxes where the spinning shaft disappeared.

"Keep in mind I said we have a *diesel-electrical* propulsion system. In the old days, the shaft from the engines would run through gearboxes to power the screws or the propellers that drive the ship. But *these* boxes are switchboards which, in turn, run a shaft through supply transformers to frequency converters that run to our electric propulsion motors. Those electric propulsion motors run through the gearboxes to azimuth thrusters, which are pods housing propellers that can rotate 360 degrees and provide optimum maneuverability."

"This whole thing is amazing," Kosters said. "I know I keep saying that but...."

"It's extremely efficient, much more powerful and very maneuverable compared to the old systems," the Captain said proudly.

Rory nodded, finally realizing the answer to a question that had puzzled him. "The azimuth thrusters you mentioned. That's why you don't need to use tugboats to dock or leave a dock, like the old days. Correct?"

The Captain beamed, "Very good, Mr. Steele. For those of us at sea for years, it is an amazing advancement that has freed us to do so much more in a short space of time. Now gentlemen, let's go this way."

Rory followed along as they continued on the tour. But after a while, something struck Rory as odd. Sal Valid had been very talkative all during dinner. And when they had been up on the bridge. But he had been very quiet during *this* tour. Even though *he* was the one who had set it up and expressed a real desire to see this part of the ship, he never asked one single question. He never made one single remark. But he wasn't quiet because he was disinterested or disappointed. On the contrary, his eyes were constantly taking in their surroundings.

Even now, Sal Valid was taking everything in and analyzing every single piece of machinery around them in a very pointed manner.

Rory shook his head. His sister Skye had been right. He had been too caught up in work, too busy seeing suspicious patterns in the most innocent of events around him. He definitely needed this vacation. Switch off the private investigator and enjoy yourself, Steele.

Chapter 7

DAY 3

07:00

Cozumel, Mexico

RORY STEPPED OFF the cruise ship onto the Punta Langosta Pier that led to San Miguel's downtown area. The scent of the salt water mixed with that of old, seasoned wood beams. Another huge cruise ship, the Ocean Queen, was docked on the other side of the wide pier, also disgorging a stream of tourists. The walk to land was interesting for a number of reasons. The sun was hot and felt good on his back. The stretch of water on either side of the pier leading to the beach was crystal clear and inviting. And the bevy of young beauties, dressed in the skimpiest of swimwear, was the crowning touch to the start of what could prove to be a most interesting day.

REACHING THE END OF the pier, Rory walked along with the crowd of passengers into a gray building. He followed the crowd to the right where they all climbed a set of stairs to an open doorway that led to a footbridge over a street. The lanes of the street were divided down the center by a line of small palm trees.

In five minutes Rory settled into a chair on the outside patio of a crowded bar and restaurant, sipping a cold and tasty, scotch-on-the-rocks. He could hear the sound of a Mexican band playing somewhere down the street and it blended nicely with the excited chatter of tourists and the call of vendors trying to hawk their wares.

AFTER HIS THIRD DRINK, a sultry voice interrupted his thoughts. "Hello, Mr. Steele, would you mind some company?"

Rory looked up. Standing there was Cassiopeia Lopez, the sophisticated beauty with a brain. She had pushed her sunglasses up on her head and flashed him a brilliant smile. Rory couldn't help himself and his eyes dropped to the semitransparent sarong she wore. Underneath was a black bikini that accentuated her voluptuous form.

"I certainly hope you approve of my attire," she said as she put a hand on her hip.

Rory felt like a little boy, caught taking a peek at the teacher's boobs. He rose to his feet and gestured to the chair on the other side of the table, "Sorry about that."

Cassiopeia smile as she sat in the chair, "No problem, Mr. Steele. I like a man who is direct. Especially in the bedroom," she added with a wink.

"I'll keep that in mind. What would you like to drink, Ms. Lopez?"

"One of those things with an umbrella. Surprise me."

Rory called the server over and ordered her a Pina Colada.

"Thank you, Mr. Steele."

"Call me Rory."

Cassiopeia Lopez nodded, "And I'm Cassie. Remember?"

"Right. Cassie."

The server was back quickly with the drink, setting it in front of Lopez

"Do you have anything planned for the day, Cassie?" Rory asked her.

"Why, what do you have in mind?" Cassie said as she picked up her drink. She placed the straw between her lips and gave Rory a wink.

Rory shook his head and laughed, "Nothing special. I just noticed a lot of the passengers were headed off on different shore excursions, that's all. I just wondered if you were going to do the same."

Cassie placed the cold glass against her cheek, "I prefer to just relax and take my time. I have enough pressure at work without coming on vacation and having to move from place to place, trying to get every ounce of sightseeing in before the ship leaves. On board at night, I like to go for a long walk at night around the upper deck. It's so peaceful and beautiful...and romantic...you should join me sometime."

"I just might do that," Rory said. He swirled the ice in his glass and it clinked against the sides as he looked out over the boisterous crowds. Then he looked back at Lopez, "If you don't mind my saying, you seem to be pretty young for a law professor at Yale."

Cassiopeia Lopez raised an eyebrow, "That's very kind of you to say, Mr. Steele. Are you trying to charm me?"

"Yes," Rory said with a slight smile, "but I'm also being serious. I always thought professors were much older."

Lopez shrugged slightly as she glanced at the passing crowd, "I just moved through school very quickly and I was always with people much older than myself. After graduation from Brooklyn Law School, I became a very successful prosecutor in New York. I like to think it was my abilities that attracted Yale...but sometimes I think being a woman, along with my Spanish heritage, did more to help me than anything else. But that's just my opinion."

"Being sexy and beautiful may have helped as well," Rory said with a salute of his drink.

"Why Mr. Steele, are you now trying to seduce me?"

"Maybe–"

An excited female voice interrupted their conversation, "Rory!"

Rory looked up to see Loretta Black, her arms wide open, shuffling towards him quickly.

Loretta threw her arms around Rory's neck and gave him a big hug, "Isn't this island just great!"

Rory grunted as she squeezed hard, her breasts nearly enveloping his head, "Yes, it is."

Just beyond Loretta were Tanya Beno and Jaimee Morrissette.

Loretta finally let Rory go and stepped back, "We've been shopping our brains out."

Rory noted all three women wore the skimpiest bikinis possible under nearly sheer sarongs. Both Tanya and Jaimee wore the expected flip-flops on their feet, while Loretta sported yellow, high heeled shoes.

Jaimee Morrissette gave Rory a wink as she pushed her chest out.

Tanya Beno, the sultry, dark-haired beauty with the golden tan lifted an eyebrow as she looked at Cassiopeia Lopez, "And how are you today?"

"I'm fine, thank you," Cassie answered, without much enthusiasm.

Despite the politeness and the heat of the day, Rory detected a chill in the air.

"It's too bad you didn't start out with *us* this morning Rory, you would've had a lot of fun," Loretta Black said.

"How do you know he's not having fun now?" Cassiopeia Lopez asked her.

Loretta Black shrugged, "Oh you know when you get older you don't party as much–"

Cassiopeia Lopez rose from her chair, a scowl on her face, "And just *who* are you calling old!"

Loretta Black just shrugged again, "No one. I'm just sayin'–"

Cassiopeia Lopez threw her Pina Colada into Black's face.

Loretta Black sputtered and wiped the drink from her face, "You bitch! Do you know who I am?"

Shaking her head, Lopez said, "Not any more than your mother *not* knowing who your father was."

Black's face became a mask of rage and she lunged for Lopez, "I'll kill you–!"

Lopez raised her hands and arms to protect her face from the looming fingernails.

Tanya Beno's arm snaked out and wrapped around Loretta Black's waist, lifting the television star off the ground and stepping back away from Black's intended target.

Rory was surprised at Tanya's quickness and strength. And there wasn't a hint of strain on her face as she held the flailing television star off the ground.

Tanya Beno smiled at Jaimee Morrissette and said something.

Jaimee nodded and began talking to Black, trying to calm her down.

Black's arms and legs continued to swing violently in the air as she tried to kick or scratch Cassiopeia Lopez.

Lopez, realizing Black couldn't get to her now, began to taunt the screaming blonde.

Rory decided retreat was the better part of valor. He dropped enough cash on the table to pay for the drinks and quietly slipped away into the crowd of tourists. A block away, he could still hear the television star's obscenity-filled tirade.

Chapter 8

RORY USED THE REST of the morning to do a little shopping. He bought a pair of teardrop earrings for Avis in the New York office, a diamond heart pendant for Mandy in the Toronto office and a Caribbean diamond charm bracelet for his sister Skye. His last purchase was a bottle of Jose Cuervo Reserva de la Familia (Extra Anejo), a 100% blue agave tequila treat for Uncle Murdock in New York.

A late lunch in the local Coconuts Bar and Restaurant was a leisurely highlight to his brief visit in Cozumel. Lounging dogs and wandering chickens on the patio added to the island atmosphere as he finished a killer margarita on the patio while looking past a marble white beach to a clear blue ocean filled with bathing beauties. But twenty minutes later, something happened to spoil the relaxing atmosphere. *Is that the voice of Loretta Black?* She was arguing with someone inside the restaurant. Rory dropped more than enough money on the table to pay the bill. He decided heading back *inside* the restaurant to the front door was not a good idea. Instead, he walked the length of the patio and skirted the far side of the building. He took a chance and glanced through the open side of the restaurant. It *was* Loretta

Black. She was gesturing wildly, arguing with a tall, good-looking young man with curly blond hair.

The young man looked amused rather than angry or concerned with her tirade. He casually sipped his drink as Loretta gave him a piece of her mind.

To Rory, it looked like a day-time soap opera, with two young television stars playing out a scene. The other patrons were amused at the unexpected entertainment but it was all too much drama for Rory. *I think it's time to head back to the peace and quiet of the cruise ship.*

WALKING BACK ALONG the Punta Langosta Pier, Rory noticed a lot of activity going on at the far end of the pier, towards the back end of the two docked cruise ships. A large number of crates were stacked up along the pier. Four forklifts were moving back and forth, hauling the crates over to an open loading door in the side of his own cruise ship, the Caribbean StarLiner. A loading door on the Ocean Queen was just closing. This had to be the restocking of provisions Captain Amundson had told them about during yesterday's tour of the lower decks. They would load the provisions through the door and then use large freight elevators to bring them down to the storage areas. Curiosity kept him moving past the gangway leading back into the Caribbean Star-Liner and towards the activity. He wanted to get close enough to see how they were doing it, without getting in the way. Despite the heat, the workers were moving swiftly, as if they were anxious to get their work done.

Rory cocked his head. He spotted Sal Valid talking to one of the workers on the pier. Sal had been the one to talk the Captain into the tour in the first place and he was no doubt interested in the inner workings of the ship, just like Rory was. Getting right into the middle of the workers was not a good idea, but he could understand the man's curiosity.

Valid turned as Rory got closer. His eyes took on a look of surprise. "Rory! How are you?" he said loudly.

"Fine Sal," Rory said. "Are you making sure they get your Stolichnaya Vodka on board?"

Valid laughed, "You're very observant Mr. Steele."

To Rory, the laughter seemed strained.

"How was your day?" Valid asked as he moved quickly towards Rory.

"It was great," Rory said. "How many crates have they–?"

"Let's get on board and I'll buy you a cold drink," Valid said quickly as he put an arm around Rory's shoulders and turned them away from the loading efforts of the workers.

"That sounds great," Rory answered. But he had the impression Sal was more interested in moving him away from the loading efforts than really buying him a drink. Was it concern for his welfare...or something else? Rory looked back over his shoulder at the restocking activity, "Maybe we could take a look first–"

"Did you see that sexy TV star, Loretta Black in that skimpy bikini today?" Sal asked him.

"Yeah...I did," Rory said.

Sal jostled Rory's shoulders and teased him, "She sure has the hots for you. I'm jealous."

"Yeah...well...make a play for her any time you want," Rory said honestly. "She might be more trouble than she's worth in the long run."

Sal laughed as he walked Rory up the gangway.

To Rory, that laugh seemed a little forced as well. *What are you up to Valid?*

Chapter 9

RORY WAS SITTING on his private balcony, sipping a scotch when a knock came at his suite door. He wasn't interested in any company and he stayed put, looking out over the moonlit sea, enjoying the soothing scent of the salt water–

The knocking persisted, now in harder, more insistent raps.

"Okay, okay," Rory said loudly as he got up and moved back inside his cabin, heading across the room. He opened the door. Standing there was a ship's officer Rory remembered seeing during the bridge tour. Larson? Thorson? It was a Norwegian or Danish name.

The officer spoke quickly, "So sorry to disturb you, sir. But the Captain wishes to see you immediately."

Rory noted the man was wringing his hands. He also detected a Danish accent and the name came to him, "Thorson, right?"

The officer gave him a brief nod, "Yes sir." He then turned and started down the passageway, looking back at Rory, "If you would follow me, sir...."

Letting out a small breath of frustration, Rory said, "Can't it wait until morning, Mr. Thorson? I'm very tired and I'd just like to relax right now."

Stopping and wringing his hands again, Thorson said, "I'm afraid not, sir."

Rory immediately feared the worse, "Has something happened to someone in my family–?"

"No, sir. Nothing like that." He gestured down the passageway, taking a step, "If you could...?"

Rory realized the officer wasn't going to offer anything more in the way of an explanation. "Okay. Just let me grab–"

The officer was already moving down the passageway.

Rory ducked back inside, snatched his key card from the kitchenette counter and stepped back into the passageway.

The officer stopped for a moment, looking back as Rory pulled his cabin door shut.

As soon as Rory began walking, the officer quickly turned and heading in the direction of the elevators.

Rory was surprised at Mr. Thorson's speedy, urgent walk and he had to hustle to keep up.

The doors to one of the elevators were wide open.

Thorson led Rory inside the elevator and stuck a keycard into a slot. The doors closed and the car started moving past all floor stops.

The open doors of the elevator - and not allowing it to stop at any floor - told Rory more than the officer did.. *Must be really serious if they are keeping an elevator out of commission for their own use*. If a crew member was overriding an elevator car and possibly irritating passengers, there had to be some kind of emergency. Then he realized something else. The bridge was only one deck down from his. But the elevator was still going down. His eyes narrowed as he glanced at the officer, "Shouldn't we have stopped at deck 8 to reach the bridge?"

"The Captain is not on the bridge, sir," Thorson said as the car finally came to a stop and the doors opened.

Rory noted they were on Deck One.

The officer was out and striding down the passageway to the left without any further explanation.

Rory hustled to keep up again as Thorson made a beeline for a closed-door halfway down the passageway.

Thorson opened the door and waited for Rory to follow him through before he closed and locked it behind them.

More alarm bells went off in Rory's head. What was happening here? He looked around as Thorson led the way to an open doorway across the room. The smell of disinfectant and the white walls told Rory he was probably in the waiting room for the ship's infirmary.

"Mr. Steele is here, sir," Thorson announced as he passed through the doorway.

The Captain was talking to a man in a white lab coat. Rory presumed he was one of the three ship's doctors his cruise information packet had said were aboard. The Captain turned, "Thank you for coming, Mr. Steele. I'm sorry I had to disturb you so late."

"Is there some problem, Captain?" Rory asked him. He was puzzled and intrigued at the same time.

"Yes. We have a *serious* problem," Amundson said, "and I must ask you to be discreet. We cannot alarm the other passengers."

"Alright," Rory agreed. He couldn't imagine where this was going.

Amundson took a deep breath, as if to steel himself, then said, "We became aware of two missing passengers our second night out–"

"Two missing passengers?" That took Rory by surprise.

Chapter 10

THE CAPTAIN NODDED AFFIRMATION, "The porters took note, that two men traveling together were absent from their stateroom, after the first night out. Their beds were never slept in. We made announcements asking for those two passengers to report their presence to the bridge but we never heard from either one. We wondered if they were simply staying somewhere else...maybe with some ladies they met, that type of thing...none of our business, of course...but...."

"I can understand your concern," Rory said.

"Then the porters reported that *another* gentleman, they positively saw in his cabin on the first day, had also disappeared. Like the others, his bed has never been slept in. The porters have never had to make it up," Amundson explained. "It was only because of the discussion of the first two missing passengers that the staff decided to bring it to my attention."

"Still..." Rory was not totally convinced.

Amundson nodded his head, "I can understand your skepticism, Mr. Steele. I felt the same way. And the gentleman traveling with the third missing passenger claims there is nothing wrong."

"Does he know where his friend is?" Rory asked.

"He insisted it was none of our business. Under ordinary circumstances. I would leave it at that. However...." Amundson turned and indicated for Rory to follow him. He opened the door at the back of the infirmary, stepped through and then held the door open for Rory.

Rory stepped into a large white room that was lined with two dozen stainless-steel locker doors at the far end. He could smell formaldehyde, along with the scent of disinfectant, telling him immediately where he was - the ship's morgue. In the middle of the room was a stainless-steel table with a white sheet over a body. He hadn't been expecting that. But an even bigger surprise was seeing Jaimee Morrissette standing beside the table with three other men. Tears were rolling down her cheeks. Rory followed the Captain across to the table.

Using a tissue, Jaimee Morrissette blotted tears from her eyes and barely acknowledged Rory's presence.

"Miss Morrissette," the Captain said, "perhaps it would be best if you waited in the other room while we discuss–"

Jaimee Morrissette shook her head vigorously no. "I need to know everything that's happening when it comes to my brother."

"Your brother?" Rory asked in surprise.

Jaimee Morrissette nodded, "I went to check on Landry–" Her grief overwhelmed her and she began crying.

Rory looked to the Captain for an answer.

Captain Amundson nodded his head in confirmation, "According to our dining staff, Mr. Landry Morrissette became ill at the end of his dinner. He complained of nausea and dizziness, but that's not an unusual occurrence on an ocean cruise."

"Seasickness," Rory concluded.

"Exactly," Amundson confirmed. "We receive complaints like this on every cruise. The staff helped Miss Morrissette take her brother to his suite and gave the usual recommendations. Dramamine or ginger to combat the nausea, eating dry crackers, bread or apples to keep liquids from sloshing around in the stomach and so on. Unfortunately, when Miss Morrissette returned from our pharmacy, she found her brother unconscious. Dr. Rodriguez here was summoned immediately."

Dr. Rodriguez was a tall, husky man with curly black hair. He had a very somber look on his face as he indicated the body on the table, "As Captain Amundson says, I was summoned to this man's suite and when I arrived... I found him in a coma."

"A coma? I've never heard of anyone with seasickness going into a coma," Rory said.

"It's possible, but there would have to be some extenuating circumstances, such as a person having diabetes," Dr. Rodriguez said. "Not being able to keep food down and ending up with low blood sugar has happened, causing death in rare circumstances. But according to Miss Morrissette, her brother had no pre-existing conditions that could explain him falling into a coma–"

Jamie spoke in a grief-stricken whisper, which trailed off, "Landry was extremely fit, he ran triathlons...."

Dr. Rodriguez looked at her with sympathy in his eyes and spoke gently, "Normally we don't perform an autopsy on someone who dies at sea. We're not set up for it." He glanced at the Captain, "But...because of the circumstances...we decided to do one in this case." He pulled back the sheet to Landry Morrissette's waist.

Rory saw Jaimee Morrissette react like she had been struck by a heavy blow. The tissue in her hand went to her mouth and she let out a brief cry. Tears filled her eyes again as she looked at her brother's dead body.

And no wonder. Very few people saw a loved one like this. A heavy 'Y' incision on Morrissette's body was evident. The arms of the Y extend from the front of each shoulder to the bottom end of the breastbone. From past experience, Rory knew the incision was very deep, extending to the rib cage in the chest, and completely through the abdominal wall below that. Rory cocked his head to get a better view of the face. Landry Morrissette looked familiar but he couldn't quite place him.

Dr. Rodriguez continued in a soft voice, mindful of Jaimee Morrissette, "I found slight acute emphysema as well as oedema of the lungs. There was also atelectasis, which occurs when the lungs don't inflate properly. The internal organs were deeply congested and showed small hemorrhages. This is an indication of blood circuit failure. Which is something I thought was occurring when I first examined this man in his suite."

Rory cocked his head, "That sounds kind of familiar...."

"These are all signs of asphyxia," Dr. Rodriguez intoned.

That hit Rory like a sledgehammer, "You mean someone strangled or smothered him?"

Jaimee Morrissette turned away and broke into tears again.

Rory looked at Jaimee, feeling badly for his sudden outburst. The death of a loved one was one thing; the suggestion of murder was something totally different.

Dr. Rodriguez shook his head no and opened Landry Morrissette's left eye, "There is no sign of petechial hemorrhaging in the eyes." He then indicated the neck, "There is no bruising or evidence of strangulation, the hyoid bone is intact –"

"Poisoning?" Rory asked the doctor.

"There is absolutely no evidence in the bloodstream that poison was administered," Dr. Rodriguez stated.

"We have no choice but to consider this one a suspicious death," Captain Amundson added, in a hushed voice.

"I can see why you would be concerned," Rory said with a nod. Then a thought struck Rory. He looked directly at Captain Amundson and spoke in a low voice, "I don't mean to be indelicate under the circumstances, but why would you involve me in this? All cruise ships have their own security officers–"

Captain Amundson made a gesture with his head to Dr. Rodriguez.

The doctor acknowledged the gesture and began walking towards the back of the room.

Turning around, the Captain walked behind the doctor, gesturing with his finger to have Rory follow them.

Rory placed a comforting hand on Jaimee Morrissette's shoulder as he passed.

Wiping her eyes with the tissue, Morrissette acknowledged the gesture with a slight glance and a nod of her head.

Dr. Rodriguez turned the handle on one of the square stainless steel doors and opened it.

Rory stepped to a position beside the Captain. He could feel the cold coming from the refrigeration unit with the door open.

Dr. Rodriguez pulled the inner table out, revealing a white sheet covering a body.

Captain Amundson gently pulled back the white sheet, revealing the pale face of a corpse, "This is Kristoffer Jensen. He is...was...our Chief Security Officer."

"What happened to him?" Rory asked in a quiet voice.

"He had the security staff working on a search of the ship yesterday for the missing passengers. During the search, several members of the security staff heard him yell man overboard at about 2 AM last night," Amundson said. "Unfortunately, those closest were one deck below. By the time they reached his position, they found him lying on the deck. He was...dead."

"He died from a massive blow to the back of the head," Dr. Rodriguez added. Then he looked at Amundson.

Rory looked from the Doctor to the Captain. He sensed both men were struggling with what they wanted to say next. Rory waited for a moment then broke the silence, "I'm sorry. But I still don't see how this concerns me –"

"You're here at the specific request of Miss Morrissette," Captain Amundson explained.

That took Rory by surprise and he glanced back towards Jaimee. She was still beside her brother's corpse, looking down at him and blotting tears from her cheeks.

"The other members of our security team are all brand-new, Mr. Steele," the Captain said. "Jensen was our *only* experienced man. We normally recruit from experienced security personnel. But our owners were trying to cut costs and figured we could hire cheap and train them during the cruise. Unfortunately, Jensen only had time to begin training the staff once we left port. So we need someone, with experience like yourself, to lead the investigation."

"So you want *me* to investigate her brother's death?"

The Captain took a deep breath and let out, shaking his head slowly, "I believe we need you for reasons *beyond* Mr. Morrissette." The Captain paused a moment, "Before he died, Mr.

Jensen voiced a troubling concern with me. I dismissed it as fantasy...but...I think he may have been right."

Rory saw a deeper, more troubled look sweep over the Captain's face. Just *where* was this going?

"Jensen was looking into the three missing passengers, as was his job," Amundson continued. "When he went back for a second interview with the traveling companion of the third missing passenger, Jensen couldn't find him anywhere. As you're aware, we had our mandatory safety training exercises, where the passengers report to their specified safety stations. Those four passengers did not make an appearance when we ran the drill. Jensen had initiated a ship-wide search. That's what he was doing when he was killed."

"Those four passengers might have just ignored the safety exercise," Rory reasoned.

"Those are the same thoughts I had," Amundson agreed. "But Jensen began to voice strong concerns that those passengers were dead, based on his past experiences. If that were true, Miss Morrissette's brother makes it *five* suspicious deaths since we left the Port of Miami. And if Jensen was yelling man overboard as reported, then there's a sixth...."

"...and Jensen himself would make seven," Rory whispered with a nod.

"And maybe Kristoffer Jensen was killed because he saw something...," Dr. Rodriguez added. His voice trailed off, hinting at something treacherous.

Rory finished the doctors thought, "Like...maybe it wasn't an accidental man overboard...maybe he saw someone *being thrown* overboard...."

Captain Amundson nodded in solemn agreement.

Everything was quiet for a moment, as each man looked at the other.

Captain Amundson's face looked grave as he finally spoke in a low voice, "We need your help, Mr. Steele - because I now believe we have a serial killer on board."

Chapter 11

A SERIAL KILLER on board the Caribbean StarLiner? A serial killer at loose in a closed environment - at sea - and far from any port and any help. Rory's mind raced at the thought. The Captain wanted an investigation but it could all go terribly bad in a heartbeat...not that this wasn't already bad. No, they had to react quickly to save more lives.

Rory rubbed his chin, thinking, and then said, "Captain, I would suggest we head straight back to Miami. We could hold everyone on the ship while the police come aboard and–"

"Sorry, but that's not possible, Mr. Steele," the Captain said.

Alarm bells went off in Rory's head. "Why not? You can't just continue on with the cruise as if nothing happened."

Captain Amundson put his hands out to calm Rory, "We will carry on with the cruise - at least in part. But that's because of logistics. We can't head straight back along our same path because of a major storm unexpectedly building in the Atlantic. We would end up sailing into the expected path of a hurricane. If we loop back around westward, we could skirt the far edge. We could even sail for another safe port, if necessary. But we also need to restock our supplies, to keep the ship functioning and the passengers fed. I'm afraid we need to continue on to our next stop at the very least."

Rory nodded his head in understanding but he didn't feel good about it.

The Captain appeared to hesitate, then he broached another subject of concern slowly, "Mr. Steele...Dr. Rodriguez and I have been wondering about alerting the passengers..." He looked over at the doctor.

The doctor nodded his head and added in a quiet, unsure voice, "I'm not sure we wouldn't be causing panic...but they have the right to know...."

"It is ultimately *my* decision," Captain Amundson said. "But I wanted your opinion, Mr. Steele. With your background, I thought you might have some insight...." His voice trailed off, hopeful someone could help him with his burden.

Rory took a moment to think, rolling all the various conflicting thoughts around in his head. "I agree with Dr. Rodriguez and his feelings," he finally said. "The passengers *should* be told."

The Captain nodded reluctantly, the concern with having to make the announcement written across his face. His shoulders slumped a little.

"However," Rory continued. "In this situation, with the fact we can't head right back to port, I recommend we *don't* tell them. Even if we could manage the initial panic and the outcry to flee the ship...we'd probably have a difficult time maintaining control of the situation for very long. That's what concerns me more."

"How do you mean?" Dr. Rodriguez asked him. His brow furrowed, "I still think they have a right to know, to protect themselves."

Rory gave him a nod, "Under normal circumstances, I would agree with you. *But*...in my experience, in a large crowd like this, you'll find a lot of people who will panic in a *different* sense. People will start looking for someone to blame for the deaths. People will turn on each other, you'll have lynch mobs forming before long. And that could happen among the passengers *or* the crew members−"

The Captain shook his head, "I can't believe my crew would ever−"

Rory held a hand up, "Sorry, Captain. But your crew are still people. They might be trained for an emergency at sea...but they're not trained for a serial killer stalking them on board. Passenger or crew - there are those who will see danger in someone who doesn't look like them - who doesn't think like them - and they'll want to take action. The next thing you know, people are being strung up or thrown overboard. A mob mentality is almost a certainty, with over 6,000 people trapped in a floating cage."

After a moment of thought, Rodriguez nodded reluctantly, "Unfortunately, I think he's right, Captain. Even if only 10% of the people aboard went into a panic...."

The Captain nodded and rubbed his forehead like he had a headache.

"So where's our next stop, Captain?" Rory asked

"Our next port of call is George Town in Grand Cayman. We dock at 08:00. Then we leave port at 17:00."

"Maybe we can get some help from the local police," Rory said hopefully.

"The Captain shook his head, "The force there is too small, with little resources. You're welcome to try, but I have my doubts about their ability to help."

Chapter 12

TEN MINUTES LATER, Rory stepped out of the ship's infirmary to see Jaimee Morrissette leaning a shoulder against the far wall of the passageway, looking down like a lost woman, dabbing at her eyes with a tissue.

Jaimee looked over and gave him a small shrug, "I hope you're not angry that I got you into this."

"No, not at all," he said, only half listening.

Jaimee stood up, dabbing at her eyelashes, "I know I have more than a missing cat...but when the Captain talked about finding an experienced policeman on board...I thought about you...."

"I'll do my best to help," Rory said in a low voice. He was too distracted to be angry. And he wasn't really sure what he could do, considering the big picture that faced everyone aboard right now. They were on a cruise in the sun...with no way off for two or three days...and the very real possibility of a serial killer in their midst. Great cruise this was turning out to be.

"Jaimee!"

It was Tanya Beno, coming down the passageway in a hurry. "I just heard about your brother," she said as she threw her arms around Jaimee's neck and pulled her close. "I can't imagine how you're feeling right now."

"Thanks, Tanya." As Beno released her and stepped back, Jaimee dabbed at fresh tears.

Beno crossed her arms, "Do they have any idea what happened?"

Jaimee nodded, "They're not positive. But from what they're saying, I think he was murdered—"

"Murdered! Are you sure? What happened to him?"

"The doctor said he died from asphyxiation. They're just not sure how yet," Jaimee answered.

"Maybe they're wrong. I'm sure it must be hard for them to figure it out," Tanya reasoned. "They probably don't have all the forensic equipment needed to really determine that. Right?"

"I don't really know about all that," Jaimee answered truthfully. "But the doctor did an autopsy and..." Her voice trailed off at that thought.

"Poor thing," Tanya said as she gave Jaimee another hug. She squeezed her tight for a moment and then stepped back again, "Do they know who did it, then? I imagine they'll wait until we get back to Miami, so the police can investigate?"

"No. I overheard them say other passengers seemed to be missing as well," Jaimee whispered.

Rory opened his mouth, to ask her not to say anything more—

"So Rory here is going to investigate," Jaimee added with a nod at Rory.

The cat was out of the bag. Rory had hoped to operate in secrecy, to ask questions without anyone being shy about answering.

Beno's face took on a look of confusion, "Rory? I don't understand...."

"Rory is a private investigator," Jaimee said.

"He is?" Tanya's eyes narrowed as she looked at Rory.

"The Captain definitely thinks he can help," Jaimee said as she patted Rory on the chest like a proud mother.

"Jaimee, I can't promise anything," Rory said quietly.

"I know," Jaimee said. "But I have confidence in you."

Beno chewed on her lower lip as she looked at Rory, "What are you going to do? Where do you start?"

"I'm not sure," Rory admitted. "Why don't you take Jaimee up to her cabin –"

"No. I want to stay with you and find the person who did this to my brother," Jaimee insisted.

"I know. But you need to get some sleep. Or at least some rest and something to eat," Rory told her. "I just have something else to do and then I'm going to get some rest myself. I'll call your cabin and keep you up to date."

Jaimee reluctantly agreed and she and Tanya Beno headed down the passageway for the elevators, ambling back and forth with the sway of the boat.

Rory looked at Beno as the two walked away. There was something odd about her reactions but he couldn't put a finger on what it was that bothered him. He shrugged to himself as the two women disappeared down the passageway. Probably just a personality thing, he thought.

Chapter 13

RORY HEADED BACK into the infirmary, closing the door behind him. Amundson and Dr. Rodriguez were back near Landry Morrissette's corpse and talking in a low, serious conversation. He approached them, "Captain Amundson?"

Captain Amundson turned from his conversation with Dr. Rodriguez, "Yes, Mr. Steele?"

"Would you have the passports for the four men who disappeared?"

"Yes. We found them in their staterooms. We put them in the ship's safe to ensure they don't get into the wrong hands," the Captain answered.

"Would it be possible for me to look at them?"

"Of course, whatever you need." Captain Amundson walked over and picked up one of the telephones for the cruise ship's internal phone system, "Mr. Kitchener. Would you step into the infirmary please?" He hung up the phone, "Mr. Myles Kitchener is working next door in the medical storage room. He joined our security department six months ago. Kristoffer Jensen told me he showed great promise. In fact, he was one of the men with Jensen that night. The others were Bern Nyhus and Kerk Bakken –"

A young, blond man, full of enthusiasm burst through the doorway just behind Rory. "Yes Captain, what can I do for you?"

Rory noted the man had a British accent. He was about 5 foot 10, four inches below Rory's height, with blond, curly hair and an athletic physique.

"This is Mr. Rory Mack Steele. He will be in charge of our security until further notice," Captain Amundson stated. "He needs the passports for the missing passengers. Also, issue him a cell phone that works through the ship's satellite connection and instruct every member of the security team to follow his instructions to the letter."

"Aye, aye, sir," Kitchener said, complete with a snappy salute. He made a brisk turn on his heels to Rory, "Follow me, mate...uh...Mr. Steele."

Rory saw the Captain smiling in amusement at the man's enthusiasm. Rory stepped through the door behind Kitchener and followed him down the passageway. Rory had a bit of difficulty keeping up with the man on the rolling floor. "Try not to go too fast, I still don't quite have my sea legs."

Kitchener turned and looked very apologetic, "I'm very sorry, sir. It won't happen again."

"No problem. And call me Rory."

"Are you sure?" Kitchener asked him.

"Yes, Myles, I'm sure. We're going to be working closely together and all this sir stuff will just get in the way," Rory explained as they reached the elevators.

"Thank you, sir - Rory," Kitchener said as he pressed the call button. "I'm from Liverpool and my family wasn't quite this formal." He pulled out a key card as the elevator doors opened and they stepped inside, "I'll override everything and take us directly to Deck 3." As the elevator began moving, Kitchener looked at Rory, "I take it you're going to be looking into the suspicious disappearances and deaths on board?"

Rory nodded, "Did Kristoffer Jensen talk to you about it? Or to anyone else?"

Kitchener nodded, "He really only started talking about it the day he died. His suspicions were triggered when we approached Mr. Moghadam about the man he'd been traveling with, the third man to disappear. He insisted there was no problem, but Mr. Jensen felt he was hiding something."

"Did you feel the same way?" Rory asked him.

"I wasn't really asked my opinion," Kitchener said.

"Well, I'm asking you now," Rory said.

Kitchener looked down at his boots for a moment and then said, "I grew up in a poor Liverpool parish, yeah? I saw lots of blokes dealing with the coppers, trying to throw them off the scent. That's what I saw with that Mr. Moghadam."

Rory nodded in understanding."One question I didn't ask the Captain, do we have full video surveillance onboard the ship?" Rory asked hopefully.

Myles shook his head, "No. We normally do, but not since we left port. There is a full surveillance system, but it went down about an hour out. Mr. Tate Nygaard, the Surveillance Manager, told Mr. Jensen one of the electronic boards had a short in it. And for some reason, there was no backup board in the storeroom."

"That's too bad," Rory said. But he took a breath and let it out slow, considering that tidbit of information. *That might be a little too convenient.*

"The Surveillance Manager has made arrangements to have one ready for pickup in George Town," Myles added. "But we don't reach the Grand Cayman Islands for a couple of days, unfortunately."

"Good, we need eyes," Rory said. "The Captain told me Jensen was conducting a ship-wide search when he was killed. How far did you get with it?"

"Everything except the top deck," Myles answered. "Mr. Jensen had gone up, while I waited for all the men to report to their assigned positions. Mr. Jensen had someone stationed at every access point to the next deck up, while the rest of the men searched from the bottom deck up."

"Why would he do that?" Rory asked.

Myles gave a shrug and a smile, "Mr. Jensen said he was always paranoid when it came to security. He wanted to make sure no one we were looking for slipped past us as we worked our way up. He said he learned *never* to take anything for granted, that you never knew what devious things humans could do next."

Rory nodded in understanding, "Smart man."

"Anyway, me and Nyhus and Bakken were at the bottom of the outer stairs, waiting for the order to move up, when we heard him yell man overboard."

"Did Jensen have a theory on what happened to the missing passengers?"

When we couldn't find the passengers - or their bodies - he felt they must have all been thrown overboard," Myles said.

"It would make sense," Rory agreed.

"Especially aboard a ship," Myles added. "It's the best way to get rid of a body, dead *or* alive."

"Why do you think Jensen's body wasn't thrown overboard, after he was killed from behind?"

Myles gave it a moment's thought and then he said, "Mr. Jensen was a pretty big guy. Someone would have to be very strong to throw his dead weight overboard that quickly. We ran up the stairs when we heard him yelling, and it wasn't more than a minute later that we found him."

The elevator stopped and Rory followed Kitchener out the door, "And no one saw anyone else when you got there?"

"Not a soul," Myles said as they moved along the passageway.

Everything Myles had said sounded plausible. But it still didn't get them any closer to figuring out who the killer was. It could still be anyone from the passengers or the crew. As he walked with Myles along the passageway, he realized he could feel larger swells under his feet, "Feels like the ship is moving more."

"Yeah," Kitchener agreed, "Ten to twelve foot swells it feels like. You get used to it after a while."

"Is it because of the storm the Captain was talking about?"

"Could be the first effects," Myles answered as he led Rory into the lobby and over to a spot that looked like a large, hotel reception area.

Rory followed the security officer past the large reception desk to a passageway behind it.

"Here we are," Myles said as he stopped in front of a door on the left labeled 'Purser's Office'. He stuck a key card into the lock and stepped inside.

Rory followed Myles into a room that had a desk, a number of filing cabinets, a gun cabinet and a large, gray safe. Kitchener spun the combination lock, pulled open the safe door and withdrew four passports.

"They all look to be American passports," Rory said as he looked at what Myles had in his hand.

"Yeah," Kitchener said as he looked through them. He passed one over to Rory, "This is the man we interviewed."

Rory flipped it open and read, "Name is...Diya al Din Moghadam."

"American passport but mid-eastern accent," Kitchener said.

"He was born in Yemen."

"This one was his traveling companion," Kitchener said as he passed another passport over to Rory.

Taking it in hand, Rory placed it on top of the other and flipped it open, "This one is...Jalal-Uddin Shammas."

"And these are the passports we recovered from the first two passengers who went missing," Kitchener said as he handed the final two passports to Rory.

Rory took them both, reading the contents in the third passport. "This one is...El-Saraya Mansour." He glanced at Kitchener for a moment, "Are we detecting a pattern here?"

Myles raised an eyebrow.

Flipping open the last passport, Rory said, "Uh huh, this one is Abdul Rehman Naser. The last three were US-born, but all the missing men have Arabic names. What do you think?"

Kitchener mulled it over as he shut the safe door and spun the combination lock, "Maybe they were terrorists...and someone patriotic took them out...?"

"If they were terrorists, why hide the fact you killed them and stopped whatever they were planning?" Rory asked.

Kitchener thought that reasoning over as he rubbed his chin. Then he raised his eyebrows and nodded, "You're right. Doesn't make sense...."

Rory looked at the Englishman for a moment and then said, "Let me ask you a question, Myles. Why did you automatically go to terrorism?"

Kitchener thought about it for a moment and then looked sheepish, "Right. Sorry. Considering all the bad news coming from the Middle East...because every missing man has an Arabic sounding name...I just thought terrorism...."

"I'm not chastising you, Myles. I'm just pointing out that you may have hit the nail on the head," Rory said.

Kitchener's forehead furrowed in puzzlement for a moment. Then he snapped his fingers, "Do you think someone had it in for them because of that? Because of their names?"

"That's one possibility," Rory said. "And that's the only one that makes sense right now. I would say we're possibly looking at a hate crime. Someone may have killed them because of what they represented in the killer's twisted mind."

"But...how does the death of Miss Morrissette's brother fit in?" Myles asked as his brow furrowed in puzzlement again.

"Maybe it doesn't," Rory said. "Or maybe he saw something like Kristoffer Jensen did. We can't rule out either possibility until we have more facts."

Myles nodded his head slowly as he pondered that thought. "So...where do we start?" he asked after a moment.

"At the beginning, like your Chief Security Officer did."

Myles rubbed the back of his neck, "Let's just hope we don't meet with the same fate, yeah?"

Chapter 14

DAY 4

MYLES KITCHENER inserted the master keycard into the key-card lock in the cabin door on Deck 7, the Verandah deck. "This is the cabin of first two passengers who went missing," he said as the door swung open.

Rory nodded as he sorted through the four passports he held, "Right. So that would be these two, El-Saraya Mansour and Abdul Rehman Naser. Both U.S. born citizens."

Myles hesitated before he stepped inside, "Shouldn't we be wearing booties, like they do in those crime shows, yeah?"

Rory nodded, "That would certainly make sense...if we had booties."

Myles grinned sheepishly, "I guess I watched too many crime shows when I was a kid, yeah?"

"No problem. You're just trying to do your job and these are difficult circumstances to run an investigation under."

Myles nodded and led Rory inside. It was a standard inside stateroom, barely 200 square feet of space with two twin beds and a single convertible sofa.

Rory stepped into the bathroom. There was a small tub with a shower head and nothing else beyond the standard ship towels.

There was no smell of soap or shampoo, so it definitely hadn't been used recently.

"Found something," Myles called out.

Rory stepped out of the bathroom to see Myles pulling a black suitcase out of a small closet. Another black suitcase was already sitting on the floor.

"Should we look in these?" Myles asked as he set the other suitcase down.

"That's what investigators do," Rory said as he squatted down beside the first suitcase. It was about 2 foot by 3 foot in size with hard polycarbonate sides, a carry handle, an aluminum telescoping handle with a push-button locking system and 2 wheels for easy rolling.

"Just not used to invading other people's privacy, I guess," Myles said as he squatted beside the other suitcase. It was the same size and configuration as the one Rory was looking at.

"Yeah, I can understand how you feel," Rory told him. "It can be really creepy when you know the person is dead, especially in the case where it's a young child. The last time they closed the suitcase, they had no idea you would be looking through it after they're gone."

Myles raised an eyebrow as he considered that Rory was saying. "You've had to do that, yeah?" he asked in a low voice.

Rory gave a brief nod of his head as he undid the latches on the suitcase and opened the lid.

Myles watched Rory for a brief moment as he sorted through the contents in the suitcase. "What exactly are we looking for?" he asked after another moment.

Shrugging, Rory said, "Anything that might help. You just never know sometimes until you see it. Right now, all I see is clothing."

Nodding, Myles opened up the second suitcase and began to go through the contents.

Rory found nothing of significance and he closed the suitcase.

"That's all I see too," Myles said. He began stuffing clothing back inside the second suitcase, "And considering some of the stuff I see passengers bring on board, these guys really traveled light."

"You're right," Rory agreed, "these guys were like monks. I didn't see any suits or formal wear." He looked up at the open door of the closet, "And there's nothing else in the closet? No garment bags? No smaller bags"

"No, nothing besides these two suitcases. But not everyone likes to get dressed up and go to the fancy dinner, though," Myles said.

"I agree. But did you see any swim trunks? Any shorts?"

Myles hesitated, thinking about what Rory had just said. Then he stood up, shaking his head, "No. That does seem strange, but...."

Rory nodded his head, "And not everyone is a sun worshiper either."

"Right," Myles agreed. "There are a lot of things you can do a cruise."

"So...what were these two passengers doing?" Rory asked as he stood up.

Myles had no answer as he looked around the room. He got down on his hands and knees and took a look under each bed. "Nothing," was all he said as he stood up.

Rory put his hands on his hips as he considered the situation. He had flown away on vacations with little more than a carry-on himself over the years, but something still didn't sit right with him in this situation. He just couldn't put a finger on it.

"I could contact the Shore Excursion Manager and the entertainment people to see if they signed up for anything," Myles offered.

"Let's go look at the cabin for the other two passengers first," Rory said after a few more moments.

Chapter 15

RORY FOLLOWED MYLES down the opulent stairway to Deck 5, the Promenade Deck, for the next missing passenger's cabin. This one was larger than the last one at just under 300 square feet. There was a small bathroom to the right of the entrance, two single beds and a small sitting area with a two seat sofa and a single chair on the far side. And just past that was a large picture window that provided a panoramic view of the ocean.

Myles stepped into the bathroom to check it out.

Rory went to the small nightstands next to the beds and checked the drawers. Nothing.

"Just towels in here," Myles yelled out. "Doesn't look like it's been used. Soap and stuff is still in their packages."

Rory moved over to the closet across from the blue sofa and opened the doors.

"And I don't see any shaving gear, no personal items at all," Myles said as he emerged from the bathroom.

Pulling out a black suitcase, Rory set it on the floor. "Check that one," he said as he reached back in and pulled out another black suitcase.

Myles slid the suitcase over, opened it and began to sort through the clothing.

Rory began to search through the other suitcase.

Finding nothing of interest, Myles tossed the clothing back into the suitcase and looked into the open closet, "Just like the other passengers. Not much in the way of clothing. No shorts or bathing trunks. And I don't see any suit or formal wear either."

"Same here," Rory said as he closed the suitcase.

Myles got down on his hands and knees, like in the other room, and looked under the bed again. He shook his head no as he stood up, "These guys were traveling really light as well. Doesn't make much sense, yeah?"

"Yeah, I agree," Rory said as he stood up.

"What now?"

Rory thought about it for a moment. He pointed down at the suitcases, "Anything look familiar to you?"

Myles srewed his face up, not sure what Rory meant. He shook his head and shrugged his shoulders.

"These two suitcases are the exact same make and model as the first two that we looked through," Rory stated.

Myles looked down in surprise, "You're right. I never noticed that. Do you think it means anything?"

"Maybe. Maybe not," Rory said. "But in an investigation, you never assume something is a coincidence until you can prove it otherwise."

Narrowing his eyes, Myles considered what Rory was saying.

"What do you think?" Rory prodded. He wanted to help Myles to learn to think like an investigator.

Myles stuck his hand out, "Could I see the passports?"

Rory drew them from his pocket and passed them over.

Myles flipped open each passport, "Mansour and Naser were traveling together, both are living in New York...this Shammas has a Philadelphia address and his traveling companion is living in Los Angeles."

"So they probably weren't shopping at the same stores where they bought their luggage," Rory reasoned.

"Unless they bought them online," Myles offered. "A lot of people do that these days."

It's a possibility," Rory agreed, "but it's a long shot that they would've bought them from the same online store."

"Maybe they bought them in Miami," Myles said. "Most passengers stay overnight, to make sure they make the cruise the next day."

"Again a possibility. But wouldn't it seem unusual for all four men to suddenly need new luggage?"

Myles nodded at the assessment as he continued to flip through the passports, "And there are no custom stamps for any other vacations or travel outside of the US for any of the men either."

"Are there any similarities in the dates of issue for each passport?"

Myles leafed back through each passport and shook his head slowly no, "All different dates between five and eight years ago."

"So, if you put it all together, what do you get?" Rory asked him.

Myles looked at Rory and raised his eyebrows, "Nothing?"

Rory picked several points off on his fingers, "All four had the same make and model of luggage. All four traveled light and didn't seem to care about formal dining...or being in the sun...or any other typical activity on a cruise. And this is the first travel outside of the US for all four men since they received their passports."

Myles gave Rory a sheepish grin as he handed back the passports, "So there are similarities. I was just too dumb to see them, yeah?"

Rory slipped the passports back into his pocket and gave him a slight shrug, "You're not dumb, Myles. You're just learning. Unfortunately, none of it may mean anything and none of it get us any closer to catching a serial killer. If there is one."

"You don't think there's a serial killer onboard like the Captain does?"

"We just need to keep an open mind on it," Rory told him. "We have a theory, but we need to let the evidence lead us to the correct conclusion."

Myles nodded his head in understanding, "Makes sense. So what do we do next?"

Rory gave his question some thought. He glanced around the room. As he had told Myles, they needed to let the evidence lead them to the conclusion. *The problem is we don't really have any evidence. That has to change quickly if we're going to prevent more deaths.* He looked at Myles, "How many people would have access to the two cabins we've looked at?"

"Normally just the steward who is part of the team assigned to each section," Myles answered.

"Do they have fingerprints on file?"

Myles nodded affirmation, "The cruise line requires job applicants to get police clearance from their country. They have to supply a certificate confirming they don't have any arrests, convictions or even criminal proceedings taking place when they're being hired. And they have to provide fingerprints so that security can verify their identity on the validity of the police clearance. The problem is all those records would be at the head office."

"That's fine," Rory said. "But we're going to need a number of things if we're going to do a half-decent investigation. Do you have a notepad?"

Myles dug into an inner pocket and pulled out a small notebook and pen.

"Good. You need to get talcum powder or baby powder...cocoa powder...a number of powder brushes, like the kind women use for makeup...."

"I can get those from the spa deck," Myles said as he wrote it down.

"We also need clear scotch tape...plastic sandwich bags...black and white construction paper...and scissors."

"What do you need all this for?" Myles asked as he looked over the list he had written down.

"It's a make-shift fingerprint kit," Rory told him.

Myles looked at the list of items again. "Really?"

Rory ticked the items off on his fingers, "The talcum powder is used to reveal fingerprints against dark surfaces, the cocoa powder against light surfaces. You lift a fingerprint with the scotch tape and apply it to the construction paper with the same color, dark or light, to allow you to examine it."

Myles nodded his head in understanding.

"We'll need to go over each room and see what we come up with. Issue instructions that no one comes into this room or the other one without your permission," Rory told him.

Myles nodded, "Okay, I'll go talk with the person in charge of the cabin stewards and secure the room. And I'll put together enough material for a dozen rooms. You never know...."

"Good thinking. We'll also need access to a computer and a scanner to digitize the fingerprints," Rory added.

"That won't be a problem."

"Good. Give me a call when you have everything on your list assembled and we'll start," Rory said. "While you're doing that, I'm going to check out Landry Morrissette's cabin. Did you get the information for that one?"

"Yes, it's on deck 14," Myles said. He wrote down the cabin number on a page in his notebook, ripped it out and passed it over to Rory. Then he headed off towards the stern of the ship.

Chapter 16

RORY STROKED HIS JAW, thinking, as Myles disappeared down the passageway. This would be a good deal of time to talk to the other security personnel that had been with the chief security officer the night he was killed. And doing it without Myles present would allow him to check their version of the story and test their trustworthiness. He pulled out his ship's cell phone and called each man, asking them to meet him at Morrissette's cabin. Then Rory headed forward, towards the central stairway. His sea legs had kicked in and he barely noticed the roll of the Caribbean StarLiner now. Reaching the staircase, he threaded his way through a group that was still laughing at their own struggles with the rolling movement of the huge ship. On deck 7, Rory saw a young security officer, hustling down the passageway towards the stairs. The man was probably 2 inches taller than Rory but appeared to be at least 20 pounds lighter. He had brown, stringy hair and a goatee. He read the name tag as the man came closer: Nyhus.

"Bern Nyhus?" Rory asked the man as he came closer.

The man looked startled, "Yes?"

Rory introduced himself and the tall, thin man apologized profusely for not knowing who he was. Rory noted the man had a Scandinavian accent.

"No problem," Rory said. "As we head up, can you tell me what happened the night the security chief, Kristoffer Jensen, was killed?"

"Yes sir," Nyhus said. The young man was quite animated and open about the investigation and the events of that night.

Rory noted the young Scandinavian seemed to be personally affected by the death of Jensen. Obviously, the chief security officer had been well-liked and had treated those under his command very well. Rory didn't find any inconsistencies or anything left out of the young man's account of things. And there were enough differences to show that Bern Nyhus and Myles Kitchener were telling things from their own personal viewpoint, rather than something that had been cooked up between the two. Once they reached deck 14 and headed for Morrissette's cabin, Rory asked Nyhus to fill him in on the particular features of this part of the ship.

The young security officer explained that the more sports-minded passengers tended to book down on Deck 12, the Sports Deck. It had a mini-golf course, a jogging track, sports courts, rock climbing, skeet and a lot of other features for the sports enthusiasts onboard. The next deck up was designated the Sky Deck. That was where families with young children tended to book a cabin. It had several kiddy pools, water parks, and other kid-friendly venues. In contrast, this deck attracted the younger, single set. It featured swimming pools, hot tubs, surf simulators and water coasters that made the entire deck a water playground.

It also included a number of adult-only areas such as nude activities.

Rory figured that was probably why Morrissette had been attracted to staying on this deck. He wondered if Landry's sister, Jaimee Morrissette was booked on this deck as well.

The other young security officer, Kerk Bakken was waiting outside Landry Morrissette's cabin when Rory and Nyhus arrived. Bakken was a few inches shorter than Rory and had a barrel chest, a ruddy complexion, and a shaved head. The man also had a Scandinavian accent.

Rory instructed Nyhus to guard the door while he went inside with Bakken to search. Rory found Morrissette's quarters to be a nice sized stateroom with the two single beds pushed together to make a queen-sized bed. There was also a small balcony area. As they searched the stateroom, Rory used the time to interview Bakken and compare his story to the one Nyhus gave and what Myles had told him.

The search itself turned up nothing out of the ordinary. But Rory did take note that Morrissette's clothing included the expected items for a shipboard cruise. They found several bathing trunks (including a skimpy Speedo), four pairs of shorts, three pairs of sandals as well as a pair of dress shoes and a suit for the more formal dining times. That made him think back to the search they had conducted in the other two rooms...and what they didn't find. Why were the other four men so different from what you would expect on a cruise? Did it mean anything?

Landry Morrissette's death was also a bit of a wild card in the investigation. The other four, plus the person who may have been thrown overboard on the night of Kristoffer Jensen's death, had all simply disappeared. If a serial killer was on board, why didn't Morrissette's body simply disappear as well? Then again, they didn't have the five other bodies. Maybe the first four had all died of asphyxiation as well and were thrown overboard, *after* they had returned to their cabins to die, like Morrissette. Then again, without the other five bodies, there was no way of knowing if they *were* dead. Still too many questions...and not enough in the way of answers.

Chapter 17

DAY 5

George Town, Grand Cayman Islands

RORY AND MYLES KITCHENER boarded the tender with nearly one hundred other passengers for the trip into the George Town Harbor. The water was emerald green and ocean spray whipped back through the open side windows as they rode the slight swells, cooling their faces against the hot sun. The smell of the salt water was exhilarating.

"I spent my last stop here talking with a cute police officer," Myles said with cocky smile. "She told me to call back anytime."

Rory smiled. "Guess you're going to find out if she really meant it."

"I'll have you know I did quite well with the birds back home," Myles chirped

"Just don't lay an egg. Like I said, we need her help," Rory said.

"Very funny," Myles replied. He watched the seagulls whirl over the gender for a moment. Then he shook his head, "I don't see why we don't just use the ship's communications system to contact her and get things going before we left."

"Because we don't know who the killer might be," Rory explained. "It could be a passenger...or it could be a crew member –"

"How do you know it's not me, then?"

"Because the Captain said you were with Bakken and Nyhus when you all heard Jensen yell man overboard before he was found dead," Rory explained. "Kerk Bakken and Bern Nyhus confirmed that. Hard to be in two places at the same time. And their version of events that night fits with yours. Each of you was consistent enough to be credible, but different enough that there was no obvious collusion."

Kitchener's jaw dropped. "You checked up on me?" he said with surprise.

"Isn't that we're supposed to be doing? Investigating and checking up on people?" Rory asked him.

Myles nodded as his face showed a red tinge of embarrassment, "I've got to get the hang of this being nosy business I guess. Yeah?"

"Yeah. Clearing murder suspects one by one is vital if we're going to narrow our focus to find the killer."

Myles blew out a breath and nodded in return. Then he was pensive for a few moments as he looked out at the sea, watching the swells break into white foam and spray as they struck the side of the tender. "Hard finding him like that," he said quietly.

"Jensen?"

Myles nodded his head slightly without looking away from the sea, "The man treated me well. He took an interest in me. That's not something a poor lad gets where I grew up...."

They rode in silence for the rest of the way, the amazing blend of Caribbean and modern architecture becoming sharper in detail as they drew closer to the old harbor city. Once they tied up at the tender dock, Myles Kitchener led the way through the crowd of locals, hawking their wares to the incoming wave of passengers near the Anchorage Center. Rory glanced back to see there were four other huge cruise ships sending tenders into the harbor. No wonder the streets were jam-packed.

"When I first came here off the ship here, I was surprised at how busy it was, beyond just the tourists and vendors," Myles said as they walked across the concrete pier to the road. "Then one of the older blokes tells me there are more than 600 banks and trust companies here. Can you believe it?"

Rory nodded, "I've had to chase money down here on a few cases. Businessmen love to hide their true wealth in off-shore accounts down here, especially when divorce comes calling."

"Really? I'll have to remember that once I get rich," Myles said with a laugh.

A quick walk through the crowds in the heat along Harbor Drive, up Shedden Road and then down along Elgin Ave, brought them to the central station for the Royal Cayman Islands Police Service. It was a three story building, decorated in various shades of browns and blues. Palm trees soared high overhead. The front entrance was busy with constables and people coming and going.

"There she is," Kitchener said. A smile broke out on his face and he waved at a beautiful, young woman just exiting the building. She had ebony skin, high cheekbones and wore a red and black police cap, black trousers with a red stripe running down the outside of each leg, a white blouse with a gold nameplate and a gold badge.

The young woman flashed a smile of brilliant white teeth in return, "Myles! You actually came back to see me."

"Why wouldn't I come back to see my favorite officer, yeah?"

"I'll bet you say that to a girl in every port you visit," she said with a mock sternness.

"Not true. Rory, I'd like you to meet Special Constable Teresa Morgan of The Royal Cayman Islands Police Service. Teresa, this is Rory Mack Steele. He's a ship's passenger who is presently acting as our head of security."

Special Constable Teresa Morgan looked directly into Rory's silver-blue eyes with intensity as they shook hands. She had obviously caught the gist of Myles' introduction and the question instantly formed in her mind. As she released Rory's hand, she cocked her head and looked directly at Myles, "Why would your ship have a passenger...?"

Myles opened his mouth to explain the situation and then looked like he thought better of it. He glanced at Rory.

Rory stepped into the conversation, "Mr. Jensen was struck by someone and killed –"

Special Constable Teresa Morgan's eyes opened wide, "That's terrible. I met him and he was so nice. Have they caught the person or persons responsible?"

"Not yet," Rory answered. "I have experience as a private investigator and was asked to lend my experience temporarily. The problem is...we don't know if it was a passenger or a crew member that was involved in the death. Because of that, I was hoping I could use your station to contact my office...."

"Instead of calling from the cruise ship's radio room?" Morgan asked. She looked at Myles again and then back at Rory, thinking for a moment. Finally she nodded, "Follow me. I'll clear it with the Chief Inspector...as a favor to you, Myles. If there is anything else you want to share...?"

When Myles gave her a slight shake of his head, she turned around and stepped back into the building.

"She knows we're not telling her everything," Myles whispered in concern as he followed her, "I hope this doesn't ruin my chance with her."

"Everything has happened outside their jurisdiction, so they wouldn't involve themselves anyway," Rory said in a low voice as they fell a few steps behind the constable. "And most of the deaths on board are still only suspicious. There's not much sense in actually using the term serial killer, until we know for sure."

"I guess that's true. But I still feel bad not saying anything," Myles whispered. "If she ever –"

"Are you two going to keep up? Or whisper like two little school girls passing gossip?" Morgan said back over her shoulder.

"Sorry," Myles said as he hustled after her.

TWENTY MINUTES LATER, Rory sat in front of a computer, using Skype to talk to his Uncle Murdock MacLeod in the New York office of Highlander Investigative Services. He explained what had happened. MacLeod turned the call over to their computer guru, Avis.

"Okay Rory, what do you need?" Avis asked when she appeared on the monitor's screen.

"I'm sending you an email attachment that contains the passenger list, the crew list and the list of dead or presumed dead.

I need you to dig into everyone's background. See if anything sticks out, any possible connections –"

"That's going to be thousands of names, isn't it?" Avis stated.

"Just do your best. I want you to start with anyone having an Arabic or middle-eastern sounding name," Rory said. "Since the missing passengers have Arabic names –"

"Could be a connection there. I'll cross reference for any reports of racism and the like," Avis said as she began keyboarding.

"Right. I've also asked a local policewoman to send a package to you by air courier," Rory added. "It has blood and tissue samples from the passenger who died of asphyxia but with no apparent cause."

"That definitely sounds suspicious," Avis said as she continued her busy keyboarding.

"It does," Rory agreed. "I'm also sending you digitized finger prints from the rooms of the victims. The captain of The Caribbean StarLiner contacted the owners and they've agreed to send you the fingerprints of everyone working on the ship. See if anything pops up."

"Okay," said Avis as she worked her keyboard. "You know, your sister Skye is not going to be too happy that you've turned her vacation surprise for you into a working holiday. You're supposed to be relaxing."

"Hey, she's the one who picked this cruise ship, not me," said Rory in retort.

"I'll be sure she knows that," Avis said as she continued to work away.

"Trouble maker."

"How do I get the info to you?" Avis asked him.

"I've sent you an email address on the ship that you can use to send me anything you dig up," Rory said. "Send it encrypted using my normal password."

"I didn't hear the magic word," Avis said as she worked away.

"Chocolate."

"And from Varsano's in Greenwich Village this time. No being cheap," Avis instructed with amusement in her voice and she closed the connection.

Chapter 18

ONCE HE WAS FINISHED, Myles took Rory back down towards the tender pier on Harbor Drive and up to the Margaritaville restaurant. The place was jam-packed with tourists that filled the place with a cheerful, party atmosphere. Myles and Rory climbed the creaky stairs to the second floor to have lunch on the outside veranda, where they had a great view out to the bay. They each had a couple of specialty cheeseburgers and tested a few of the 52 flavors of margaritas available. After they were finished, they headed back downstairs, discussing the English Premier soccer league and Myles' favorite team, Liverpool, who continually referred to them by their nickname; The Reds. As they neared the bottom of the wide stairs, a large group of people came up the stairs, heading up to the second floor.

Rory moved to the side of the stairs as he continued down. Myles moved to the side as well and just behind him. Half a dozen steps from the bottom, Rory and a young lady accidentally bumped shoulders. Rory turned sideways and smiled in apology to the young lady, "Sorry–"

Crack.

Rory's brain instantly registered the gun shot.

Someone grunted in pain.

Rory pushed the young lady down as he yelled, "Down! Everybody down!"

Crack.

A tall, thin ceramic pot, on the apron next to the stairs, exploded into sharp, jagged pieces.

Screams of terror filled the air of the restaurant as tourists dove for the floor.

Rory crouched on the stairs. From the corner of his eye, something over at the entrance caught his attention, something that stood out as unusual in a tropical setting.

A figure in dark clothing and wearing a black ski mask was on the far side of the restaurant, striding purposefully across the floor between the tables and obviously headed towards the bottom of the stairs. Some people screamed and cowered, while others dropped from their chairs and skittered away on their hands and knees.

Knowing he had to act fast, Rory glanced back. Myles was lying on his back on the stairs, two steps up, holding his shoulder. Rory slid up to him, "You hit?"

Myles nodded as he grimaced in pain.

Rory just grabbed the man's uniform, pulling him down the remaining six stairs and off to the staircase to the left, looking for cover.

Crack.

Splinters of old wood exploded as the bullet buried itself in the side of the stairway, just above Rory's head.

People who had been frozen in fear by the first gunshots, were now fleeing in two masses of hysteria, some towards the front door and some towards the back door of the restaurant.

Myles slid to the floor, sitting on his butt as he held his shoulder in pain.

"No, no, no, no! We have to keep moving," Rory said. He grabbed Kitchener's shirt and hauled him to his feet.

Crack.

A bullet whined close overhead and shattered a wall ornament.

Both Rory and Myles ducked and fell to their knees in reaction. Rory grabbed Myles by the shirt again, pulling at him and urging the man to keep moving. Together they began scrambling as low and as fast as possible to the back door of the restaurant, along with dozens of other fleeing vacationers.

In moments, the hysterical crowd burst through the back door, scattering in every direction.

Rory and Myles moved outside with them. Myles turned to the left but Rory grabbed his arm and stopped him.

Crack.

A bullet tore wood splinters off the door casing, close to Rory.

Myles ducked and swore. He turned to run and stumbled over someone's discarded shoe. He grimaced in pain when he broke his fall using his wounded arm.

Rory pulled Myles to his feet and steered him directly away from the building. "That way," he urged. He guided Myles across a dirt parking lot to a weather beaten wood building. Rory pulled Myles around the far corner just in time.

Crack.

A bullet clipped off the corner of the building, sending wood splinters flying.

Rory kept Myles moving, angling their run towards a line of building across a dirt lot and the street he could see between them. Rory spotted police officers running far to the right and towards the Margaritaville chaos. Within moments, Rory and Myles were on Cardinal Ave and moving quickly past a line of colorful shops.

Myles stepped on the edge of the cement sidewalk, now hobbling on a sore ankle and he grunting in pain with each step, holding his shoulder as well.

Rory moved Myles between two of the shops to take a look at the wound. "You're fortunate, the bullet just grazed you."

"How much pain do you get when the bullet actually goes in?" Myles asked through gritted teeth.

"Let's hope you don't find out." Rory kept Myles behind him while he peered around the corner, looking to see if the shooter was still in sight.

"Never heard of terrorism in a place like this before," Myles said as he leaned back against the green building and held his shoulder.

"I don't think that was terrorism," Rory said.

"Are you kidding? I saw the shooter," Myles said. "Dark clothing and a black ski mask...."

Rory glanced back at Myles, "You're right. But with all those people in the restaurant, how many were hit?"

Myles blinked his eyes several times, thinking, "I...."

"*We* were the target, Myles. Every single shot was in our direction. The shooter pursued us out the back of the restaurant and shot at us as we ran," Rory said. "There were no shots at anyone else." He peered around the corner again, looking up and down the street.

Myles frowned, "But...why would we be targeted?"

Rory was quiet for a moment, thinking deeply about each step of the attack. Then he turned and looked at Myles, "Actually...I don't think *we* were targeted at all. Every one of those shots came closer to *me* than to you...."

Myles held a hand on his wounded shoulder as looked at Rory for a moment, thinking back to the attack. Then he nodded his head, "When that young woman bumped into you on the stairs, you moved, yeah? That's when I heard the shot and I felt the pain in my shoulder. The bullet would've hit you right in the forehead. Instead...."

Myles was right. He hadn't realized how close death had actually come to him back there. That stirred a little anger inside and he clenched his fists, wishing he could get his hands on the shooter right now.

"Do you think it was the serial killer from the ship?" Myles asked in a quiet voice.

Rory nodded slowly and thoughtfully, "The person or persons responsible for the deaths must have found out I was helping with the investigation."

"That should narrow down our hunt," Myles suggested.

"Maybe," Rory said quietly as he considered who it might be. He looked at Myles, "Is your ankle okay to go?"

Myles pulled himself erect and nodded, looking angry, "I should be okay. With your help, we can get back to the ship fast. Then we'll talk to the crew and see who came off or went back on the tender, dressed like that. *Someone* is going to pay for all this pain."

Chapter 19

DAY 6

The Caribbean Sea

EARLY THE NEXT MORNING, Rory visited the infirmary. Myles Kitchener was having the dressing on his wound changed by Dr. Gonzalez. The first thing that struck Rory was the easy skill Gonzalez exhibited in gently caring for the wound while the floor underneath them was rolling.

"Morning mate," Kitchener greeted Rory cheerfully.

"Good morning." He was amazed at the resilience Kitchener exhibited, despite what he had gone through yesterday. "How does that feel this morning," Rory asked him, indicating the ugly red gash on Kitchener's left shoulder.

"Hurts like the blazes, but I'll live. Surviving the doctor's methods might be different though," Kitchener grumbled.

"Good morning, Mr. Steele," Dr. Gonzalez said. He smiled and winked at Rory.

Rory nodded a greeting in return.

"Anything?" Myles asked him hopefully.

Rory shook his head, "No. Kerk Bakken and Bern Nyhus kept watch until we sailed and nothing. And I was finally able to talk to the every staff member working the tenders yesterday. No one saw anyone dressed in dark clothing, coming or going. And someone dressed like that, would've stood out like a sore thumb, considering the heat. I even talked to the crew members working the lower doors while they restocked the provisions and other supplies. No one saw anyone –"

Myles cursed under his breath and then added with a bitter tone, "I knew they wouldn't. I was hoping, but...."

Rory's brow wrinkled in confusion, "Why do you say that?"

"Because I got an angry call from Special Constable Teresa Morgan on my cell phone before I came down here," Kitchener grumbled. "They found a black ski mask along with a black pullover and black trousers stuffed in a bag in a waste bin after the shooting."

That startled Rory."Why would she call you about it? She must have been guessing–"

"One of the responding coppers saw me struggling with the bloody wound when we got back to where the tender was docked. He recognized me from the station, from when we were using their computer."

"And she put two and two together," Rory said in understanding.

"Her superior is *not* too happy we brought a killer into port with us and gave no official notice," Myles added. "He's put in an official protest with the Captain...although Amundson is happy we didn't talk about a serial killer with them either, so he's okay with us. But...poor Teresa. Her superiors stripped the hide off her...."

"I'm sorry I dragged you into this," Rory said sincerely.

"No, it's fine mate. It's my job," Myles replied. "It comes with the territory, yeah?"

Rory nodded reluctantly, "Yeah, sometimes it just does."

Dr. Rodriguez finished the dressing, "See me again tomorrow, Mr. Kitchener. I think everything looks fine. But let's make sure you don't get infected while we're at sea. All right?"

"Yeah. Thanks doc," Myles said. He climbed off the table. "Oh!" he said suddenly. "I almost forgot, Rory. Morgan told me they found the handgun as well."

"The shooter dumped it? Any luck on prints?" Rory asked him hopefully.

Myles shook his head, No, sorry. She said there were no prints."

Rory felt deflated at that news.

"But get this," Myles said, as he paused a beat for emphasis. "She says...it was a plastic gun."

That surprised Rory. "A *plastic* gun! Are you sure?"

"That's what she said. Took them by surprise too," Myles said. "It was a 9 mm. Everything, except for the firing pin, was made from what their firearm's expert called an ABS plastic...whatever that is...."

"I'm familiar with it," Rory said as he mulled over the news. "Acrylonitrile butadiene styrene is a tough, strong thermoplastic material. It's readily available...and this changes things. Maybe it even helps us narrow down our pool of suspects."

"How so?" Myles asked him as they left the medical center.

"Think about it Myles," Rory said. He wanted to use this as another teaching point. "To this point we were just assuming someone tossed those passengers overboard...."

Myles raised an eyebrow, "You think they were shot?"

"It's a possibility."

"But if they *were* shot, then it could be anyone. How does that narrow things down for us?" Myles asked as they walked down the passageway.

"If they were shot, there was no guarantee the body would always fall overboard," Rory said, "If they were shot and fell on the deck...it would take some strength to lift the body...."

"Okay...so someone big enough or strong enough. That narrows things down," Myles said.

Rory let him think as they walked.

"But they would have to clean up the blood as well," Myles added as they reached the elevators.

"Right. An additional problem for the killer," Rory agreed. "But you're missing something important."

Myles tilted his head to the side as he looked at Rory.

"It's premeditated, Myles. Planned. The killer didn't just come aboard and go crazy because he saw some Arab looking people or whatever he's thinking in his sick mind. The killer even smuggled a weapon on board."

"Are you sure?" Myles asked, the skepticism quite apparent in his voice. "That wouldn't be easy...."

"Think about it, Myles. I highly doubt the shooter would have had time to buy a gun illegally once we docked at George Town before he attacked us –"

Myles snapped his fingers as he nodded his head in understanding, "And it's not likely you'd find a plastic gun like that on the islands either."

"Exactly. A standard gun maybe, but not something that exotic," Rory agreed. "But think about this...how many people would have the contacts to even buy a plastic gun before they boarded in the United States?"

"Not many I imagine," Myles said. "Maybe he printed one of those 3-D guns I've been hearing about in the news," he added after a moment of thought. "You know, the kind where they print it out of plastic or some other material, yeah?"

Rory nodded, "Possible. But how many people have access to that kind of technology?"

Myles nodded his head, thinking, "That would narrow the suspect pool, as they say."

"Exactly," Rory agreed as he pulled out his cell phone. "I'll call my office and have them add that to the parameters to search through."

"Do you think this might stop the killing?" Myles asked him. "If the killer doesn't have his weapon any more...."

"Unless he or she smuggled more than one on board," Rory said.

"But the firing pin was metal," Myles protested. "Our metal detectors –"

"Easy enough to remove the firing pin and place it in a set of nail files in your luggage or something that would pass by without a second look," Rory argued.

Myles took a deep breath and let it out in frustration, "So...if the killer *does* have another one, it's not likely we find it, even if we search the ship with metal detectors."

"Probably not," Rory said. He looked at Myles for a moment, "Both Bakken and Nyhus told me they haven't talked to anyone about the case...."

Myles nodded and then put a hand to his chest, "You don't think I did–"

"I just had to ask," Rory said. "Just like I asked them."

"Honest. I didn't–"

"That's good enough for me, Myles," Rory said as he put a re-assuring hand on the man's shoulder. "But that's what we have to do, ask questions. Right?"

Myles visibly relaxed, "Yeah. It's just the way you were looking at me...."

"You look for signs of deception when you ask questions," Rory explained. "You have to think like an investigator...or like a lawyer. Look for facial tics, lack of eye contact, body language...."

Myles nodded in understanding, "Mr. Jensen had some books on security and investigating. I guess I better start cracking those books, yeah?"

"When you get the time," Rory said. "Which reminds me, did Jensen do a report on his investigation? The first thing I did was check in his quarters and I didn't see anything."

Myles shook his head, "No. He was reluctant to start anything like that until he knew for sure. Public relations on a cruise ship and all that."

Rory nodded his understanding, "Too bad. Well, the Captain says he didn't say anything either. And I called Dr. Gonzalez last night and he hadn't said anything either–"

The elevator doors slid open and Jaimee Morrissette stepped out. Her eyes went wide, "Rory! Are you okay?"

"Of course. Why...?"

"It's all over the ship. They said you were shot at on the island and someone was wounded...."

"That was me, ma'am," Myles said as he lifted his wounded arm slightly.

"Are you okay?" Jaimee asked him as she stepped forward. The elevator doors closed silently behind her.

"Just a flesh wound as they say in the movies," Myles answered a little proudly.

"Thank god. You could've been killed," she said as she looked from Myles to Rory.

Rory took the opportunity to ask her the same question he had asked the others, "Jaimee...did you say anything about the investigation to anyone..?"

Jaimee Morrissette shrugged, "Just to some of the people who were at the table when Landry took sick. They saw me crying and I just told them what had happened. And that you were looking into it. Why? Was it wrong?" She put a hand to her mouth, "I'm sorry, I didn't realize...."

"It's okay. It's understandable under the circumstances," Rory said.

"I'm so sorry," Jaimee repeated.

"That's okay. And maybe it'll work out for the better," Rory said, trying to ease Jaimee's sense of guilt.

But Jaimee didn't look convinced as she took a darting glance at Myles.

"He's right ma'am. It's okay," Myles said.

"Actually, you can help us with that part of our investigation," Rory added, trying to get her to forget about her faux pas.

"How?" Jaimee asked. She bit her lip.

"We need to know everything that happened that night," Rory explained. "Can you give that information to Myles?'

Jaimee nodded, "Yes, of course."

"Myles, why don't you go with Ms. Morrissette and make sure we have an accurate list of *everyone* who was at the table with Landry Morrissette that night. Then find a quiet spot and invite everyone there for a quick interview. Call me when you're ready."

Myles nodded affirmation.

Rory held up his cell phone, "Meanwhile, I'll make that call to my office that we talked about."

Chapter 20

TWO HOURS LATER, Rory entered the lounge Myles had commandeered on the Upper Promenade on Deck 11. He was immediately impressed with the rich, redwood and golden overtones of the large space. A large, upscale bar filled half the room on the right-hand side, The wall on the far side was sheer glass and allowed an amazing panoramic view of the white capped ocean the cruise ship was plowing through. The beauty of the place was also a reminder of what he was missing because of the deaths on board. But there wasn't much he could do about it now. There would be time for pleasure later, once he insured no more people would die.

He spotted Myles across the rolling floor. He was at a long table surrounded by plush chairs. Nine of them were filled with people in casual attire. Those would be the passengers who were sitting at dinner with Landry Morrissette the night he died. Rory didn't recognize any of them.

Myles stood up at the end of the table as Rory approached, "Mr. Steele. I was able to find everyone, sir."

Bakken and Nyhus stood up at the other end of the table.

"At ease gentlemen," Rory said with some mirth as he motioned for them to sit.

Myles moved to another chair, leaving the one at the head of the table for Rory to use.

But Rory preferred to stand. He put his hands behind his back as he stood at the head of the table, "I want to thank everyone for coming here."

"What's this all about?" an elderly woman asked him. She gestured to Myles, "This officer said you wanted to talk to us about the night that young man took sick. We really don't know anything, you know."

"She's right," the elderly gentleman sitting beside her said. "Surely you can't think one of us had something to do with his death?"

"It's just part of our investigation," Rory told them. "We just need to know what happened that night, the sequence of events—"

"All I know is that he said he was feeling sick at the end of dinner," offered a buxomy redhead.

Her tight, low-cut T-shirt told Rory the woman knew what her assets were and how to play them up. Especially when she jutted her chest out a little more and offered the hint of a smile as he looked at her.

Rory tore his eyes from the double-D's and addressed everyone at the table, "This won't take long, I assure you. First question. This is *everyone* that was at that table with Landry Morrissette that night. Correct?"

The passengers looked around and everyone nodded after a moment of reflection.

"Good. Now...was there anything unusual that happened that night during dinner? Any little thing you can think of?" Rory asked them.

Everyone looked around again and they all shook their head no.

"It wasn't any different from any other night," a younger man said. He had a blue-dyed, faux-hawk haircut.

The young, dark-haired woman beside Mr. Faux-hawk spoke up, "Other than you-know-who showing up." Her eyes had a look of delight in them.

Rory noted several of the other younger ones around the table nodding eagerly. "Who would that be?" he asked.

"Loretta Black," a young woman announced. She had a spike hairdo and an amazing peacock sleeve-tattoo on her upper right arm.

"Who?" the elderly man asked.

"The television star. It was really her," peacock sleeve-tattoo said as she looked at the others in excitement.

The elderly man looked to the elderly woman beside him and they both shrugged their shoulders. They still didn't know who the young woman was talking about.

Rory interrupted the excited chatter around the table, "Why did she stop by?"

"She stopped to talk to the young man who died. She seemed to know him *very* well," the buxomy redhead said, with a touch of sarcasm.

Mr. Faux-hawk nodded, "Yeah, she knew Landry alright...was that his name? Yeah, she knew him by name." He sat forward, as if he was offering some confidential, juicy gossip, "I asked him about it, when we both went to the washroom during dinner. Apparently they had met at one of the dance clubs the second night out of Miami...and then she simply showed up at his cabin with a bottle of champagne."

The elderly couple wasn't too impressed with the implications but the younger ones took it in stride.

"Way to hook up on a cruise," said the young woman with the peacock-sleeve tattoo. She gave a fist pump.

Rory felt a little foolish. Loretta Black's visit to his own cabin wasn't quite the special occasion he had assumed. Then a thunderbolt struck him. Landry Morrissette was the young man Loretta Black had been arguing with at Coconuts Bar and Restaurant back in Cozumel, Mexico! Black's argument with Cassiopeia Lopez took on more meaning. Loretta Black definitely had a volatile temper. If she was angry at Landry, how far would she go?

"Was there anything else that happened?" Myles asked the passengers around the table after a moment. "Even the *smallest* thing could be important."

Rory looked at him and nodded, glad to see him trying to become a real investigator.

Once again, everyone around the table looked at each other and each shook their head no.

"Were there any changes in the seating assignments for the table that evening?" Myles asked.

That question received another negative response from the passengers around the table.

"I checked with the server and the assistant server assigned to your table that evening," Myles said, as he pulled out his notebook from his jacket and looked at it. "According to them, Mr. Morrissette had the surf and turf. Do you know if that's accurate?" he asked as he looked around the table.

"Yes it is," the elderly lady said. She gestured to the man beside her, "He offered my husband a taste of the lobster because he said it was so good. But my husband is allergic to seafood."

The elderly man nodded, "I break out in hives like you can't believe. One time–"

"He did have that extra dessert," interjected a young brunette who had been silent to this point.

"True," the buxomy redhead agreed.

"Why does that stand out?" Kerk Bakken asked. Then the man shrunk back as he looked at Rory, as if he was overstepping his boundaries.

Rory gave a quick nod of appreciation, "That's a very good question."

Kerk Bakken's countenance brightened with the praise.

Rory looked directly at the young brunette, "Why do you remember the extra dessert?"

"Because one of the servers was offering it around," she answered. "That Landry had just finished his cheesecake, when the server came around with a piece of Black Forest cake. Landry grabbed it before I could. I just *love* Black Forest cake–"

"And you didn't miss anything, because you ordered a second piece of your own right after that," teased the buxomy redhead.

The young brunette gave her a big smile, "Yes I did. Two in fact."

Rory and Myles exchange glances.

"Anything else you can remember?" Rory asked them.

Everyone shook her head no at this point.

"Okay. Thanks for coming everyone. If we have any other questions, one of us will contact you," Rory said.

The passengers rose and headed off, quite talkative amongst themselves as they left the lounge.

"Do you think that means anything, the extra dessert?" Myles asked Rory.

"I'm not sure," Rory answered honestly. "But it doesn't hurt to follow up on it." Something else came to mind and he asked Myles, "Did the Surveillance Manager get the video surveillance working? He was supposed to pick up a new electronics board in George Town...." His voice trailed off when he saw Myles shaking his head no.

"He did pick up the board, but the video surveillance system is still not working for some reason," Myles said. "He has someone going through the software now with a fine tooth comb. And he's checking every part of the system across the ship, looking for the problem. He can't figure out what's wrong."

Rory didn't like that. It was too convenient. But at this point, there wasn't much they could do about it. "Okay. Check with the staff working the dinner that night. See if you can find out who was offering that Black Forest cake around," Rory instructed the officers. "It's all we have to go on right now."

"Okay. I'll take Kerk and Bern with me, unless you need them," Myles said.

"No, that's good," Rory agreed. "Your search for the server among all the staff working that night will go faster if you share the task. We need to find the killer or killers before someone else innocent dies. While you're doing that, I'll try and find Jaimee Morrissette. I need to ask her something."

"After we talked, she told me she would be up on the Sun deck, where her cabin is, if we needed her," Myles said.

"Okay, thanks."

Myles turned to Bakken and Nyhus and spoke with a sense of urgency, "Okay mates, let's go find that server and learn what he has to say."

As the three members of the ship's security team left the lounge, Rory's thoughts went back to Loretta Black. And her temper. Or was it jealous rage? He remembered a line from Shakespeare. In modern vernacular it went 'Beware of jealousy, my lord! It's a green-eyed monster that makes fun of the victims it devours.'

Chapter 21

RORY STEPPED OUTSIDE onto the Sun deck into glorious sunshine. The scent of salt water mixed with the chlorine from the large onboard swimming pool. The laughter and chatter that carried across the deck, was a stark contrast to the task he and his small team of security officers were engaged in. It emphasized the need to find the killer before one of these innocent people lost their life. They were only here because they wanted to enjoy a cruise. Even Rory's appreciation of the bevy of young beauties, dressed in the skimpiest of swimwear, was muted. Hard to enjoy yourself when you're tasked with the responsibility of keeping them all safe.

Rory began walking among the passengers. Jaimee hadn't answered his knock on her cabin door, so he assumed she would be out here in the hot sun somewhere. Although he found it difficult to believe the young lady would be back to sunning herself so soon after her brother's death.

As he wandered through the sunbathing passengers, Rory spotted Tanya Beno lying poolside. Her black, skimpy bathing suit left little to the imagination. But it also confirmed something else. Rory remembered her firm handshake that had suggested strength. And her ease at lifting Loretta Black off the ground with one arm back in Cozumel testified to that strength. Her near nakedness revealed the truth. She looked like a competitor in a professional fitness contest, complete with the requisite six-pack abdomen and guns for arms.

"Are you just going to stand there staring...or will you join me?" Tanya asked him as she patted the deck chair beside her.

Rory flashed an embarrassed smile, "Sorry about that."

"No problem. And especially no problem with a good look-ing man checking me out," she replied coyly as she pushed her sunglasses up on her head. "You never know where it might lead."

"I wasn't—" Rory decided a denial would just sound hollow since he *had* been checking her out. He gave her a half-smile of acknowledgment, "Actually...have you seen Jaimee Morrissette?"

"Lucky girl," Tanya said with a raised eyebrow.

Rory shook his head no, "I just need to talk to her about her brother."

Tanya considered him for a moment and then lowered the sunglasses back over her eyes. "I left her up on the Observation Deck. There's a lounge at the bow of the ship. She just wanted to sit alone for a while."

"Thanks."

There was no further comment from Tanya.

Rory turned and made his way back across the crowded deck and back inside to the central staircase. Climbing the stairs to the observation deck, he made his way through the chattering crowd to the front of the ship. He found Jaimee Morrissette sitting at a small table in the front lounge. There were only two other peo-ple sitting on the far side of the room. Jaimee was staring glumly through a glass wall that offered a spectacular view of the ocean.

Rory stopped a few steps away, not wanting to interrupt her. And yet he needed information if he was to stop a killer. He finally stepped closer. "Do you mind if I join you?" he asked in a quiet voice.

Jaimee was startled out of her thoughts and she lifted her sunglasses. There were tears in her eyes. She set the sunglasses down on the table and self-consciously wiped the tears from her eyes, "Sure."

Rory sat in the chair on the other side of the small table, "You're sure I'm not bothering you?"

"No, it's fine. I was just thinking about...." Her voice wandered off as she gazed out over the sea through the glass wall again.

A bar waiter wandered by the table, offering colorful drinks on a tray.

Jaimee shook her head no and went back to staring at the sea.

Rory took a green colored drink and sat quietly sipping it.

Jaimee finally spoke after a few awkward moments, "Have you found anything out about Landry? Did the passengers he sat with that night give you any help in figuring out what happened?"

Rory set his drink down on the table and shook his head, "No. We're still working on it. I have three men from ship's security talking to the staff who were on duty that night."

Jaimee just nodded her head as she continued looking out over the sea. It was a beautiful sunny day and the sea was fairly calm but she obviously wasn't enjoying any of it.

Rory ran a finger through the condensation on the outside if his glass, "Would you mind if I asked you a question about that night?"

Jaimee glanced at him and gave a small nod after a moment.

"The other passengers at your brother's dinner table said that Loretta Black stopped to talk to your brother that night. How long did they know each other?"

"They didn't really," Jaimee answered. "Loretta Black was sitting at the table I was assigned to for dinner. We just struck up a friendship from the beginning. She met Landry when we went to the disco on the promenade the second night out. They danced a little and had a laugh, but other than that...."

Rory nodded, not wanting to say anything further at the moment.

"And speaking of Loretta, that brings up that episode that happened on Cozumel when we saw you," Jaimee added. "Loretta is really sweet but...she *does* seem to have a tendency to blow up over men. When she saw you with that other lady...well...I'm sorry that it happened Rory, I really am."

"That's fine. It wasn't your fault," Rory told her.

Jaimee shrugged, "I know. But...I just wanted you to know how sorry I was."

Rory decided he needed to broach the subject. "Were you aware that Loretta Black also had a heated argument with Landry on Cozumel that same day?"

"She did?" Jaimee seemed genuinely surprised.

Rory nodded, "I saw them myself at a place called Coconuts. You weren't there?"

Jaimee shook her head no. She looked genuinely confused. "Tanya Beno and I ended up on our own." Then Jaimee rolled her eyes, "Loretta latched on to *another* young man from the ship and wandered off, batting her eyes at him."

Rory chewed on his lip for a moment, thinking. "Do you know who he was?"

Jaimee shook her head no, "I saw him on the Sun Deck a few times. Good looking, college-kid type. But I don't know his name. Sorry."

Rory wondered if there was a way to find out who he was. It might give him a timeline for Loretta–

A moment later, Jaimee spoke, her eyebrows knit together in thought, "I have no idea what Loretta and Landry would be arguing about. That doesn't make any sense. Unless she had designs on him...."

Rory involuntarily raised an eyebrow.

Jaimee caught the gesture and grimaced, "That's kind of dumb of me, isn't it? Loretta had designs on *every* man she met. Why would my own brother be any different." She looked out over the sea, shaking her head.

Rory stayed mum, waiting for any further revelations or information.

"The little bitch," Jaimee whispered under her breath. She looked directly at Rory and cocked her head, "Do you think she had anything to do with...?"

Rory just shrugged, "I have no idea. I'm just asking questions and trying to figure out what happened. The more pieces I can fit together–"

"Do you want me to talk to Loretta?" Jaimee said, her nostrils now flaring with anger. "Do you want me to find out why she and Landry were arguing?"

"No, that's fine–"

"But...we can't get let her get away with it," Jaimee insisted.

"We're not letting anyone get away with anything," Rory assured as he sat forward. "An argument is not proof of anything."

Jaimee puffed her cheeks out and blew out a breath, obviously frustrated.

"Do me a favor," asked Rory, "just keep an eye on her. Let me know if she does say anything about it. Can you do that?"

Jaimee nodded but she didn't look too happy about staying silent.

Rory wondered if this conversation might not turn out to be a bad idea. She had already rolled through a gamut of emotions in just this short conversation. His thoughts were interrupted when his cell phone rang. He pulled it out and answered, "Hello?"

"Mr. Steele, it's Myles. We have a problem."

Chapter 22

RORY HURRIED into the Promenade on Deck 5 and threaded his way through the other passengers, looking for the signs pointing the way to the Guest Relations desk. He saw it midway down the Promenade and spotted Myles standing beside a long counter with two other men in ship's uniform. All three had a look of concern. "You sounded like it was urgent," Rory said as he approached them.

"It is. Me and Bakken and Nyhus didn't make it to the galley yet like you asked," Myles said apologetically.

"That's fine," Rory assured him. "You said there was a problem...?"

Myles nodded and gestured to the two men beside him, "Mr. Larson here is the Chief Purser. Mr. Nystrom is the Passengers Service Desk Officer. The service desk acts like the front desk of an upscale hotel. It provides all kinds of guest services like exchanging traveler's checks, we have safety deposit boxes, banking services for passengers–"

"One of the other things I also care for is the lost and found service," Nystrom interrupted in a heavy Norwegian accent. His brow was furrowed.

"Okay," Rory nodded, wondering where this was going. All three men were obviously worried about something,

"One of the porters found this on the top deck early this morning, just after the sun came up," Larson added as he extended a hand and held out a woman's black, clutch handbag that glittered with sequins. "It was just lying on the deck in the open," he added ominously.

That didn't sound good in light of recent events on board. Rory took the handbag and clicked it open, looking inside.

"Take a look at the passport," Myles prompted him.

Rory took out the dark-colored American passport and flipped it open with one hand. Rory felt his blood run cold and he whispered, "Cassiopeia Angelica Lopez." He handed the handbag back to Larson, as he continued to stare in shock at Cassie's face. Like all passport photos, she wasn't smiling and that only seemed appropriate, considering the circumstances and what this might mean.

"We were naturally concerned," Larson continued, "Mr. Nystrom attempted to return it personally to Ms. Lopez but–"

"There was no answer when I personally went to her cabin," Nystrom said. "Under the circumstances, I was extremely concerned. So the steward and I entered the cabin. The bed was still made up, Mr. Steele! There was *no* indication anyone had been there during the night."

"On a normal cruise we don't care if someone stays in their own cabin...or with someone else," Larson said. "But under the circumstances...considering what's been happening, we decided to contact Mr. Kitchener immediately."

Just then a three note chime sounded and a female voice made an announcement, "Would Cassiopeia Lopez please con-

tact or go to the Guest Relations desk on deck five, the Promenade. There is a message waiting for you." The message was repeated once more.

Rory looked at the other men, wondering why someone was
looking for Lopez.

"I sent Bakken to have that announcement made," Myles said.
"And I sent Nyhus back up to Ms. Lopez's cabin in case she shows
up there."

Rory nodded, deep in thought, "Okay. Good. That's good
work, Myles. And thank you, gentlemen. If you do hear from
Cassiopeia Lopez, please let one of us know immediately."

Nystrom and Larson acknowledged the instructions and
stepped away into a small office behind the Guest Relations desk.

Rory was torn. With this turn of events, there was someone
they had to talk to...and right now. But he felt foolish. Once
Myles realized the contact Rory and the next target of their investigation had the first night out...he just hoped it wouldn't un-
dermine his credibility and have Myles think less of him - or trust
him less - which could be a problem in the ongoing investigation.

Myles watched Rory, aware he was going through some internal struggle and he simply waited patiently

"Myles," Rory said finally, "come with me. There's someone we
have to talk to *right now*."

Myles nodded and then had to rush to keep up with Rory.

Chapter 23

RORY STAYED QUIET as they climbed the opulent stairs to the Vista deck. The next person they needed to interview had invited Rory to stop by her penthouse suite anytime. He was sure this was *not* what she expected. Rory led the way through the passageways and finally stopped outside cabin #91008. He pounded on the door, "Loretta Black, open up!"

Myles stood beside him, eyes wide in surprise, "Why...?"

Rory pounded on the door again, "Loretta! Are you in there?"

Myles looked nervous, "Maybe she's out...?"

Rory shook his head firmly, "No way. It's far too early for this one." Rory put his hand on the door handle as he said to Myles, "Open it up."

Taking the master keycard from his pocket, Myles slipped it into the lock.

Rory opened the door a crack, calling out loudly, "Loretta? Loretta Black?"

There was no answer.

Pushing the door open, Rory stepped inside.

These quarters were more luxuriant and much larger than Rory's penthouse suite. There was an amazing glass wall on the far side, leading to a good-sized balcony. And there was Loretta Black, in a skimpy bathing suit, lying on a lounge chair outside on the balcony and sunning herself.

Rory strode across the floor purposefully and roughly slid open the balcony door, speaking firmly, "Loretta? Didn't you hear me calling you?"

Loretta calmly pushed the sunglasses up on her forehead and sneered, "*What* are you doing in my room? I didn't invite you in here–"

"Get in here *now*," Rory said loudly.

Loretta Black got up in a huff, threw her sunglasses down on the lounge chair and took a step towards Rory, "How dare you!"

"I do dare," Rory said firmly. He stepped back inside, picked up a robe and threw it at her as she stood just outside the sliding door, "Put this on and get in here. *Now.*"

Loretta Black caught the robe and glared at him as she put it on. She tied the belt sharply as she stepped back inside the penthouse, sulking, "You were more fun when I visited *your* cabin."

Rory saw Myles turn his head and look at him with a start.

"Sit," is all Rory said as he pointed to a chair.

"You can't tell me what to do. I'm an American citizen–"

"We're in international waters," Rory replied sternly, "I'm the law here."

Loretta sneered as she sat down in a huff, crossing her legs and her arms. The robe parted, revealing her shapely, tan legs.

Rory wasn't having any of her tactics distract him. He reached down and flipped the robe over to cover her.

"You didn't mind looking at my legs before," she said with a sneer.

Rory decided the direct, blunt approach would be best. And the quickest...before she sidetracked this whole interview. Lives were at stake. "You were arguing with Landry Morrissette back in Cozumel. What were you arguing about?"

"Is that what this is about? Are you jealous, Mr. Steele?" she said as she raised an eyebrow. "I'm sorry if you took our little bit of fun as anything serious."

Rory could see Myles look in his direction again. "Answer the question," Rory said firmly.

Loretta sneered again.

He turned to Myles, "Which deck did you say the jail was located on?"

Myles raised an eyebrow, "The holding cells are below, on deck one."

"You can't do that," Loretta protested as she sat up straight. She looked at Myles, "I'm an American citizen and he can't treat me like this."

"We're not in America, we're in International waters. And he can, because he *is* the law on this ship," Myles simply said. "That's the law of the sea."

Loretta frowned and sat back, crossing her legs and arms again. The robe fell open and she reached down and roughly covered her bare legs again. Her mouth twisted this way and that until she said, "He was two-timing me with that little *bitch* and I wasn't having *any* of it...." Her voice trailed off, and her face reddened, realizing how it sounded, considering what had happened to Landry Morrissette. She let out a huffy breath and looked away, angry.

"And which little bitch would that be?" Rory asked her.

Loretta was quiet for a moment and then shrugged, "I don't really know her name."

"Really," Rory said sarcastically.

"Yes, really," Loretta answered. Her foot started bouncing.

"You only met Landry on the second night out from Miami. Isn't that right?"

Loretta didn't answer.

"You're extremely possessive, aren't you? Every man you meet belongs to you, isn't that true?" Rory prodded.

Loretta remained silent but her jaw clenched in annoyance.

"And you have quite a temper. I saw that when you tried to it attack Cassiopeia Lopez," Rory reminded her.

Loretta's knee began to bounce as she looked up at Rory, "I didn't *touch* your little girlfriend."

"Only because someone intervened and pulled you away in a blind rage."

Loretta's knee bounced faster as she bit her lip, trying to maintain control.

Rory was aware Myles was looking at him again, obviously wondering what had happened behind the scenes. "And you know very well she's not my girlfriend. We met at the Captain's table, just like you and I did on the first night out. You know that."

"If you say so," Loretta said sharply.

Rory paused his questioning for a moment, narrowing his eyes as he looked at the famous television star. "How far are you willing to go when you don't get what you want?"

Loretta's knee continued to bounce. Then it stopped suddenly and her eyes blinked, "You...you can't suspect *me* of doing something to Landry?"

Rory shrugged, "How far are you willing to go, when that temper of yours ignites in full flame, Loretta?"

"That's ridiculous," she said in a huff.

"I *saw* your rage, remember? You said you were going to kill Cassiopeia Lopez–"

"It's just an expression,'" Loretta grumbled as her knee bounced again.

"You're a television star," Rory said as he spread his arms wide, "your whole life is on view. Are we going to find other incidences on the Internet of that temper of yours igniting?"

Loretta was taken aback by that comment. "That doesn't mean anything," she said in a harsh whisper.

"It doesn't look good for you *Mz. Black*," Rory said sarcastically. "When this goes before the judge–"

"'That's ridiculous. You can't do that," she protested loudly.

"Were you with Cassiopeia Lopez last night?" interjected Rory quickly.

Loretta looked puzzled, "No–"

Rory's voice was harsh, "Are you sure? Are we going to find witnesses who saw you two together last night?"

"No!" protested Loretta loudly. "I'm telling you, I didn't see her. What does she have to do with–?"

"She disappeared last night," Rory yelled. "We found her handbag on the upper deck."

Loretta Black looked stunned.

"Did you lose your temper again? Maybe it was an accident? You lost your temper and–"

"No," Loretta Black said. Her voice was suddenly very subdued, "I'm telling you, I didn't see her last night."

"Where *were* you last night?"

Loretta answered quickly, "I went to a show on the Upper Promenade...and then I spent the rest of the evening in the casino on the Promenade."

"You do realize we have security cameras on every deck? In the passageways, in the casino...?" interjected Myles, letting his voice trail off with the implications that they would know if she was lying.

Loretta shrugged a little and held her arms tighter around her upper body. "I *may* have slipped into a small backroom with someone for a minute," she said in a quiet voice.

Rory looked at her. She didn't look so sure of herself right now. Rory pushed harder, "With who?"

Loretta fidgeted with the tie on her robe and shrugged, "I was drinking a lot last night, having fun...I don't remember much...."

"Very convenient, wouldn't you say," Rory remarked to Myles.

Myles nodded, "And very suspicious, under the circumstances. When a person doesn't have an alibi...."

Rory looked hard at Loretta, "He's right."

Loretta uncrossed her arms and legs and held her hands out to Rory, "Look, I admit I have a temper. I admit I get angry when...but I didn't do anything to Landry. Honest. It's the truth. And I *didn't* do anything to Cassie. I swear to you."

Rory narrowed his eyes as he considered Loretta Black and her truthfulness. He decided he wasn't going to get any further at this point. He stabbed a finger directly at her, "*You* are confined to this cabin until I say otherwise–"

"But–"

"It's either here or down in a cell. Your choice."

Loretta Black sat back angry, crossing her arms and her legs.

Rory glanced at Myles, "Have one of the security men stand guard outside this cabin. She doesn't leave until I say she can, understood?"

Myles nodded once.

Rory looked back at Loretta and said in a firm, quiet voice, "You better hope we find another answer because it doesn't look too good for you right now. On *both* deaths. If you have *anything* else to tell us, I would advise you to do it now."

Loretta just took a deep breath and let it out as she stared off into the corner, obviously not happy.

"Let's go." Rory turned and headed for the door.

Myles followed him.

Outside in the passageway, as Myles closed the door, Rory turned to him. "Any questions? Anything you need to know about her and me–"

"No," Myles replied quickly. "I can understand the situation and how things developed. I just wish you would've told me before we went in there."

Rory nodded. "Since I left the army ten years ago, I've gotten used to working on my own. And to tell you the truth, I wasn't sure how you would take it. But that's no excuse. I guess we're all learning - or relearning."

Myles nodded, accepting the explanation.

Rory thought back to Myles' threat about the security cameras showing where Black would have been that night, "We don't have video surveillance yet, do we?"

Myles gave him a sly smile, "She didn't know that."

Rory smiled and nodded approval at the ploy. He looked at the cabin door and then back at Myles again, "Better make that two men on guard. Ms. Black has a way of manipulating men and those two will have to look out for each other if you know what I mean?"

Myles nodded as he took out his cell phone. "I'll explain the situation in no uncertain terms. No lookie and no nookie."

Rory smiled again, "Something like that."

"Do you really think she did it?" Myles asked as he looked through the list of numbers on the phone for the one he wanted.

Rory half shrugged and shook his head, "I have no idea. She has a temper, that's for sure. I've seen it in action. And anyone is capable of anything. After all the years of being involved in the investigative business, that's the one thing I *am* sure of."

"Now what?" Myles asked him as he hit speed dial and waited for someone to answer.

"After you get things set here, have Bakken and Nyhus meet you in the galley and continue your search for the server," Rory instructed.

Myles nodded, "What are you going to do?"

"I'll go check out Loretta's story about being in the casino and slipping into a room. Maybe her new beau, whoever he is, will give her an alibi," Rory said sarcastically.

Chapter 24

RORY ENTERED the casino on the Promenade. The place was very busy and the sounds of laughter and chatter, interspersed with the whirling sounds of the slot machines, reached his ears. The decor was gold and glitzy, with varying shades of brown accents. The staff was dressed in dark brown pants, dark sleeveless vests and white shirts with brown bow-ties. Rory walked past a line of passengers playing Roulette. A number of other passengers were crowded around the craps table, shouting encouragement as someone rolled the dice. A cheer went up. Rory continued on and then saw two men he recognized playing at the blackjack table. They had both been at the Captain's table the first night out and on the tour below deck. Adriaan Kosters was the Dutchman who was running the American division of a European high tech company. The other was the Englishman, Blake Smallridge. He was the one who had talked a lot about the various gambling establishments he had frequented in Europe. As Rory suspected, he didn't just talk about gambling.

Kosters glanced over as Rory approached, "Mr. Steele. That was the name, wasn't it?"

Rory nodded and shook the man's hand.

"Ah, Mr. Steele," Smallridge said as he glanced over. He set a card down on the table. "Hit me," he said to the dealer.

The dealer gave him a card.

Smallridge took a peek at the card, his face brightened and he flipped them over. "Blackjack!" he announced as he threw his arms in the air.

Kosters laughed and shook his head.

Having finished the more important aspect of gambling, Smallridge reached around and extended his hand to Rory, "So nice to see you again, Mr. Steele."

"You can both call me Rory. No need to be formal," he said as he shook the man's hand.

Smallridge nodded. "Are you going to join us? I haven't seen you in here at all."

"What's your poison, Rory?" Kosters asked.

"Poison?"

"He means what game do you like to play," Smallridge said with a chuckle. "I keep telling him, people on this side of the world could also answer that question by telling you what they like to drink, like a bourbon or a shot of whiskey." He looked at Kosters and jostled him with an elbow, "You're going to have to learn the speak American if you're going to deal with them."

Kosters smiled and nodded, "Very true, I guess."

"Well, my poison is Scotch," Rory said, "gambling...not so much."

"So, you're just coming in here to watch us lose our money then," Kosters said.

"No. Actually, I was just wondering if you saw Loretta Black in here last night," Rory said in an offhanded manner.

"Yes...we saw her," Smallridge said as he looked at Kosters, wondering why Rory was asking the question.

"Did you see her with a young man?" Rory asked him.

Smallridge leaned over and grinned, "Jealous are you?"

Rory didn't rise to the bait, "No. I'm just helping her look for something."

"Right," Smallridge scoffed, obviously not believing that story.

Kosters looked around and then pointed at a young man walking on the other side of the room with a drink in his hand, "That young man there. The one with the curly black hair? That's him."

Smallridge leaned over and said in a low voice, "They disappeared into a small room the dealers use for their supplies. She came out looking like she had been ridden hard."

Rory nodded, "Thank you, gentlemen." He rapped his knuckles on the wooden table, "And good luck in here." Rory approached the young man, not sure exactly how he should broach the subject. The young man didn't owe him any answers and he could easily clam up. "Excuse me, sir? Can I speak to you for a moment?"

The young man turned, an impatient look on his face, "Make it fast, I have things to do."

The nasal, short-a accent pegged him as a New Englander, probably Rhode Island. And his attitude spoke old-family money. Which meant Rory had to be extra cautious or the young man would dismiss him quickly. He decided to play the servant. He put his hands behind his back and nodded his head once, "Yes, sir, I understand. My name is Rory Mack Steele. I'm the Chief of Security for the ship–"

"Security? Am I in trouble?" the young man asked facetiously. A stupid, lop-sided grin creased his face.

"No," Rory said, trying to figure out how he should approach this. "I understand...."

The young man's eyebrows raised as Rory's voice trailed off.

Rory decided he would play to the young man's ego. He leaned in and said in a low voice, accompanied by a lecherous grin, "Just keep your bit of fun...like last night...out of the crew areas please, sir...if you know what I mean? Stupid regulations that I have to enforce...you understand, sir."

The young man shook his head softly and then finally understood what Rory was referring to as a 'bit of fun'. He leaned in with a pompous look on his face, "That little blonde thing dragged me in there. What could I do?"

Rory had his answer. "Just take her up to your cabin and...." Rory made a suggestive gesture, pumping his fist.

The young man imitated the fist pump, "Bent her over a chair in there and didn't take me much time. She went off like a firecracker." Then he straightened up and glanced away dismissively, "A nice piece of tail, but not worth it in the long run."

"What do you mean, sir?"

"She started complaining after we came out. Every time I looked at another female that walked by, she went crazy on me."

"Really?"

The young man nodded, "Dumped her ass real fast."

"So you weren't with her the whole night?"

"No. Moved on. Too many fish in the sea," the young man said. Then he laughed. "Hey, that's a funny joke on a boat isn't it?"

Rory forced a laugh and nodded. He patted the young man on the shoulder, "Well, good luck with your fishing. Just take your catch back to your cabin," he added with a tap of a finger on the side of his nose and a wink.

The young man laughed and sauntered off.

The conversation confirmed Loretta's account of being with the young man. But it still left the question of what she did after getting bent over a chair in the supply room. *And* after getting dumped. To a volatile person like Loretta Black, *that* could really set off a firestorm. Rory wandered back through the casino, wondering what he should do next.

Adriaan Kosters approached him, a tall, dark-colored drink held in each hand. The ice clinked against the glasses as he gestured, "Was the young man able to help you with what you were looking for?"

"Somewhat," Rory said.

"That's good," Kosters replied. He lifted one of the glasses, "Excuse me, but I have to get this over to Blake. I'm hoping to get him drunk enough to take all his money in a card game later." He laughed at his own joke and headed off.

As he left, Rory decided to join the security team in the search for the server of the Black Forest cake—

"Oh Rory," Kosters called out.

Rory turned to see the man was about twenty feet away, standing near a boisterous crowd clustered around another blackjack table.

"You might...oops." Kosters pulled back as he nearly had the drink knocked out of his hand when a couple of passengers jostled him. After a moment of apologies between him and the passengers, Kosters turned back and talked a little louder, to be heard over the crowd noise, "You might also want to talk to that dark-haired lady. Tanya is it?"

"Tanya...?" Rory realized he had to raise his voice when Kosters shook his head, "You mean Tanya Beno?"

Kosters raised a glass, "Yes, that's the one."

Rory was puzzled why he said that.

"She was with that Black woman later on in the evening," Kosters called out in explanation. "After Black was with that young man."

"Tanya Beno was here too?"

Kosters nodded and then called out, "Yes. She came in here with that law professor that was at the Captain's table. I don't remember her name, but it was her."

That took Rory by surprise and he didn't say anything in return.

Kosters raised one of the drinks in a goodbye gesture and disappeared into the crowd.

"Thanks," Rory said, more to himself. He went back outside onto the Sun Deck where he had left Tanya Beno lying poolside earlier. He walked through the crowds, anxious to see if she was still here. She wasn't. Just an empty deck chair. He would have to scour the ship—

"I take it your little tête-à-tête with Morrissette didn't work out?"

Rory turned to see Tanya Beno walking towards him with a drink in her hand. He couldn't help but take another glance at that firm, athletic body in the black, skimpy bathing suit

"Or are you back just to enjoy the sights?" she said with a coy smile as she stepped past him. In one smooth, confident motion, Tanya sat down and lay back on the deck chair. She lifted one knee as she settled down, "Are you going to join me this time?"

Rory shook his head as he took a step towards the end of the deck chair, "No. As much as I'd like to...."

"But duty calls," she replied and she took a sip of her cold drink. Condensation ran down the outside of the glass.

Rory glanced off to the sea for a moment, then looked back down at Tanya, "I understand you met up with Loretta Black in the casino later in the evening last night?"

"Yes," she replied simply.

Rory couldn't see her eyes because of the sunglasses. He wanted to ask her to lift them, so he could gauge every nuance of expression, but he didn't want to push it.

"How long were you with her?"

"Not long. Maybe a half hour," she said. She took another sip of her drink. "She was quite inebriated and started having problems staying on her feet because of the rolling deck. I walked her to her cabin. Very nice suite, by the way. When I left her, she was passed out on the sofa."

Rory nodded.

"Why are you asking? Do you believe she had something to do with the death of Jaimee's brother?" Tanya took another casual sip of her drink.

Rory didn't reply.

"She does have quite a temper, that one," Tanya remarked in an offhanded way.

Rory decided to throw her a curve. "Did you see Cassie Lopez last night?"

Tanya lifted the sunglasses and placed them on her forehead. She looked up into Rory's silver-blue eyes, "The fact that you're asking me the question, tells me you already know the answer, Mr. Steele."

Tanya Beno was no fool. A look into her dark, calm eyes told Rory this woman wasn't easily shaken.

"I take it Cassie Lopez is missing?" Tanya asked him.

The question surprised Rory, "Why would you think that?"

Tanya raised an eyebrow, "The recent ship-wide announcement, asking for Cassiopeia Lopez to report in - coupled with the fact that you're running an investigation into murder and missing passengers - well, it doesn't take a genius to figure it out."

This woman definitely wasn't stupid.

"I left Cassie on the top deck late last night. She likes to go for a walk around the top deck before she goes to bed. I didn't stay very long because - frankly - I prefer my walks in the moonlight with a man."

Rory just let her talk.

"And that's when I met Loretta. After I helped her to her cabin, I went directly to my cabin, where I went to bed - alone, unfortunately."

Rory looked into her dark eyes. She didn't appear to be hiding anything.

Tanya Beno lifted her other knee and then opened her legs just a little, "Would you like to examine me personally as part of your investigation, Mr. Steele? Maybe pink handcuffs...?"

Rory's cell phone rang, diverting his attention.

"It's Myles," said the voice on the other end, "could you meet me in the main galley on deck 4 right away?"

Chapter 25

RORY PASSED THROUGH the double-doors into the cruise ship's main galley. The place was huge and the definition of noisy, controlled chaos. Stainless-steel equipment stretched as far as he could see and there were chefs, assistants and servers working feverishly to prepare an amazing variety of dishes. The air was rich with the mouth watering scents of sea food and a wide variety of deserts. Off to the side he saw Myles. He was standing next to a short, white haired Filipino server who looked to be about fifty years old. Rory headed across the galley deck towards them.

Myles gave Rory a nod as he approached and gestured to the Filipino server, "This is Jaypee Andrada, Mr. Steele. He was assigned to a table, near where Mr. Landry Morrissette was sitting that night."

The Filipino server wrung his hands together and looked very nervous as he stared at Rory.

Myles spoke in a quiet voice, placing a comforting hand on the Filipino server's shoulder, "It's okay, Jaypee. Like I told you, you're not in trouble."

The Filipino didn't look convinced, but he nodded his head in understanding.

"Good. Now tell Mr. Steele what you told me about that night," Myles prompted.

Jaypee swallowed and nodded. He began speaking in broken English, "I bring the dessert you ask about out to one of the passengers. But he said he no order it, that it was a mistake. No one at table said they ordered it. And no one wanted it, so I offered it to other tables–"

Rory cocked his head, "Hold on. It was *your* table. You must have taken the order."

Jaypee shook his emphatically, "No, no, no. I *not* take order." He gestured to a long line of stainless steel counters on his right, "But it *was* on ticket there for that table and that passenger."

"That's where finished orders are set for pickup by the servers," Myles explained.

Jaypee nodded emphatically, "It *was* there for that passenger. I not make mistake."

"And Jaypee asked his assistant about it. But he denied taking the order as well," Myles added. "Right?" he asked Jaypee.

Jaypee nodded affirmation.

"*But,*" Myles said as he held a finger up for emphasis, "Jaypee still wasn't satisfied. He was determined to find out why the ordering system under his responsibility broke down. He was finally able to get his assistant to tell him that one of the pastry trainees gave him the dessert to take to that table and that passenger specifically–"

Rory held his hands up, "Hold on." He pointed at Jaypee, "You just said *you* took the dessert out to the table." He pointed back at Myles, "Now you're saying it was this *assistant* who took it to the table. Which is it?"

Myles held his own hands up, "Just hear me out." He looked at Jaypee, shrugging, "Actually, maybe I should just let you explain it."

Jaypee Andrada nodded vigorously, "Yes, yes." He looked seriously at Rory, "Assistant was given ticket and dessert by one pastry trainee and told it was for that passenger." He held a finger up, "But assistant see order not taken by one of us. And he *know* I would not approve." He wagging his finger emphatically, "Not how it is done. It *must* be done properly. I've worked on ships since I'm fifteen years. Must always be done properly and he know that. So assistant put ticket and dessert there for *me* to pick up and take out to table, so he not blamed."

Myles looked at Rory, "I interviewed Jaypee's assistant and he says the same thing. I can go get him, if you like."

Rory shook his head, "No, it's fine. Do we know the name of this pastry trainee?"

Myles nodded as he pulled out his notebook and referred to it, "His name is Saeed Jan."

Rory looked at Myles, wondering if he had heard right. *Another Arabic sounding name?*

Myles nodded, "I know what you're thinking. Strange, yeah?"

"Yeah," Rory agreed. "Have you talked to this Saeed Jan yet?"

"No," Myles said. "We checked his quarters right away, but he wasn't there. His shift won't start for another few hours–"

Just then Kerk Bakken and Bern Nyhus came hustling into the galley. They both looked extremely concerned and were out of breath.

Bakken shook his head no at Myles.

Myles cursed under his breath.

"What's wrong?" Rory asked.

Myles looked at this notebook again, "The passenger who was supposed to receive the dessert...his name is Sunbool Raad."

Rory rubbed the back of his hand under his chin. *Another Arabic sounding name? Where is this going?*

Bakken spoke up, his breathing heavy, "Mr. Kitchener sent us to look for him and Bern and I just came from his cabin. He's not there."

Bern Nyhus read from a piece of paper, his breathing raspy as well, "And neither is the person staying with him. I checked and a passenger registered as Matak Sarror was staying with this Sunbool Raad."

"And while he did that, I checked with the cabin steward," Bakken added. "He says they didn't have to make up the bed or clean the room this morning. It doesn't look like either one were in there last night."

Everyone looked at each other, wondering if the death toll was adding up.

Rory took a deep breath, considering what to do next. He looked at Myles, "Did you get a chance to search and process the pastry trainee's room yet, like we did with the others?"

Myles shook his head, "No, not yet. We didn't have the kit with us."

"Okay," Rory said, "We can go search it to start." Then he turned to Bakken and Nyhus, "I want you gentlemen to go back to the cabin for these two men. Do a complete search and gather fingerprints, like we did in the other three cabins. Then go down to the pastry trainee's room and do that one as well."

Bakken nodded

"You'll find the fingerprint kit in my quarters," Myles told him.

"What if the two passengers *do* show up while we're in there?" Nyhus asked.

"Detain them. Lock them in the bathroom if you have to," Rory said firmly. "One of these three guys has to know something about what's going on. I'm convinced of it. Let Myles know when you're finished with all three rooms."

Kerk Bakken and Bern Nyhus moved off at a quick pace.

Rory turned to Jaypee Andrada, "If the trainee shows up here, while we're down in his room, *detain him*. I don't care if you lock him in a freezer. You hold him and call Mr. Kitchener immediately. Do you understand me?"

Jaypee Andrada nodded vigorously, eyes large, wondering what he had gotten himself into.

Chapter 26

MYLES LED RORY out of the galley and down to the crew quarters on Deck 1. This deck was more functional in tone and not anywhere near the opulence of the passenger decks above. The first stop was the general crew bar that served as the favorite off-duty staff spot for the crew to relax and socialize. The crew bar was noisy and alive with music and it looked like the booze was flowing freely, with a number of members looking tipsy.

"Saeed Jan?" Myles called out as he stepped into the entrance-way. He watched for a reaction from the men and women sitting or standing around the bar. But no one said anything. They simply looked at each other.

"The same reaction the coppers used to get when they came looking for someone back home," Myles muttered to Rory.

"Comes with the territory, I guess," Rory said. "I can try...."

Myles shook his head, "No, I got this." He took a deep breath and yelled across the bar, "This is not a game. I'm about to take down the name of every bloke in here. I'm sure the Captain will be interested in your lack of cooperation."

The men and women looked at each other in a more serious manner. But still no one spoke up.

After a few moments a meek voice called from the far side of the bar, "H-he's not here." A young Filipino man, looking very nervous sat rigid on a stool.

Myles beckoned him forward.

The young Filipino looked scared as he stepped across the rolling floor. The others in the bar looked at him for a moment and then went back to talking and drinking.

Myles stepped back in the passageway as the young man stepped out of the bar, "What's your name?"

"Edenjevy, sir. I'm Saeed's bunk mate."

"Do you know where he is?" Myles asked him sternly.

Edenjevy shook his head, "No sir. I haven't seen him since early this morning, sir."

"You're sure?"

"Yes, sir."

Myles looked at Rory and then took the young man's elbow, turning him around, "All right for now. Take us down to your quarters."

"I...I have to go with you?" The young man looked scared.

"We may need to ask you more questions," Myles said. "Let's go."

Edenjevy walked just ahead of Rory and Myles, winding his way through the passageways to the quarters he shared with the pastry trainee.

"Have you known this Saeed for very long?" Myles asked as they walked along the rolling deck.

"No, sir," Edenjevy said as he looked back nervously, "only on this trip."

"Do you spend a lot of time with Saeed?"

Edenjevy shook his head no again, "Just see him in our room at night."

Does he have any close friends?" Rory asked. "Anyone he spends time with?"

Shaking his head no again, Edenjevy said, "Not see him with anyone. I sorry."

When they reached the quarters, Myles had the young man wait in the passageway as he opened the door with his master key-card. He then led the way inside, leaving the door open. The room wasn't very big and it smelled of damp clothes and old soap, covered slightly by an old air freshener hanging from the ceiling. Dead ahead was a small closet, with two bunk beds on the left and built-in wooden shelves with four lower drawers next to a door on the right side.

Rory went for the closet.

Myles went to the drawers.

Edenjevy leaned in the doorway, "The top two drawers are his."

"Fine," Myles said as he slid open the first drawer, "but I'll have to search them all, okay?"

Edenjevy nodded, afraid not to cooperate.

"Not much in here," Myles said as he opened and closed each drawer and looked through the sparse clothing he found.

Rory looked through three small shoe boxes on the top shelf and found a number of personal items and loose change, but little else. He patted each piece of clothing hanging from a thin rod across the closet but still found nothing of any significance.

Myles closed the last drawer and headed for the doorway. It led to a small bathroom with a sink, a toilet and a cramped, stand-up shower.

Rory crouched down to check the items on the floor of the closet. Most of the shoes were plain white with rubber soles and black laces. There were a three pairs of running shoes and two pairs of sandals but little else he could see. Then his eye caught something on the floor at the back of the closet. He reached up, parted the clothing and then leaned forward on one knee. He wasn't 100% positive about what he saw...but he wasn't going to take any chances. "Myles," he called out over his shoulder, "do you have any gloves on you?"

There was muffled 'no'.

From the doorway, Edenjevy said, "One minute, sir. I get you."

Rory looked around but the young man had already disappeared.

Myles stepped out of the tiny bathroom, walked over to the closet bent over behind Rory, trying to see what he was looking at, "What did you find?"

"I'm not sure," Rory said as he chewed on his lip, thinking and waiting for the young Filipino to return.

"I have them," Edenjevy called from the doorway.

"Bring them here," Rory said as he gestured for the man to enter the room.

Myles took a pair of latex gloves, used for handling food, from Edenjevy and passed them down to Rory, "Will these do?"

"Perfect," Rory said as he slipped the gloves on and snapped them into place. Then he carefully reached to the back of the closet and pulled out pieces of a three foot plant that had a green stem with hooded, purple flowers at the top. Holding the pieces in one hand, he reached back in and pulled out a small clay pot filled with dirt.

"What's that?" Myles asked in wonder. "I've never seen a plant that looked like that before."

"It's a member of the buttercup family," Rory said. He set the pot down and looked over the pieces of the plant.

"That belong to Saeed," Edenjevy said. "He bring on board ship in George Town. I ask him why." Edenjevy shrugged, "But he just say it was pretty."

"Pretty...but deadly," Rory said quietly.

"What do you mean?" Myles asked him. "What is it?"

"It's called Monkshood," Rory told him. "It's been used by assassins for centuries."

"Assassins? You mean...?"

"It's poisonous...and virtually undetectable. In fact, it can poison you just by touch. That's why I asked for the gloves."

"Why is it in pieces?" Myles asked. He leaned over more and pointed towards the pieces, "The thickness of the stem for those two sections don't look the same. It looks like some of it is gone."

Rory nodded, "And I can only think of one reason why pieces of a deadly plant are missing."

Myles swore under his breath, "Don't tell me he put it in that dessert, meant for that passenger, that Sunbool Raad guy."

Letting out a low breath, Rory nodded, "I think that's exactly what he did. But Raad rejected it for some reason and it was accidentally eaten by Landry Morrissette."

"But why would this pastry trainee do that?"

"That's a good question. One best answered by Saeed Jan. We need to find him," Rory said as he stood up. "*Now.*"

Chapter 27

RORY STOOD ON THE BRIDGE of The Caribbean Star-Liner, the sea rolling gently beneath his feet as he looked at Kitchener's notebook. Myles stood patiently next to him. Captain Tor Amundson, his second in command, Staff Captain Lars Thorson, Jon Magnuson, the First Officer and Tate Nygaard, the Surveillance Manager, all stood off to the side, talking in low voices as they discussed the onboard situation. The other two navigation officers, normally in charge of minding the computerized autopilot, had been sent for a break. Dr. Thiago Rodriguez stood in silence, watching through the large, curved window of the bridge as the ship plowed through the Caribbean Sea.

Kerk Bakken and Bern Nyhus came hustling onto the bridge, a number of papers in their hands. "We got the information packets made up," Bakken said.

"Good," Rory said as he closed the notebook and handed it back to Myles.

The ship's officers all stepped over to stand beside Myles and Rory.

Rodriguez turned his attention away from the sea and back to the serious matter at hand.

Bakken gave Rory a set of papers stapled together and then he and Nyhus handed a set to each other person present on the bridge.

Rory then flipped through the pages as he talked, "We've put together a picture and the information we have on each person."

The sound of paper rustling sounded over the soft hum of the electronic equipment on the bridge.

"The first one is a picture of Diya al Din Moghadam, taken from his American passport."

"American passport but born in Yemen," Kitchener said.

"Correct," Rory said.

"The next pictures are Jalal-Uddin Shammas, El-Saraya Mansour and Abdul Rehman Naser," Rory continued. "All three are missing passengers. All had American passports which *show* they were US born."

Staff Captain Lars Thorson looked up at Rory, "The way you say that Mr. Steele...implies you believe otherwise...."

Rory nodded slightly, "I'll get to that in a moment. The next picture is Landry Morrissette. He's the passenger who died in a suspicious manner. Which brings us to the pastry trainee, Saeed Jan."

"Yemeni born, with an American passport," Nyhus said.

"Coincidence?" Myles asked no one in particular. No one replied.

"The next picture is the plant found in Saeed Jan's quarters," Rory said. "It's known as Monkshood and we have to keep an eye out for any others, just in case. Dr. Rodriguez, have you had a chance to consider the plant's properties?"

"Yes," Dr. Rodriguez said. "This plant is classed as an alkaloid toxin. In fact, it's one of the deadliest and most formidable, poisonous substances known to man."

The room was silent.

"The effects of the toxin found in the plant is *consistent* with the symptoms leading to the death of Mr. Morrissette," Rodriguez reported. "I don't have the facilities here to make a definite scientific link at this point but...I'm sure this is what caused the young man's death. A very agonizing death, I might add."

Myles glanced at Rory, "You said this plant was used by assassins, yeah?"

Rory nodded.

Myles flipped the page, "So this pastry trainee was really trying to assassinate this other passenger...Sunbool Raad...another Yemeni with an American passport."

"Why would someone want to assassinate this man?" Jon Magnuson, the First Officer asked. He looked at the others, but no one had an answer.

Tate Nygaard, the Surveillance Manager spoke in a quiet voice as he looked at one of the pages, "This other passenger, the one staying with Sunbool Raad...his name is Matak Sarror...." He glanced up, "He's *another* Yemeni with an American passport. Are we seeing a pattern here or is it just a coincidence?"

There was silence in the room as everyone considered the implications.

"How many are missing overall?" Staff Captain Lars Thorson asked in a low voice as he flipped through the sheets of paper.

"Six passengers are missing," the Captain said. "And Mr. Landry Morrissette, a passenger, is dead. We also have Kristoffer Jensen, our Chief Security Officer, dead...."

"And Cassiopeia Angelica Lopez is also missing," Rory said in a subdued voice. "Her handbag was found on the upper deck."

"That makes nine people in total then, either missing or dead," Thorson said.

"And a pastry trainee, Saeed Jan, is implicated in the death of at least one of them," Kitchener added.

Magnuson looked at Rory, "Do you think he might be responsible for them all?"

Rory looked at Bakken, "You were looking into the man. What did you find out?"

Bakken took out a notebook and flipped it open with one hand, "Not a lot really. I talked to his cabin mate and other members of the staff who had contact with him. The man is 5' 10" tall...around 180 lbs...first joined the crew in Miami...was quiet...kept to himself. But one thing stood out to everyone. He was quite fit, always doing push-ups or pull-ups on door frames. That kind of thing."

"Sounds more like someone who should have been working in your fitness center than as a pastry trainee," Rory remarked as he looked at Captain Tor Amundson and Staff Captain Lars Thorson.

"Or security," Myles added.

Captain Amundson nodded, "True. But he would have had to apply specifically for either job."

"So he *wanted* to be in the galley then," Myles Kitchener reasoned.

Rory narrowed his eyes as he thought, "When you're doing an investigation, especially when you're trying to solve a series of crimes, you look for patterns–"

"That's the M.O., the modus operandi, yeah?" Myles asked him. "The criminal's method of working?"

"Exactly," Rory confirmed. "We're all creatures of habit. And criminals are no different. And they rarely change what works. If this pastry trainee was responsible for the other deaths, where we have no bodies, it's probably because he threw them overboard. The question is...why would he risk poisoning someone? Why would he change what was working for him?"

Everyone was quiet, obviously thinking about the situation.

Myles Kitchener spoke up first, "Maybe the passenger he made that poison-laced dessert for, he didn't put himself in a position to be killed and thrown overboard. He had to kill him in a different way."

Rory nodded his head thoughtfully, "That's a very good possibility."

"But...," Myles said slowly, "what would be his motive for killing this Sunbool Raad? Or any of the others for that matter? There has to be a reason, yeah?"

"You would think so," Rory said, "but you never know with some killers. It could be just for the thrills of killing."

There was a visible shudder from several of the men.

"The other possibility would be a hate crime," Rory said. "The only connection we have so far between the victims seems to be the Republic of Yemen. It appears Morrissette was killed accidentally, so we can remove him from the equation. And it looks like Jensen was killed because he saw something. I would imagine we'll find the same thing happened to Ms. Lopez. So both of them are also outside the pattern. All the others had Arabic names as well, which again points back to the Middle East.

Which is why I'm suspicious about those passports showing those men are US born."

Everyone was silent as they considered what Rory was saying.

"The other possibility is...we could be seeing some type of fight based on cultural differences, regional differences, maybe even a political fight," Rory said. "But the connections are still too tenuous, so I could be totally wrong. We would need deep background checks for all of the missing passengers to confirm a link between them, beyond what we see on the surface." He looked over at Captain Amundson, "Are we still cut off from returning to Miami by that storm?"

Staff Captain Lars Thorson spoke up, "The storm has swung north over the Bahamas, but it's still too dangerous for us to try and navigate our way through."

"He's right," Captain Amundson said. "If we turned back now, the seas will still be very rough. But we are scheduled to land in Montego Bay, Jamaica tomorrow morning. If we leave at the end of the day, that will give the storm another day to move northward. If it looks good, we could head back through the Windward Passage between Cuba and Haiti. Depending on the weather, we could get back in another two or three days at the most."

"Okay. Monitor the weather and set sail back to Miami at the earliest opportunity," Rory instructed him.

"What do we tell the passengers?" Captain Amundson asked him.

"Tell them that there are mechanical difficulties that require that you return to Miami," Rory offered.

"That should make a lot of them happy," grumbled the Staff Captain.

Captain Amundson grimaced and nodded, "You're right. I'll call the owners and have them authorize refunding every passenger or offering them another cruise. Under the circumstances, the owners will be glad to get away with no bad publicity."

"Perfect," Rory said. He turned to Tate Nygaard, the Surveillance Manager, "Any possibility of getting the ship-wide surveillance system going again?"

Nygaard shook his head as he rolled his eyes in frustration, "No. And I can't figure it out. It actually doesn't make any sense. We've gone over every piece of it and we still can't figure out why it simply won't work. There's a possibility it's a software glitch, but we can't trace it. We tried to run the surveillance system mechanically but it won't work without the computerized software for some reason."

"Aren't computers just wonderful," Bern Nyhus said.

Kerk Bakken snorted derisively.

"Keep working on it," Rory told Nygaard. "Captain, please let me know if anything changes and we can set sail for Miami sooner."

Captain Amundson nodded his head in agreement.

Rory turned to Myles, "How many security staff are there?"

"There are only seventeen of us who reported to Mr. Jensen."

"That's it?" Rory said in surprise.

Myles shrugged and glanced at the Captain.

Captain Amundson didn't look too happy as he shook his head slowly, "The owners didn't feel we needed any more members than that reporting to the Chief Security Officer. Passengers pay and provide the profits, so there are a lot more of them than us in the crew and staff. Plus the owners didn't feel the need to cut into the profit margin for experienced men with military or police training." Amundson cursed under his breath. "I remember hearing about some ships that had ex-Gurkhas or other ex-military types on board as members of the security team. Now I know why and I wish I had pushed harder...."

"Well, we can't do anything about it now," Rory said. He thought for a moment, "Do you have firearms onboard, Captain?"

Captain Amundson nodded "They are under lock and key. But I can't believe this man would have a firearm. There's no way he could smuggle it onboard–"

"The evidence strongly suggests Myles was shot in George Town with a 9mm *plastic* gun created by one of the new 3-D printers," Rory revealed. "The Royal Cayman Islands Police Service found it back in George Town, dumped in a waste bin, along with the dark clothing the shooter wore."

Everyone's head turned quickly to stare openly at Myles.

Myles self-consciously placed his hand on his wounded arm and nodded.

"I thought that was just science fiction stuff," whispered Jon Magnuson, the First Officer.

"Only the firing pin was metal," Rory said. "And that could have been removed and hidden with other nondescript items in a suitcase when the shooter went through your security check to get on board."

Captain Amundson give a slow, disbelieving shake of his head as he spoke, "I can't believe all this is happening." He cleared his throat and looked at Rory, determination on his face, "We have Glock 26 subcompact 9mm pistols onboard that we can provide you with. We *also* have Glock 18 machine pistols with a shoulder stock –"

"The Glock 26 pistols will work nicely," Rory said. He didn't say it, but he felt too much fire power in the hands of inexperienced men could prove to be deadly.

Captain Amundson nodded, "I will break them out, along with holsters, for each man you want to arm."

"Thank you, Captain," Rory said, "Myles, work with Kerk and Bern to get the printouts of Saeed Jan's picture and his vital statistics to each member of our security team. And I want you to work out the details on a ship wide sweep. Let's see if we can find this pastry trainee before he kills anyone else. There are sixteen of us and we're going to work in pairs. You and I can work together. Make sure *everyone* knows this man is dangerous and *no one* takes any chances. Arm each man with a Glock 26 pistol in a *concealed* holster. And they *must* keep it concealed. We can't alarm the passengers in any way. Understood?"

Myles gave Rory a single, firm nod of his head.

"Find a quiet, secure location when you have everybody armed and ready and give me a call."

"We can use the security office below deck," Myles said.

Captain Tor Amundson turned to the First Officer, Jon Magnuson, "You can work with me to get the weapons and ammunition ready for the security staff. Mr. Thorson, you have the bridge."

Thorson nodded acknowledgment of the order and turned to the ship's communication system to recall the navigation officers to re-man the bridge.

Tate Nygaard, the Surveillance Manager, addressed Rory, "I'll continue to work on getting the security system running again. I'll keep you updated on my progress." With that said, he hustled off the bridge.

Dr. Thiago Rodriguez headed for the exit as well, "I'll be down in medical if anyone needs me. And from the sound of it, they might."

As Kerk Bakken and Bern Nyhus followed the Captain and the first officer out, heading for the armory, Myles hung back. He stepped up beside Rory and spoke in a quiet voice so no one else could overhear, "What about our detainee up in cabin #91008, Loretta Black?"

Rory ran his fingers through his black hair as he considered the hot-tempered blonde. "As much as I'd like to keep her locked up, just to spare the rest of the passengers from that temper of hers...there's not enough evidence to suggest she's involved."

"She would have the motive, and the money, to hire someone," Myles suggested.

Rory pursed his lips as he nodded, "I thought of that as well. The problem is...other then Cassiopeia Lopez, the rest of the missing passengers don't fit in with that theory."

"Maybe the rest are just to throw us off the trail," Myles said.

Rory shook his head slowly, "That would only work if she knew Landry Morrissette and Cassiopeia Lopez *before* she came on board. Jaimee Morrissette told me she introduced her brother to Loretta Black in the disco on the promenade the second night out. And I was there when Black and Lopez met at the Captain's table the first night out of Miami as well. If they had met before, they hid it well."

"Do you want me to go up there and let her out?" Myles asked him, not really looking like he wanted to go.

"No, I'll do it. I'm the one that put her in there," Rory answered reluctantly.

Myles took out his master key card and handed it to Rory, "You can let yourself in. I'll call the two men on guard detail to head down to the armory. That way, they won't be in the line of fire. We can't afford to lose any more men."

"Very funny, Kitchener."

"But not untrue, Steele."

Chapter 28

RORY INSERTED THE MASTER KEYCARD into the door for Loretta Black's suite and cracked the door open. He knocked hard against the door and called out, "Loretta? It's Rory. I'm coming in." There was no reply and he stepped carefully into the suite, fully expecting something to come crashing down on his head.

Loretta Black was standing on the far side of the room, near the sliding glass door to the balcony. She was dressed in a skimpy yellow bikini that left little to the imagination. The world-class beauty stood there with her arms crossed tightly over her chest and a scowl on her face, "Were you afraid I wasn't *decent*? Well I am, but I'm not sure about *you*."

"Fair enough," Rory answered as he closed the door behind him. "But I was investigating a murder. Someone lost their life–"

"And I wasn't responsible. I keep telling you that."

"And the evidence suggests that you weren't responsible," Rory admitted.

"Suggests!" Her foot began tapping as she crossed her arms tighter across the yellow material barely capable of holding her breasts in.

Rory took a deep breath and let it out. There was no sense in arguing. He turned and waved a hand, "You're free to come and go. The guards have been taken away." He opened the door–

"Rory!"

Rory turned to look back from the doorway.

Loretta Black ran in her high heeled shoes, taking small, rapid steps across to him. She stopped a couple of feet away from him, "I'm sorry."

Rory just nodded once and turned to leave.

"We could have had fun," she said quickly.

Rory looked back at her. He nodded after a moment, "You're right. And we did. Briefly. But you're so competitive in your personal relationships...." He let his voice drift off as he decided not to say anything further. He stepped out of the suite, pulling the door closed behind him.

Loretta Black said something sharp in anger on the other side of the closed door.

RORY ENTERED THE SECURITY office on deck 2. The space was large but Spartan looking. Because the room was below the water level, there weren't any portholes. The room felt humid and the smell of the sea was heavy. There were a line of built-in cabinets on the left-hand side and a number of desks on the right, some of them with computers sitting on top.

In the center of the room, Myles was handing out information packets and a Multiband Inter-Team walkie-talkie to each member of the security staff

Rory could see the men were somber and their bodies were stiff with tension. Lacking any military or police training and experience, their first brush with a serious security problem and tracking a killer would no doubt be scary. Rory felt for them.

Myles acknowledged Rory with a brief nod and continued with his task

Rory spotted the brig at the far end of the room and walked across the rolling deck to take a look. There were four cells with iron bars, like any jail. Each cell had white gloss walls, green floor paint, a bed attached to the wall and a stainless steel toilet, attached to the wall, opposite the bed. Rory spotted a potential security problem in the first cell. He was about to call Myles over when his thoughts were interrupted –

"Here you go, sir."

Rory turned to see one of the security men handing him an information packet and a walkie-talkie. The top page of the packet showed a picture of Saeed Jan and his vital statistics.

"Everyone has a packet of information and a walkie-talkie," Myles said as he stepped over to join Rory and the other man. "The packet also has a printout with the search grids each of us will take."

The remaining men gathered behind Myles, looking concerned and ready for instructions.

"Very good. And everyone has a Glock 26 pistol?" Rory asked Myles. He glanced to the men behind Myles.

"Yes sir," Myles replied crisply. "Oh," he said and reached to a desk where he picked up a Glock 26 pistol in an ankle holster and handed it to Rory, "Sorry about that."

Rory took it in hand and set it on the desk. The ankle holster, with a nylon leg strap, was the only way they could conceal the weapon in the heat and not alert the passengers.

"All I've ever done is shot at paper targets on a shooting range," one of the security officers said quietly.

"Then pretend you're shooting at a paper target," Rory said with a smile.

That broke up the tension in the room and everyone smiled.

Rory addressed everyone in a quiet, but confident voice, "Look. This is not going to be easy for any of us. I *have* had experience in gun battles and I can assure you, it never gets easy. That's why we're working in pairs, because we need to watch each other's back to stay safe."

That seemed to relieve the pressure the men were feeling even more.

"We're going to assume several things about this man," Rory said as he tapped the picture of the pastry trainee. "One...consider him dangerous. We're told he was always doing push-ups and pull-ups, so he's fit and he can probably handle himself in a fight. But we have no idea if he has any military training or martial arts training, so it could be more than just a street fight if you corner him. Don't hesitate to call for help if you spot him. We don't need dead heroes."

The men listened intently, the tension ratcheting up again as they considered the dangerous man-hunt they were about to begin.

"Two," Rory continued, "consider this man *armed* with a 9mm plastic gun –"

"You mean like one printed out by one of those new 3-D printer things?" one of the security men asked. "I've heard about in the news but...it's real?"

"Yes," Rory said. "But don't consider it to be simply a toy. He can easily kill any one of us with it."

The men around the room nodded their heads but the rising tension was etched on their faces.

"Three" Rory added. "Consider he may be working with someone else onboard. And I'll be blunt...it could be a passenger...it could be a member of the crew. Don't talk with *anyone* about this operation. Right now, the only friends you have are in this room."

The men glanced at each other.

"Don't get lured into any situation where you can't retreat or get cut off from help, even with your partner," Rory continued. "If you're unsure about *any* situation, call for another team to back you up. Or several, if necessary. Again, I prefer cautious security men rather than dead heroes."

The men looked at each other and nodded.

"Any questions?"

The man glanced at each other but were silent as they shifted on their feet several times in anxiety.

Rory looked at Myles and nodded.

"Okay men," Myles said as he took charge. "We're going to start at the top, Deck 16, the Observation deck. We'll work our way systematically down through each deck. Each team has sections to search on each deck. Mark them off on your sheet and report to me every time you finish a section. We'll coordinate our search all the way down to the bottom hold. Any questions?"

The men stood still, anxious and waiting.

Rory added one other thing, "Keep in mind that we don't want to panic the passengers by being overly officious. Keep your guard up and be alert, but try to smile and be friendly. We want to make sure everyone feels secure while we search. Understood?"

The men nodded.

"Let's go."

Chapter 29

RORY AND MYLES BEGAN their part of the search in the forward section of the ship. The sun was hot and brilliant as they worked their way through each section of their assignment slowly, checking every nook, cranny and possible hiding spot. All the search teams checked in without finding anything. Myles directed everyone down to the Sky deck for the next part of their search. Deck 15, the Sky deck, had a number of families with children of various ages using the variety of kid-friendly pools and game areas. A number of younger children stopped Myles to ask him about the ship, his uniform, and a hundred other questions.

Myles did his best to accommodate them all while Rory kept watch for anyone trying to slip by them in this section. After 20 minutes Myles was finally able to break away and they finished searching the area.

Once again, all the search teams checked in without finding anything. The next deck down was the Sun Deck. It catered more to the adults and singles. Rory and Myles slowly moved through their area, keeping an eye peeled for their quarry while trying to avoid being distracted by all the young ladies in bikinis.

"Hello, Rory. Back to see me, are you?"

Rory looked down and saw Tanya Beno on a lounger beside him. She had moved from beside the pool, where she had been the last time he saw her, to the edge of the deck, obviously following the sun. Her body glistened tantalizingly with lotion.

"Why the coordinated search patterns?" Tanya asked him.

That comment startled Rory. "I'm not sure what you mean," he replied.

Tanya cocked her head, "I saw several teams of men on my way back here. If you were simply looking for Cassie, you wouldn't have teams of men working together to protect each other."

"I think you're reading too much into it," Rory said, trying to deflect her curiosity.

"Uh-huh," she replied as she straightened her head and gave him the hint of a smile.

Rory wondered how she knew about search patterns.

"From a former boyfriend," Tanya said.

"Pardon?"

"Isn't that what you were wondering about? How I knew about search patterns?"

"I wasn't–" Rory shut his mouth. There was a lot more to this woman than met the eye. He wondered–

"It looks like your partner wants to perform his own search pattern on me," she said with a coy smile.

Rory wondered what she meant and then glanced over at Myles.

Myles self-consciously rubbed the back of his neck and cleared his throat, clearly trying to hide the fact that he was blushing.

"Don't be shy," Tanya said as she lifted her knees and spread her legs across the lounger. "I'm always willing to cooperate with the law. Look where you want."

"I don't think that'll be necessary," Rory said as he took Myles by the elbow and guided him away.

"I'll here if either one of you changes your mind," Tanya called after them.

Myles was obviously embarrassed, "I wasn't...."

"Don't worry about it. I've had my own personal run-in with that one. She wound me up a bit too," Rory said. "And she is a looker."

"I'm not sure if I ever actually looked at her face," Myles confessed with a sheepish smile.

Rory laughed, "Let's finish up with our section and get out of here. If we meet up with her again, she just might convince you to start a cavity search."

His eyes lit up and Myles grinned broadly, "Never thought of that. But I'm always ready to do my duty."

"How noble of you, Kitchener."

THE SEARCH TEAMS MOVED down deck by deck, searching each section thoroughly. Rory noted the tension among the search teams was increasing. Sooner or later, one of them could confront a possible serial killer. Unless, of course, he managed to slip past them. That was the one possibility that concerned Rory more. And especially due to the fact they were now on deck 2. There were only two more decks below this one.

Static hiss interrupted his thoughts.

Myles snatched his walkie-talkie from his belt, "Go ahead."

"This is Nyhus. We found Saeed Jan. I need you and Mr. Steele in the aft storage freezer right now! And I need some men sent to the central staircase to work with Bakken. I'll explain when you get here."

Kitchener looked at Rory, waiting for his instructions.

Rory gave him a nod, "You know the men, split them as you see fit."

Licking his lip, Myles issued orders into the walkie-talkie, "Anderson, Helvig, Thorp. I need your teams to head to the central stairs to meet with Bakken. The rest of you, head for the aft storage freezer, deck 2. Now!" That done, Myles Kitchener turned and led the way at a run through the passageways, yelling at people to move out of the way as they made their way towards the stern of the cruise ship. The other teams joined them along the way.

They were all starting to breathe heavy when Myles announced finally, "We're almost there. The aft storage freezer is just ahead."

Down the passageway Rory could see a massive door that was wide open, Dense clouds of condensation were rolling into the passageway, caused by the cold air inside the freezer colliding with the warmer air outside the open door. A shadowy figure emerged through the clouds as their pounding footsteps came closer.

It was Nyhus. "In here!" he yelled urgently and then disappeared back into the rolling fog.

Rory wondered why he didn't have his weapon in hand. Then he assumed they must have the pastry trainee subdued. That was good work, he thought as he ran through the cloud of condensation into the freezer. Through the foggy mist, Rory estimated the freezer space was at least forty feet wide. But most of the space dead ahead was hidden from view by clouds of mist and he couldn't tell how far it extended. He glanced over his shoulder to see Myles and the other members of the security team following close behind. Every one of them had drawn their weapon once they had gotten inside the storage freezer.

Rory finally spotted Nyhus - barely a shadow through the mist on the right. The man was walking in a hurry and Rory took off at a jog after him.

Nyhus came to a stop near a cardboard container on the floor. It was four-foot x eight-foot in size and as high as his knees.

As Rory approached, Nyhus flipped open one of the top flaps. "We found him like this," he reported.

That took Rory by surprise. He peered into the box as the others crowded around.

A man with Middle Eastern features, wearing the white uniform of the kitchen staff, was lying inside the box. His body was twisted in an S shape.

"That's definitely Saeed Jan," Myles said as he held his papers with the man's picture close to the head of the body.

"Is he dead?" asked one of the men in surprise.

"Yes, but it hasn't been long," Nyhus replied.

Rory reached in and touched the man's face. It was still warm. "He's right," Rory said. He looked around, the clouds of condensation swirling around them, "Considering where we are, it can't be more than fifteen minutes."

"That would make sense," Nyhus said. He gestured for Rory and the others to follow him and he began walking quickly back towards the still open freezer door as he talked. "Bakken and I were just coming out of one of the rooms down the passageway when we saw the flash of a figure running out of this storage freezer."

Rory and the others followed behind Nyhus, wondering where he was going.

"Bakken and I ran down the passageway, chasing the figure," Nyhus said. He walked through the mist in the doorway, turned right and hustled down the long passageway, "Whoever it was went this way."

Rory and the others continued to follow close behind.

After a short walk, Nyhus turned right down another short passageway and stopped at the end, next to an open porthole. He gestured for Rory to look through it, "Take a look...."

Rory stuck his head through the porthole, wondering why. Then he saw it. A thin nylon rope was hanging on the left, next to the hull of the cruise ship. Rory twisted his head to look upward, trying to see where it disappeared.

"We saw the rope swinging back and forth in front of the open porthole when we reached this passageway," Nyhus told him.

"Someone was climbing up to the next deck," Rory said as he pulled his head back in.

Kitchener moved forward to look through the open port-hole. He whistled his amazement.

"The person had disappeared by the time we looked out. So Bakken headed up to the next deck, while I went back to the freezer," Nyhus explained. "That's when I found–"

Static from their radios interrupted and Myles answered, "Go ahead."

"This is Bakken. We're up two decks and still no end of the rope. We're going to the next deck up."

Rory and Myles looked at each other.

"The person has to be a bloody ninja to climb several decks outside the ship like that," Myles exclaimed.

Rory narrowed his eyes, thinking. *Or a trained assassin.* He didn't want to vocalize his feelings and create more tension, but this thing was turning out to be far more dangerous than he could've ever imagined. A serial killer was one thing. But a trained assassin–? Rory suddenly realized the men were standing around and watching him lost in thought. They were starting to look very concerned and he knew he had to get them busy to break the tension.

Rory turned to Myles, "Put two men on the storage freezer door. No one goes in until I say so. Then take the rest of the men and head up to join the search for the end of the rope and whoever climbed it. Start interviewing passengers. Somebody had to see something. While you're doing that, I'll go and get Dr. Rodriguez. Hopefully, he can tell us what happened to our pastry trainee and maybe we can find some clues to his killer."

Myles issued instructions as Rory headed off down the passageway.

Chapter 30

DR. RODRIGUEZ WAS SHIVERING as he bent over the body. The pastry trainee had been taken out of the cardboard box by several of the security men gloves after an initial examination. Rory had sent two men to get parkas that were used by the crew who worked in the storage freezer and they now returned. They carried a gurney holding a number of the parkas. They set the gurney down. "Here you go, sir," one of them said as he handed Rory a parka.

Rory passed it over to Dr. Rodriguez instead, "Here you go doc. Sorry I didn't think of it sooner."

Dr. Rodriguez gratefully took the parka and put it on, "No problem. We had other priorities, didn't we?" He rubbed his hands together briskly.

Rory nodded as he donned his own parka, "So what's the verdict? Any ideas what happened to our pal here?"

Rodriguez zipped up his parka, "My initial examination says this man died of a broken neck. I'll have to do an autopsy, of course, but I would say the hyoid bone is broken." He knelt down beside the body.

Rory did the same.

Dr. Rodriguez reached down to the dead man's right arm. He lifted it slowly, saying, The flesh is starting to freeze and I have to be careful." Getting it up to where Rory could see, he ran his fingers lightly over the hand and said, "There are no abrasions or indications of a fight on the knuckles. The left is the same." He pointed at the forearm, "And I don't see any signs of defensive wounds on the arms either. Of course, the autopsy may show bruising under the skin. The cold could be preventing me from seeing them right now, but...."

"So the initial examination tells us he was either taken by surprise," Rory surmised. "*Or*...he knew his attacker."

"I would say so."

A static hiss interrupted them and Rory answered his walkie-talkie, "Go ahead."

"Rory, it's Myles."

"What did you find?"

"We're on deck five. We found the end of the climbing rope tied to the bow winch for one of the lifeboats," Myles reported.

"That means the person climbed 3 decks on the outside of the ship?"

"It looks like it. We've checked with passengers and any crew nearby, but no one says they've seen anything," Myles said, sounding dejected. "At this time of day, most people are inside the main dining room or in one of the restaurants."

"Keep checking," Rory said. "And see if you can find anyone where the line passes the other two decks. The killer could've jumped off anywhere on the way up. I'll be up in a minute myself."

"Never thought of that. Will do," Myles said.

Rory set the walkie-talkie back on his belt, "Anything else you for me right now, doc?"

"No, Mr. Steele," Rodriguez said. He stood up and gestured to the men, "Let's get this body to the morgue."

Rory stood up as well and stepped back, watching as the two men lifted the body onto the gurney. *He shook his head softly.* This was not good. Someone was one step ahead of them. Someone *knew* they were searching and *who* they were searching for. Which meant someone also knew *why* they were searching for the pastry trainee.

"Once I get more information from the autopsy, I will contact you, Mr. Steele," Rodriguez said.

"Okay, thanks Doc. I'm headed up to Deck 5."

RORY USED THE CREW stairway to reach deck 5 and then stepped through a door to the outside deck area. He knew immediately why the killer had tied the end of the rope off on this deck. This specific outer deck area around the ship also served as a jogging track, with three marked lanes for the more athletic-minded passengers. Myles had said they found the end of the climbing rope tied to the bow winch for one of the lifeboats. Rory could see a long line of yellow, sixty foot long, enclosed lifeboats, each one marked on the side with the lettering 370 PERSON RESCUE VESSEL, mounted on the outside wall. Anyone jogging along this track wouldn't be paying attention to the lifeboats. And they wouldn't be paying any attention to the limited view of the sea between the lifeboats either. The meant the killer either knew the ship very well or was highly trained in setting up his entry and exit point for the kill.

Walked along the outer deck, Rory felt his concern rise as he mulled over the mounting evidence that they were facing a formidable foe in this killer.

Myles was just up ahead, talking with two of the security men beside one of the large lifeboats.

Rory highly doubted they would find much. Myles turned to him as he approached.

"This is where the line was tied," Myles said as he pointed to an area between two of the lifeboats.

Rory looked at where he was pointing and saw a heavy winch, complete with a gearbox and a motor, at the stern of the lifeboat. Another winch, at the bow, would allow the lifeboat to be lowered by heavy cable to the sea. A metal stairway, set in place over top of the winch, allowed entrance into the stern of the lifeboat for the passengers and crew during an emergency. Rory could see a black, nylon line tied to the metal stairway. He stepped up onto the stairway to examine the knot. It was a figure 8 knot used by experienced climbers. He looked down into the lifeboat.

"We checked inside the lifeboat, in case someone was hiding in the wheelhouse or the toilets. Or maybe left something behind. Nothing there," Myles explained.

Rory stepped back down onto the deck.

"I've sent some men back inside the ship, asking questions of anyone they come across. Others are talking to the joggers along the deck. But so far, nobody saw anything," Myles said. "Most passengers stay off this outer deck, because of all the jogging and running going on."

"I can understand that," Rory said. He stepped back at the heavy sound of running and a moment later a small pack of joggers thundered past them.

Once they passed Myles said, "I'll go work with the men in-side and see what we can find out."

"Okay," Rory said.

Myles walked across the deck to a door leading into the ship.

Rory watched as Myles opened the door, stepped off the jog-ging track and back inside the ship. Now Rory understood why this particular lifeboat was used. Stepping across the deck, he looked through the brass and glass porthole in the door as it closed behind Myles.

Rory had a direct view down the short passageway to the cen-tral staircase. It offered the optimum entrance and escape route for a well-planned operation. The possibility of someone seeing the killer was remote. Whoever had killed the pastry trainee had the skills of a *professional*. Which added a whole layer of complex-ity to whatever was happening on the ship.

Chapter 31

DAY 7

Montego Bay, Jamaica

STANDING SIDE-BY-SIDE against the railing, Rory and Myles watched groups of passengers leave The Caribbean Star-Liner one deck below, walking down the ramp to the pier, lively conversations discussing what they had planned for the day. The centuries-old city spread its arms invitingly east and west around the harbor and the unique strains of reggae music carried across the air from the old buildings not far away. It was a warm and beautiful day but neither man was enjoying it.

Myles stopped looking through his high powered binoculars and set them down on the railing, "Normally I'd be looking forward to going ashore for a change of pace from shipboard duties. Four of us had even taken up golf. We talked about playing the Half Moon Golf Course the next time we were here." He pointed to an open green space evident in the distance on the left side of the harbor, "It's just off the coast up there."

Rory didn't say anything. He simply watched the passengers, excited to get on with their day of sightseeing and exploring the second largest city in Jamaica.

Myles shook his head, "A little selfish of me, yeah? All those people dead and I'm lamenting the fact I can't go golfing."

"Don't beat yourself up about it. It's just human nature," Rory answered quietly.

Myles gave a half-hearted nod as he looked down at the passengers walking along the pier, "Yeah. Still...."

Rory changed the subject, "Once the passengers get back onboard, let's restrict our security patrols to the outside of the upper decks. I want them visible in their uniforms, but the men still have to keep their weapons concealed. Maybe we can prevent someone else from being thrown overboard at least."

"Sounds like a good plan," Myles agreed.

Rory said as he placed a hand on Myles' shoulder, "Now, let's head down to see what Dr. Rodriguez has found with the autopsy on our pastry trainee."

DR. RODRIGUEZ DRIED his hands on a towel as Rory and Myles stood next to Saeed Jan's corpse. "Mr. Jan died from a broken neck, as I had expected," Rodriguez said. "It was the result of a severe twisting motion."

"You mean like this," Myles asked as he pantomimed holding the head and twisting it violently as if he was screwing it off the body.

"Exactly."

Myles looked at Rory with raised eyebrows, "That takes training, like the military or martial arts. Yeah?"

Rory nodded, "And strength as well as surprise."

Dr. Rodriguez set the towel down and stepped over to the body. He pointed at the hands, "As I mentioned in the freezer, there were no abrasions, contusions or wounds on his hands. And the autopsy didn't reveal any bruising *under* the skin to indicate he was in a fight either." He pointing along the forearms, "And there were no signs of bruising under the skin on either arm, so there are no indications of *any* defensive wounds."

"If he didn't defend himself, and he didn't fight with anyone, that means he was either surprised or he knew his attacker," Myles surmised. He looked at Rory, "Right?"

"That would seem to be the logical conclusion," Rory agreed. "What it doesn't tell us is *who* did it." He looked at Dr. Rodriguez, "I don't suppose you have any way of getting fingerprints off the body?"

Dr. Rodriguez shook his head as he set the arm down, "No, I'm afraid not. Our onboard capabilities are pretty basic. The only other thing I can tell you is that this man was physically fit and quite capable of defending himself."

Rory used his fingers to tick off his points, "So...he either knew his attacker...or he was surprised. Which points to *two* different scenarios. One...someone knew he had poisoned Landry Morrissette and took revenge."

"But if they knew he had poisoned Mr. Morrissette, why wouldn't they just tell someone?" Myles. asked

"Some people prefer to take matters into their own hands," Rory said.

Myles considered that for a moment. "That's true. Maybe his sister...?"

"I don't get the impression she could have killed a physically fit person like Saeed Jan with her bare hands," Rory said.

Myles nodded his agreement with a slight nod of his head as he pondered the situation.

"Maybe it was another passenger," Dr. Rodriguez offered. "Or...a member of the crew." Rodriguez didn't look comfortable with having to suggest that possibility.

Myles grimaced at that thought as well.

"Both are possibilities," Rory agreed. "*But*...the fact that the poison was meant for someone else, that Morrissette was killed *accidentally*, can also point to another scenario." He looked at Myles and Dr. Rodriguez, waiting to see what conclusions either man would draw.

Myles narrowed his eyes and focused internally, considering the facts, trying to determine where they led to.

Dr. Rodriguez crossed his arms and pondered the question as well.

Myles' head jerked to attention, "Someone must have known he was *actually* trying to kill Sunbool Raad."

Rory nodded.

Dr. Rodriguez snapped his fingers, "Add the fact that he didn't fight back, that he didn't defend himself because he knew the killer –"

"He had someone working with him," Myles interjected.

"But it's rare for serial killers to work together," Dr. Rodriguez said.

"That's true," Rory said, "But not out of the realm of possibility. Some serial killers work with a partner, one dominant and one submissive."

"And that could be what we have here," Myles said, "and the dominant one kills the submissive one."

"It's possible," Rory said. "But we still don't have enough evidence to come to one specific conclusion. But the possibility of a partner means we have to stay on guard. There could be more deaths yet."

"But...if he did have a partner...why would he turn on him?" Dr. Rodriguez asked.

"That's another question I can't really answer," Rory said with a small shrug. "Maybe this man killed someone he wasn't supposed to. Or maybe the partner is panicking. He or she sees us searching the ship and figures we're closing in. There were members of the staff and crew who saw us searching this man's quarters –"

"Maybe it's his bunkmate," Myles said quickly snapping his fingers.

"It's possible," Rory agreed. "But there were a lot of other people down there that day. It could be any one of them."

Myles chewed on his lip as he considered the situation. "We could start interviewing the crew," he suggested, "see if we can find a lead."

Rory looked at Myles. "Possibly," he conceded. "But there is one other possible lead," he suggested in return.

Myles narrowed his eyes as he looked at Rory. Then it dawned on him, "You mean George Town? Where his bunkmate said this guy picked up that plant? But how can we–?"

Rory waited silently for Myles to understand *how* they could follow that lead.

After a few moments, Myles got it. He grimaced and shook his head, "No, no, no. I'm not sure Special Constable Teresa Morgan will be too happy if I call again."

Chapter 32

"WHY ARE YOU CALLING ME?" Constable *Teresa Morgan yelled into the phone. "Are you totally trying to single-handedly destroy my career!"*

"I know you're mad," Myles replied.

"Mad! I'm not mad. Being mad would simply imply I'm upset with you," Morgan stated. "What I am is righteously indignant! That's anger with a real sense of injustice, in case you don't have a dictionary handy. You used me–"

"That's not really true–"

"Yes, it is! You didn't have the decency to fill me in, did you? You let me convince my superiors to help you. You bring a killer onto the island and you don't tell me. Thanks to you, I'm permanently inside now."

"Teresa–"

"I am Special Constable Morgan to you! Do you understand me?"

The line went dead as she hung up.

Myles looked at the phone, "That went well."

Rory patted him on the back, "Try again. It's only lead we have right now and –"

"I know. More people could die if Saeed Jan did have a partner," Myles said.

"And we don't know the extent of his connection to the person he got that plant from on the island," Rory added. "It could be innocent or...."

Myles nodded, "I know, I know. How many people would be selling something as dangerous as Monkshood as a decorative plant."

"And we don't have any fingerprints that could lead us to Saeed Jan's killer," Rory said. "And the fact the killer was able to scale the outside of the ship to escape, tells us how dangerous –"

"I know, I know." Myles took in a breath and let out a low sigh. He didn't have much choice.

Rory placed a comforting hand on Myles' shoulder, "Just do the best you can."

Myles took another deep breath, held it and then let it out in frustration as he hit speed dial. Placing the phone to his ear, he looked at Rory as he waited for the Special Constable to answer again, asking, "Can someone on the other end kill you through the phone? You know, electrocute you through your ear or something?"

RORY AND MYLES STOOD side by side on the bridge with Captain Tor Amundson. The Caribbean StarLiner was plowing slowly through the rolling swells of the Caribbean Sea. Jamaica was beginning to recede away to their right.

"The storm is moving north slowly, so we'll take it slow as well," Amundson said. "Not much sense rushing into heavy seas and putting ourselves at risk."

"Sounds good," Rory said. "At least we're on the way back–"

"Why are we not on course!"

Everyone turned to see Salman Valid rushing across the bridge, eyes wide in concern as he descended on the Captain.

"What's wrong Mr. Valid?" the Captain asked with concern,

"Why are we not headed to our next port of call?" Valid demanded to know. "We should be skirting along the north side of the island. It should be along our starboard side. This way, we're headed to the Windward Passage between Cuba and Haiti!"

"It's all right," the Captain said as he held his hands up to placate the man.

"No it's not all right," Valid insisted. "We're halfway through our cruise! We should be heading to–"

"We've had mechanical difficulties," Myles Kitchener interjected.

Valid turned on Myles, "I wasn't talking to you, was I?" He gave Myles a long, hard look and then turned back to the Captain, "I *insist* we continue on."

"I'm afraid that's not possible, sir," the Captain said politely but firmly. "The rest of the passengers will be notified shortly. Everyone will be given a full refund or upgraded passage on another cruise if that's what you're worried about."

"That's not the point," Valid said. He clenched his jaw and stood silent and sullen for a moment. Then he turned abruptly on his heels and strode angrily back across the bridge.

"That was weird," Myles said as they watched Salman Valid disappear out the bridge exit.

"To say the least," Rory murmured, trying to make sense of the whole thing.

"Some passengers don't take change very well," Captain Amundson commented with a wry smile. "After years of doing this, you realize some people never like anything to disrupt their plans–"

The sound of a cell phone ring-tone interrupted their conversation. The tune was Rule, Britannia!

Myles reached for his cell phone and looked at the caller ID, "Sorry about that."

The Captain had one eyebrow raised, "Really? Britannia, rule the waves, Mr. Kitchener? On a ship operating under the Scandinavian flag?"

Myles' face turned a slight red. "Excuse me," he said and he moved to a corner of the bridge for privacy.

Captain Amundson turned to look back at the sea with a smile on his face, "I may need to use your brig, Mr. Steele."

"I don't blame you," Rory said. They needed a bit of the comic relief to ease the tension –

"Rory!"

Amundson and Rory both turned to see Myles beckoning them over with a wild swing of his arm. Both men walked over.

"Hold on, hold on!" Myles said into his cell phone. "I'm going to put you on speaker phone." He pressed a button on the cell and held it up between all three men. "It's Special Constable Teresa Morgan," he said. "I have Rory and the Captain listening, go ahead Teresa."

"We took the picture of your suspect, Saeed Jan, down to the Port Authority of the Cayman Islands and accessed a number of Webcams they run for tourism in George Town," Morgan said in an ex-

cited voice. "They actually keep the feeds on computers for a short time for security purposes. Checking on the time frame for the arrival of the tenders from your cruise ship, we found him coming ashore."

"Was he alone?" Rory asked her.

"Yes," Special Constable Morgan replied. "It was tricky, but we were able to track him across town to the back door of a wealth management company. And we only saw him going in the back door...because we had already been monitoring the company."

"Why were you monitoring them?" Myles asked her.

"We've been working with the British government on an international case," Morgan replied. "We are a British overseas territory and have close connections, obviously. But we're also one of the world's largest offshore financial centers. The British government contacted us when their investigation into terrorist activities in the United Kingdom appeared to have connections with this particular wealth management company where your man visited."

"How are they connected to terrorism in the United Kingdom?" Rory asked her.

"We were only able to figure that out because of what happened on board your cruise ship. And because of the shooting here," Morgan explained, "It allowed us to legally raid the wealth management company and search the entire location. It appears they have been laundering money and financing terrorist activities around the globe."

Myles whistled in astonishment.

"Any idea how our man is tied in with them?" Rory asked her.

"Not yet," Morgan answered. "We are just in the preliminary stages of going through all the records we seized. But I can tell you this; someone at the company had a small greenhouse area where they were raising plants similar to the one you described. We assume

they were going to use them for assassinations. But that's only a guess at this point...."

All three men looked at each other in astonishment.

"I just wanted to thank you for the lead. It has helped me get back into the good graces of my superiors," Morgan said. *"And apparently there is a big promotion in line for me."*

"Congratulations Special Constable Morgan," Myles said.

"You can call me Teresa again, Myles. And once I get my promotion, you'll get something in reward the next time you visit," Morgan added, with an evident smile in her voice.

Myles got a big smile on his face, "What will –"

"I'll call you if I get any more information." Special Constable Morgan hung up.

Myles continued smiling as he slipped his phone back into its holder.

"That doesn't sound very good at all," Captain Amundson said in a serious tone. "Having a man connected to terrorism on board...."

"The passenger who was supposed to receive the dessert...this Sunbool Raad...why would a possible terrorist assassinate *him*?" Myles asked rhetorically.

Both Rory and the Captain pondered the question.

"He didn't have a diplomatic passport," Myles added, as he pondered his own question. "And I would assume a prominent person or political figure wouldn't be sharing a cabin."

"Have you found any indications that the *other* missing passengers would be the type of people you would assassinate?" the Captain asked them.

Rory pondered the question and shook his head, "No. Not really. The only other thing that would make sense...is...if they're members of a political party or rebel group trying to overthrow a government in their homeland."

"Their only connections were to the United States...and to Yemen," Myles said.

"Maybe the missing passengers are part of some group from the Sudan that Saeed Jan came on board to eliminate," the Captain said.

"If that's the case...and Saeed Jan *did* have a partner, there definitely could be more killings," surmised Myles.

"It's also possible one of the people who was targeted, figured out what was happening and killed Saeed Jan before he could act," Rory offered.

All three men looked at each other for a moment, pondering the possibilities.

"Keep the men on their toes, Myles," Rory said. "We still have more questions than answers. I have a feeling this is not over yet."

Chapter 33

DAY 8

IT WAS EARLY MORNING, just before sunup and Rory joined Myles and Captain Amundson on the bridge. The seas were heavier this morning but Rory found himself navigating the rolling deck a lot easier than he had anticipated. The sky was dark in the far distance and the air felt humid and smelled of more salt, the ocean no doubt stirred up by the storm they were following.

Captain Amundson was on the other side of the bridge, sitting in one of the high, comfortable chairs bolted into the deck. He raised a hand in greeting, "Good morning. Mr. Steele. I hope you had a good night's rest?"

Rory nodded once, "Morning. I tried, that's all I can say."

Myles was walking across the bridge with a covered coffee cup in his hand. He looked a bit subdued in manner, "Morning, Rory,"

"Morning, Myles." Rory looked enviously at the coffee cup.

"Nothing to report from last night. Everything was quiet," Myles said. "This is yours," he added as he passed the coffee cup to Rory.

Rory took it eagerly.

Myles stepped over and took another covered coffee from the cup holder in a chair on this side of the bridge.

Rory noted there were a couple of extra men on the bridge if his memory of Amundson's bridge lecture was accurate. Jon Magnuson, the First Officer was here, no doubt acting as Officer of the Watch. Karlsson was an able seaman who would be keeping watch, Jesson was here as the pilot and Breckenridge was another able seaman who was at the navigation table. Karlsson and Breckenridge would be the two extra. He wondered why as he looked out at the sea, "Where are we?"

"We passed through the Windward Passage during the night," Jon Magnuson answered. "We're nearing the Inagua Islands and headed for the Turks and Caicos."

"That dark sky in the distance is the tail-end of the storm," Myles said.

"We eventually plan to sail north-west along the Bahamas at a slow pace, matching the storm's movement," the Captain explained from his chair. "But if the storm changes direction and the sea gets too rough, we may have to set into a port temporarily. So we're staying on alert."

That made sense. Rory looked out to sea as the crew went about their work efficiently and quietly. The waves ran from four feet to eight feet in height and looked much grayer than the inviting blue color he had witnessed the first few days out of Miami. *If I didn't know better I would say this is a bad omen. If I believed in those things.*

Breckenridge called out to the Captain and Magnuson, "We'll be approaching Great Inagua in about twenty minutes."

"Very good Mr. Breckenridge," Magnuson replied, standing a few feet away from Rory and watching the sea through binoculars.

"I've heard of the Turks and Caicos Islands but I've never heard of the Inagua Islands," Rory said between sips of his coffee.

"It's not very well known –" The First Officer never finished his sentence.

Gunfire erupted and bullets ripped through his chest, caused him to fall backward onto the rolling deck. Dead.

"Don't move!"

"Hands up!"

Rory turned to see two men on either side of the entrance to the bridge. They were dressed totally in black, including black ski masks with holes for their eyes and mouth. Two more men burst through between the other two and onto the bridge. Each man had a tactical shoulder mic for combat communications and was brandishing a submachine gun with a long, straight magazine.

The strange looking weapons didn't look like any recognizable make or model Rory was familiar with – Rory suddenly realized why – each submachine gun was a 3D printed weapon made from ABS plastic, just like the weapon the shooter had left back in George Town. All that useful (but still useless) information ran through his mind in the blink of an eye. Then his thoughts were broken by movement to his right.

One of the other ship's officers on the bridge was stupid enough to lunge forward. It was Jesson.

One of the gunmen swung his plastic weapon swiftly around at Jesson and fired without hesitation.

Jesson was knocked backward violently as bullets ripped through him. He fell to the deck hard, bloody and dead.

Captain Amundson came out of his shock and he rose from his chair, yelling, "What are you doing on my bridge?"

"Don't," Rory yelled as he raised his hands in the air and glanced over at the Captain.

That caused Amundson to stop dead in his tracks. Realizing the weapons had swung towards him, he licked his lips, understanding how close he had come to being killed like the others.

The four black-garbed gunmen spread out and gestured for Rory and the remaining crew members to move towards the front window of the bridge.

Rory feared they were all going to be murdered on the spot, but he moved slowly back to the spot they indicated.

Myles, Captain Amundson, Karlsson, and Breckenridge all backed up slowly, with their hands, up to join him.

Two more black-garbed gunmen entered the bridge. These men had their weapons slung over their shoulder and they carried a large silver-colored box between them. It had a number of switches, dials and four, foot-long, rubber-coated antennas. They set it down on one of the large flat tables on the bridge. Then one of the men began flipping switches and turning dials on the box. A low hum sounded across the bridge.

A second set of gunmen entered the bridge. They carried a large cardboard box and set it down at the foot of the large, flat navigation table. That done, they stood up, un-shouldered their weapons and turned to guarding Rory and the crew with the others.

Another lone, masked gunman entered the bridge, his weapon carried in one hand. He looked clearly to be the one in charge, the leader of the others.

Rory was startled. He could hear automatic weapon gunfire coming from other parts of the cruise ship.

Myles tilted his head towards Rory and whispered, "That sounds like –"

"Quiet!" One of the gunmen took a step forward, weapon pointed at Myles and glared.

Rory could feel his heartbeat rise, wondering...

"I've got it working." It was the man who had been working on the large silver box. The low hum coming from it faded to a whisper as he turned a dial. Then he simply turned and left the bridge.

Rory realized what the box was...a large signal jamming device. It would put an electronic blanket over the cruise ship, preventing anyone from sending or receiving any help messages, including cell phone calls. Clever.

The leader moved to one of the other large electronic boards on the bridge where he set his weapon on top and began doing something. The large sound of a foghorn erupted across the cruise ship. It sounded twice more.

Rory remembered the Captain telling him that specific flat board was the navigation system.

The leader then picked up a hand mic from the side of the table and spoke in a loud voice, "This is an announcement from the bridge. I repeat. This is an announcement from the bridge for all passengers and crew. You are all instructed to stay in your quarters. If you are not in your quarters, return to them now. Anyone who deviates from these instructions will be shot." He sounded the horn several more times and went through the same announcement twice more.

Rory took note of the fact the man had an Arabic accent. The same was true with the other man who had set up the jamming equipment. Where they connected to the Yemeni passengers?

The distant sounds of gunfire erupted from time to time.

Rory could see the Captain flinch and clench his fists in anger at the thought of someone being killed on his cruise ship.

But there was nothing they could do.

One of the gunmen took a walkie-talkie from his belt and spoke in a fast, Arabic language.

"Terrorists?" Myles whispered to Rory.

One of the gunmen turned quickly, "Quiet! Anyone who talks again will be shot dead. No more warnings. Do you understand me?"

Myles turned white.

Rory glanced at Myles and gave him a quick nod that everything would be okay as long as they cooperated. But he wasn't so sure about that himself.

"Sit," another gunman said to them as he waved his weapon.

Rory and the others slowly sank to sit on the rolling deck, backs against the front window.

More gunfire erupted in the distance, somewhere on the cruise ship.

The foghorn was sounded again and the announcement to stay in your quarters or be shot was repeated several more times over the next hour.

Rory and the others sat in quiet shock, watching a group of terrorists taking complete control of The Caribbean StarLiner.

Chapter 34

RORY WENT OVER THE SITUATION in his mind as the time passed. The terrorists had struck quickly and efficiently and the operation had been well planned. They all had a tactical shoulder mic for combat communications, but one of them had just used a walkie-talkie. They had used the tactical mics to coordinate the start of the attack, then had to switch to short-range lower-frequency walkie-talkies once the signal jammer started. These guys weren't amateurs. And striking before sunup would ensure the majority of the passengers and crew would be in their quarters, possibly sleeping. That would make the takeover of a large cruise ship, with thousands of passengers, a lot easier. But there was no doubt some of the passengers or members of the crew would fight back or stumble into a bad situation. That was probably the gunfire they could hear. Rory wondered what the end-game might be for these gunmen. Whatever it was though, he had to find weaknesses in their command structure or plans, so he could escape or get a message out. He wondered how many terrorists there might be –

A static hiss sounded and the gunmen who had made the announcement spoke into his walkie-talkie, "Go ahead."

"All secure," came a faint voice.

"Good," the leader said.

Another black-garbed gunman, his weapon slung over his shoulder, entered the bridge carrying a heavy, white sack. "The weapons," is all he said as he set it on the floor against the far wall.

The leader simply nodded and then stepped around towards Rory and the crew. He pointed at the Captain, "I want you to set course for your next scheduled port of call."

Captain Amundson lifted his chin in a defiant gesture, "I won't help you. You can steer the ship on your own."

The leader stood still, without any reaction for a moment. Then he gestured, "Stand up, all of you."

When no one moved, one of the other gunmen stepped forward and pointed his weapon menacingly.

"Do as they say," Rory suggested as he rose to his feet, with his hands up to show compliance.

Captain Amundson, along with Myles, Karlsson, and Breckenridge, cautiously rose to stand beside him.

The leader pointed to the large bridge windows behind them, a hard tone in his voice, "Turn and look."

Rory reluctantly turned along with the other men, fully expecting to be shot from behind now. He heard a gasp from one of the crew members and realized why.

Four decks below them they could see the open deck at the bow of the cruise ship. Toward the front of the deck was the large green circle that was the helipad, used by a helicopter to remove passengers that required emergency treatment. A steel wire guide had been secured at the ship's prow and ran over the top of the helipad and was secured somewhere on the wall below. Each member of Rory's security team was hanging by the neck along the wire. Kerk Bakken and Bern Nyhus were the two closest bodies.

Myles cursed at the sight of the men he had worked alongside.

Rory assumed it was the security team's weapons that were in that white sack delivered by one of the terrorists.

Captain Amundson turned and swore at the leader.

One of the other gunmen stepped forward, aiming his weapon at Amundson.

Rory turned his upper body, "Captain, don't." The next few moments were tense.

Then the leader took a step and placed his hand on the weapon, urging the man to lower it. His eyes through the ski mask were hard as he looked at the Captain, "If you don't want anyone else aboard to die, do as I say. We can always turn from killing your crew to the passengers –"

The Captain spat out his words, "You'll probably kill everyone anyway."

"Not if we get what we want," the leader calmly assured him.

"And what is it you want?" the Captain asked after a moment.

The leader's voice was calm as he said, "Please change the course of the ship, as I ask, and all will be well."

The Captain glanced over at Rory.

Rory nodded slightly. It was the best course of action right now. Stay alive and wait for a better time.

The Captain seemed to read his mind and he nodded reluctantly, looking back at the leader, "I'll need these men to help –"

"You don't need all of them," the leader said. He pointed at Karlsson and Breckenridge. "These two men will work with you. Now go sit in that chair, before I *do* lose my patience."

The Captain began to walk across the bridge.

"You move from there, you die," the leader threatened him.

The Captain sneered slightly but he looked shaken.

Karlsson and Breckenridge slowly walked across the rolling deck to join the Captain.

The leader then pointed at Rory and Myles. "Have these two put with the others."

The gunman nodded once and then spoke briefly into his walkie-talkie in Arabic.

Next, the leader turned to one of the terrorists who had carried the large, cardboard box onto the bridge. "Get everything set up and hooked into the system."

The terrorist went into action, moving over to the large navigation table. He reached down, opened the flaps on the cardboard box, pulled something out and set it on top of the table.

Rory was surprised to see the object looked like a large remote control for a radio-controlled airplane. It looked to have a screen, like the GPS in his car. Rory wondered if they were going to use that to steer the cruise ship. But that didn't make sense if the Captain and his crew cooperated and navigated the ship for them. A back-up system just in case? That made more sense.

"You've cut off the system," Karlsson said. "We can't set course —"

"Yes, you can," the leader said. "The Captain knows what to do."

Rory wondered if that meant using charts to navigate. He watched intently as the crew talked to the Captain in low voices, discussing something. Then a noise at the entrance to the bridge drew Rory's attention.

Three more masked gunmen walked into on the bridge, their weapons at the ready.

The leader gestured to Rory and Myles.

Two of the three gunmen stepped across the bridge to Rory and Myles and gestured with their weapons to move to the exit.

Rory consider fighting for a moment, then decided against it. He began walking slowly towards the exit instead.

Myles followed closely behind.

The lone gunman at the exit turned and led the way out, the other two following at a distance behind Rory and Myles.

As Rory left the bridge he heard Captain Amundson issuing instructions to Karlsson and Breckenridge.

Chapter 35

RORY AND MYLES were herded side-by-side along the passageway and away from the bridge. The terrorist in the lead kept a good twenty-foot distance, leaving little chance he could be taken by surprise. The other two followed far enough behind to ensure the same thing.

"Did you see the weapons?" Myles whispered to Rory.

Rory nodded discreetly, "Plastic."

"Like the handgun they found back in George Town."

"Easy to smuggle onboard—"

"Quiet!" yelled one of the masked gunmen behind them.

Myles glanced discreetly back over his shoulder, took in a small breath and let it out slowly, obviously trying to maintain his composure.

Rory just gave him a nod, trying to ensure him everything would be fine. Inside, he wasn't so sure.

The terrorists took them to a cross passageway and then over to the central staircase. Once they started moving down the stairs, the terrorists continued to keep their distance, both in front and back, removing any possibility of their prisoners taking them by surprise.

Rory kept his eyes open for any chance to escape as they approached the landing for deck 7. But masked terrorists were standing guard off to either side of the landing, making escape impossible. The same thing happened on deck 6. On deck 5 the terrorists marched them out into the promenade.

Myles caught Rory's attention with a soft, "Psst."

Rory glanced at Myles.

Myles indicated with his eyes to look to the right.

Rory spotted a bloody body lying in the doorway to one of the gift shops. One of the ship's staff had paid for an early start to the day with his life. Rory clenched his jaw in anger, but there was little that could be done at this point.

The terrorists marched Rory and Myles to the doors for the main dance floor. The lead terrorist held the door open. His eyes were hard and challenging as he watched the two prisoners pass like he wanted them to try something.

Rory didn't take the bait. And he hoped Myles wouldn't either.

Passing through the doorway and between two terrorists on the inside, Rory realized he and Myles wouldn't be alone in the large, open room. He estimated there were at least one hundred passengers sitting on the floor, including a number of teenagers and small children. A number of the passengers had bruises on their face, indicating they had resisted in some way. Adriaan Kosters, the Dutchman and Blake Smallridge, the Englishman, were two of the passengers he recognized. They were sitting side by side on the floor. Tate Nygaard, the Surveillance Manager was another familiar face. He was sitting behind Kosters.

"Sit," instructed one of the terrorists.

Rory took a spot beside Kosters.

Myles asked one of the passengers to scoot over and took a spot beside Rory.

Deadly silence settled over the large room.

Rory glanced around to see if there was a way out. Four masked terrorists with those plastic automatic weapons stood guard just inside the double-door entrance. Four more stood guard at the exit. They weren't taking any chances.

"Any idea what they want?" Adriaan Kosters asked Rory in a quiet voice; as he stared ahead, trying to hide the fact he was talking.

"Not really," Rory admitted.

"They've taken over the bridge and turned the ship towards Oranjestad, Aruba," Myles said quietly.

"That was our next port on the cruise anyway, wasn't it?" Kosters asked him.

"Yes," Myles said. "It'll probably take us a couple of days from where we are," he added.

"But if we were having mechanical difficulties, wouldn't that put us in danger?" Kosters whispered harshly.

One of the men near the exit, yelled at someone on that side of the room to stop talking. There was silence from everyone for a few moments until there was a whisper behind Rory.

"Mr. Steele."

Rory did his best to turn his head without drawing attention to himself.

Tate Nygaard, the Surveillance Manager had shuffled over to sit just behind Rory. "I know why we couldn't get the surveillance system working. They had an inside man –"

"Who?" Myles whispered a little too loudly in his surprise.

Everyone held their breath and watched the terrorists in silence for a reaction. But none came.

Nygaard leaned toward Rory as he kept an eye on the terrorists at the front doors and said, "Rajvir Siddiq. He was a new team member, working as my electronics technician. When the terrorists took over the surveillance room, they took us all away except Rajvir. They gave him one of those funny looking weapons. He was the man in charge of looking for flaws in the circuit boards–"

"Didn't you check all the components yourself?" Myles whispered harshly.

"No," Nygaard said defensively, "that was his job and I never suspected–"

"How did a terrorist become a member of your team?" Myles asked harshly.

"Ask head office! They hired him, probably because he came cheap," Nygaard whispered back harshly.

Rory put a calming hand on Myles' arm. "It doesn't do us any good to fight. And keep in mind your head office also skimped on your security department."

Myles closed his mouth, his jaw flexing and grinding away in suppressed anger.

"And this was well-planned. We have to work together," Rory whispered.

Myles calmed himself and then gave Nygaard a small nod of apology.

"So they can watch us now?" Adriaan Kosters asked as he looked around for a surveillance camera.

"No," Rory answered. "The system is wireless and they've jammed all signals from the bridge." After some thought, Rory

asked Myles, "Any idea why they would want to go to this Oranjestad specifically?"

"Not really," Myles admitted.

"Oranjestad is the capital city of Aruba," Blake Smallridge
said. "I've been there before because of the casinos. Besides
tourism, offshore banking is an important part of the economy.
Maybe they're going to hold the ship and all of us for ransom?"

Rory considered the possibility.

Myles leaned his head close to Rory, "Do you think there's
a relationship between the offshore banking in Aruba and what
Teresa told us about that wealth management company in
George Town laundering money and financing terrorist activities
around the globe?"

"That's a possible connection," Rory agreed. He gave it some
thought, mulling over everything they had learned from the information Special Constable Morgan had given them. "Isn't Aruba a Dutch island though?" he asked in a low voice.

"I believe so," Myles said.

Adriaan Kosters spoke up, "Aruba, along with the Netherlands, Curaçao and Sint Maarten form the Kingdom of the
Netherlands. They all have the Dutch nationality, like me."

"Would the Dutch government be willing to pay a ransom
to free all the passengers on this cruise ship?" Blake Smallridge
asked him.

Kosters opened his mouth to say something and then closed
it, obviously not sure of anything.

Blake Smallridge didn't look too encouraged by his friend's
silence.

Myles leaned discreetly closer to Rory and whispered, so the
others wouldn't hear, "Did you see Bakken and Nyhus?"

Rory nodded.

"They just...strung them up...the bloody bastards," Myles whispered forcefully.

Rory felt the same anger and anguish but stayed silent.

"I still have my cell phone," Myles whispered. "I guess they didn't think about that. I could try and call –"

Rory shook his head no discreetly, "They didn't take our cell phones because that large box they brought to the bridge is jamming all the signals. No calls can be made in or out."

Myles cursed in frustration.

Rory couldn't blame him. This didn't look good.

"So...what do we do now?" Myles whispered.

"Stay observant and watch for an opening," Rory said. "We'll find a way out of this yet."

Chapter 36

DAY 9

THE NIGHT WENT LONG AND SLOW for Rory. He got a little necessary sleep as he and Myles split the time keeping watch for any new developments or a possible way out of the situation. But everything remained the same. Four armed terrorists in ski masks continued to guard the front doors and four guarded the exit doors. Rory saw them change shift at least once during the night. And every one of them had a similar plastic weapon. But one thing Rory expected to see - but didn't - were explosives. He knew from seminars he had attended that terrorists often strung explosives on or around their hostages. That would serve several purposes. They could use that as a threat to keep SWAT teams from invading. But that wasn't likely to happen in the middle of the ocean. At least not yet. They could also take video of the hostages wearing explosive and use it as a tactic in negotiations. But no explosives - no videos taken that he knew of - and no indications negotiations were going on yet either. Maybe later?

Another purpose for the use of explosives by terrorists was to keep the hostages themselves in line, through the threat of detonations and death if anyone tried anything. But nothing like that had been done here either. At least, not in this room. And none of the terrorists seemed to have strapped bombs to themselves either. None of this made any sense.

The only possibility was that the terrorists couldn't send out messages or video either because of their own jamming equipment. Maybe they were waiting until they docked. All Rory could do right now was sit, wait and watch.

Myles stirred on the floor where he had flopped over. His eyes opened up and he went to move, then froze. Obviously, he didn't want to make any sudden moves that could get him killed. He slowly turned his head and looked up at Rory.

"Morning sunshine," Rory said quietly.

Myles slowly rose to a sitting position, rubbing the sleep from his eyes, "I can't believe I actually fell asleep."

"It's a good thing, though. We want to keep our strength up," Rory said.

"Any changes?"

"No."

Myles looked around, "I wonder if they're going to feed us?"

Rory looked around too, considering the possibility, "Not sure how they would do that logistically. Keeping everyone in their cabin makes more sense. But I doubt they would have the manpower or the willingness to deliver food to each hostage on the ship."

"Breakfast in bed, delivered by your local terrorist," Myles joked with dark humor.

"As long as you don't die from the lead in your diet," Rory whispered.

Myles snickered.

"Quiet!" one of the terrorists yelled.

"Are we going to get something to eat?" a young woman called out.

One of the terrorists near the main double-doors lifted his weapon and took several strides towards the questioning woman, aiming at her head.

The woman burst into tears and buried her face in her husband's chest as he wrapped his arms around her.

The terrorist stood there menacingly for a moment and then lowered his weapon. He took several steps backward and leaned back against the wall beside the double-doors, still staring coldly at the woman.

"Guess that answers my question," Myles whispered as he glanced at the terrorists from the corner of his eye.

The double-doors opened at the front and two more terrorists in ski masks entered. There was a brief conversation and Rory assumed they were here to relieve two of the guards.

There was a noise at the exit doors and everyone turned to see two more terrorists entering. As they closed the door behind them, sharp words were exchanged with the other four and within moments a heated conversation erupted between all six terrorists at the exit.

One of the terrorists at the front double-doors shouted something towards the exit. One of the terrorists standing next to him said something in reply in a harsh tone and now all six at the front began arguing as well. Some type of heated confrontation was now taking place at both sets of doors.

Rory wondered if he could take advantage of the situation. The terrorists at the front doors were the closest, but he was still too far away to reach them and grab a weapon. And six men instead of four made the odds even greater. But the fact that there were now twelve terrorists armed with weapons and in a foul mood, made him very nervous. There was no telling what could happen if they started firing on each other. And that began to look more and more like a possibility as the voices became louder.

"What do you think is going on?" Myles asked him in a low voice, so as not to attract attention.

"Not sure," is all Rory said as he glanced around the room, looking for a possible escape route.

A number of the passengers began to fidget nervously.

"If these guys get too worked up we could pay the price," Adriaan Kosters said. His voice was shaky but loud and he rubbed his hands together.

"Just stay calm," Rory said as he gestured with his hand for the man to keep his voice down.

"Stay calm! We could get killed," Kosters hissed. He began rocking as he sat on the floor, obviously anxious as he looked from the argument at the front doors to the one taking place at the back exit.

"Adriaan. Don't attract attention to yourself," Blake Smallridge said as he placed a hand on his friend's arm.

Kosters pulled his arm away roughly.

Rory realized the Dutchman's agitation was getting out of hand. If Kosters jumped up or did something foolish, all twelve agitated terrorists could turn and open fire in a heartbeat. He doubted many of the hostages would survive. Rory felt a tightening in his own chest.

"Control yourself," Myles hissed harshly across to the Dutchman.

Kosters turned with anger blazing in his eyes, "Don't tell me–!"

Enough!" a loud voice commanded.

The bickering terrorists shut up and turned quickly, weapons raised–

The firm voice had come from another terrorist, who had just stepped through the front double-doors and now stood firmly planted, weapon held loosely at his side as the doors closed slowly behind him.

The weapons of the twelve slowly lowered as this new terrorist stood his ground.

A few angered words of protest sounded from one of the terrorists at the back exit.

The new terrorist yelled something again. Then he began a long string of harsh words in a fast, clipped Arabic language.

The body language of the other twelve terrorists told Rory this newcomer was a leader and they seemed to fear him. But he appeared to be taller than the leader who had been in charge up on the bridge. This had to be *the* leader of the terrorist group.

The leader gestured firmly and curtly issued instructions to the others.

Two terrorists at the front doors left, grumbling as they did, as did two terrorists at the exit doors.

The leader dressed down the remaining terrorists and then abruptly turned on his heels and left through the front doors.

The body language of the terrorists left to guard the room told Rory they were not happy with what had just happened. There was definitely some group dynamic going on. If he could figure out what it was, maybe he could use it to his advantage –

"Quiet!" one of the terrorists yelled as he raised his weapon and walked towards the murmuring hostages.

Several of the children broke out in tears. The adults tried to comfort them and get them to quiet down under the intense glare of the gunman.

Rory prepared his body to jump for the terrorist if he started to fire.

The gunman took another menacing step.

Silence finally settled over the room.

After another moment, the terrorist finally stepped back to the double-doors.

Rory's thoughts returned to what it happened. There was definitely personal anger among a number of the terrorists and he wondered if he could use it to his advantage. But how could they figure out what it was? He turned to the men on either side of him and whispered, "Does anyone know what they were saying? Does anyone know why they were arguing?"

The men all shook their head no.

Rory leaned back discreetly and whispered the same questions to a man just to the side of Smallridge.

The man shook his head no, glancing up in case he was noticed by the terrorists.

Rory asked the woman beside the man.

She shook her head no as well.

"Ask the others around you," Rory whispered. "If we know what they were arguing about, maybe we can use it."

The woman looked nervously at the terrorists at the front and then discreetly whispered to the woman beside her.

The man turned slightly and whispered to the person behind him.

Rory's saw heads shaking no again and again. After a few moments, he decided it was a futile effort. He turned his attention back to the large dance hall, looking for a way out. If he could find a way out, maybe he could get away, if someone caused a distraction. He whispered to Myles, "Do you know of any other way out of here, besides those doors?"

Myles looked around discretely for a moment. Then he shook his head no, "Not that I know of–" Myles cocked his head.

"What's wrong?" Rory asked him.

Myles closed his eyes, "Do you feel that?"

"Feel what?" Rory could feel the normal rocking motion of the boat and wondered if that was what Myles was referring to.

Myles glanced at the floor, "We've...stopped."

Rory wasn't sure how we could tell that. "Why would we stop? Maybe we've reached port?"

Myles shook his head as he chewed on his lips, "No. We're still a day away."

"Are you sure?"

Myles sat quietly for a moment, obviously gauging the movement of the deck underneath him. Then he nodded, "Positive."

Rory considered what he was saying. It didn't make any sense, "Why would we stop in the middle of the ocean?"

"I have no idea," Myles said. He looked somber as he continued to try and sense what was happening.

Rory's attention was diverted as someone tapped him lightly on the shoulder. Rory turned.

A woman behind him leaned forward just a little. She must have crawled closer. "One of the passengers speaks Arabic and he told me what he could," she whispered.

Rory kept his eyes on the terrorists at the front doors, as he leaned back slightly to hear better.

"He couldn't fully understand their dialect, but it sounded like some type of division between the terrorists," the woman whispered. She glanced at the terrorists for a moment and then continued, "He said it could be religious but it sounded more like a family squabble. He's not totally sure but there was some definite cursing and personal attacks going on." The woman sat back and glanced over at the terrorists at the exit again.

None of the terrorists reacted so they hadn't noticed the exchange between Rory and the woman.

Rory thought about what she had said. Could this be an entire family of terrorists? That didn't seem possible. And without knowing *exactly* what their disagreements were, there was no still way he could leverage this information against the terrorists. All he could do at this point was to continue watching and waiting.

Chapter 37

SKYE STEELE PRESSED SPEED DIAL for the New York office and waited impatiently as the rings sounded on the other side of the call. Skye was three years younger than her brother Rory, but at 6'-2" tall, she was the same height. With sparking, green eyes and fiery red hair, her grandmother used to say she took after the Highland lassies of the MacGillivray family, than the Steele or MacLeod side. She had started working as a private investigator in the family business while her brother was still serving in the Canadian military and she had worked hard to become an expert in several martial arts disciplines, including Wing Chun, a form of Kung Fu, specializing in close-range combat and practiced by proponents of the art like Bruce Lee, as well as more esoteric forms like Brazilian Jiu-Jitsu, a self defense system that focuses on grappling and especially ground fighting. Unfortunately, all that was useless right now as she worried about her brother.

The Gulfstream G650 private jet banked to the right, the deep blue of the ocean filling half of the round window beside her. Blue skies and ocean views normally soothed her but Skye was too worried to even notice the view right now. Her brother was out there somewhere. And she was personally responsible for him being there, setting up the cruise as a surprise. She would never forgive herself if –

"Avis speaking."

"Hi Avis. It's Skye. Any word?"

"No. Uncle Murdoch has been in touch with the owners of The Caribbean StarLiner again and they still have no idea where it is. They've had no calls from the ship and they haven't been able to reach it at all. It's like it simply disappeared off the face of the earth."

"I tried to call Rory's cell phone a number of times again and I can't get through either," Skye said. "It goes straight to voice mail."

"Where are you now?" Avis asked her.

Skye looked out the window, "We're not far from Sangster International Airport in Montego Bay."

"Then what?"

"I have no idea," Skye admitted, "but I'm closer here than in New York, if Rory needs me."

"I agree. Keep your phone handy in case we hear from Rory," Avis said and she hung up.

Skye looked out the window and scanned the swells of the blue ocean far below. Where are you Rory? Where are you?

SOMEWHERE IN THE CARIBBEAN Sea

Myles Kitchener's body visibly stiffened as he went on alert.

Rory noticed the reaction, "What's wrong?" he asked in a low voice.

"We're starting to move again." He looked at the deck, gauging the movement.

Rory wasn't sure he could feel it. To him the ship's rocking felt the same as always.

"We're turning," Myles whispered urgently after a few moments.

Rory concentrated on the motion of the ship. Yes. He could feel it now. The massive cruise ship was making a wide turn to the left.

The other passengers murmured. They could feel it as well.

"Quiet!" a terrorist yelled.

The hostages complied but they kept looking at each other, their faces looking pallid, fearing the worse.

"Any idea why?" Rory whispered to Myles.

Myles shook his head no.

Rory could feel the cruise ship beginning to move faster as he concentrated on the movement of the deck underneath him. Why would they head for the port in Oranjestad, Aruba...stop in the middle of the Caribbean Sea...and then turn around?

"Maybe someone knows about our situation," Myles whispered. "Maybe the U.S. Navy is closing in."

Rory considered the thought. It was possible.

The rocking motion of the cruise ship increased as time passed.

"They're running the ship at full speed now," Myles whispered.

"Are you sure?" Rory asked him.

"Positive," Myles said. "We've only run a few times at 22 knots. Usually it's only half that speed. But we've done it enough for me to tell. The terrorists are in a hurry to get somewhere. They weren't doing that when we were headed to Aruba. So why now? Are they running from someone?"

Rory wondered the same thing. Where were they were going so fast and why? His mind ran through various scenarios but without more information, everything was just a guess. He waited and watched for more changes or a way out.

Chapter 38

TIME PASSED SLOWLY as the prisoners sat on the rolling dance hall deck. As the cruise ship plowed through the seas, Rory continued to go over everything in his mind. Nothing new popped up. Nothing that would get them out of this. He glanced around. The passengers were looking haggard, especially the younger ones, and the room was beginning to smell stale. Fatigue from the constant tension of staying on alert and watching for a break was beginning to affect Rory as well. His head sagged as his eyelids grew heavier. A few hours later, a changing of the guard broke into Rory's half-sleep.

Two terrorists in ski masks entered the front double-doors and one of them said something in a low voice to the two on guard.

Two more terrorists entered at the back exit.

As he watched them talking, Rory realized one of the new terrorists at the front was female. There was no mistaking the shapely, athletic body of a female under the black garb. This was the first and only female terrorist he had seen since the cruise ship had been taken over.

Rory waited to see if an argument would break out again. Maybe it would give them an opportunity to learn more. But there was no animosity or flare-up this time. The four at the back stood quietly, while a few pleasant words passed between the four at the front.

Rory was suddenly struck by something odd and he was now wide awake. All four terrorists who had just entered weren't carrying plastic weapons like the others. Instead, they carried Argentine-made MK-3 submachine guns with a curved 40 round magazine. Was that why they had stopped? To get conventional weapons? But why not replace *all* the plastic weapons with conventional firearms?

He mulled the new information over. Terrorist more commonly used AK-47s or any other number of mass-produced weapons. But considering they were in the Caribbean Sea, and just north of South America, using weapons manufactured in Argentina made sense. Probably easier to source locally on the black market. And the 9×19mm Parabellum cartridge the MK-3 used was one of the most popular cartridges in the entire world. But none of this information seemed to have any significance or helpful their predicament–

Static hiss came from back at the exit.

One of the terrorists who had just come in, took a walkie-talkie from its holster and said something into it.

There was more static hiss and Rory could hear the faint voices of terrorists over the walkie-talkie. It sounded like they were reporting in - one after another.

Clearly something was about to happen beyond a simple guard change. But what?

After a few moments, the terrorist said something final into the walkie-talkie and slipped it back into its holster. Then he looked across the deck, to the female terrorist at the other set of double-doors, and gave a subtle nod.

This female terrorist returned the subtle nod, looked to the terrorist who had entered with her and casually lifted her FMK-3 weapon to her waist.

Rory went on high alert. This was it. Every passenger in here was going to be shot dead and thrown overboard. Maybe the Navy *was* chasing them. He moved his hands into position to spring off the deck and fight back. As he waited to react, he was conscious of the up and down motion of the ship. Would burial at sea be his fate –?

The female swung her weapon around swiftly and opened fire.

The two terrorists who had been standing guard before she had entered began to dance. Bullets ripped though their bodies and tore holes in the wall behind them.

Screams from the hostages in the room filled the air.

Rory heard the roar of automatic weapons gunfire at the back doors as well.

And then it stopped.

Two terrorists as the front and two at the back lay dead on the deck, blood seeping through the dozens of wounds on their body. Their plastic weapons had been ripped apart as well and lay in jagged pieces.

The four remaining terrorists now stood still, calmly waiting as they looked at the frantic, screaming hostages.

Automatic weapon gunfire sounded in the distance around the cruise ship.

"Quiet!" one of the terrorist v from the exit doors. He stepped forward and yelled twice more, calling for quiet in the room.

The hostages were finally able to stop their panicky screaming but they weren't calm. Parents trembled as they wrapped their arms around their children. Passengers whimpered uncontrollably, many looking ready to panic and run.

Rory couldn't understand any of this. Terrorists attacking terrorists? Maybe it *was* a family squabble. Or some philosophical differences between the terrorists themselves. Rory's mind raced, trying to stay calm as he wondering how he could use this to escape. Then something else struck him. The man who had yelled for quiet had a *Russian* accent, *not* middle-eastern like the others. What was going on here?

The male terrorist at the back spoke into his walkie-talkie again, "Go ahead."

A faint 'all secure' comment came through the walkie-talkie.

Two more terrorists, dressed in black and wearing ski masks, entered the front exit and nodded at the terrorist at the back who had received the all clear message.

The terrorist nodded in return and stepped away from the exit and began skirted around the passengers, heading towards the front entrance.

Sounds of concern rose from the men, women and children as he passed near them.

The terrorist swung his weapon up casually and set it on his shoulder as he neared the front of the dance hall. He stopped in front of the female terrorist and said something to her. Then he turned on his heels, his weapon still casually lying on his shoulder, and he slowly walked across the rolling deck towards the group of passengers sitting on the floor.

Actually, Rory had the impression the man was heading directly for him.

The female terrorist started walking behind the man, her weapon held loosely her side, her eyes sweeping confidently over the hostages sitting on the floor.

Rory could hear sounds of concern behind him...and he could understand why. No one had any idea on what had just happened...or what was about to happen.

Both of the terrorists stopped ten feet away from Rory, their feet set apart as they stood silently side by side on the rolling deck.

Rory could see Myles tense. And he felt himself do the same. It didn't look too good for him right now–

The male terrorist reached up and pulled off his ski mask in one motion.

Rory was shocked.

The female terrorist beside him did the same. She pulled off her ski mask and smiled, "Hello, Rory."

Chapter 39

SALMAN VALID stood looking down at Rory, a slight smirk on his face. He cradled his FMK-3 submachine gun across his chest in a move that showed full confidence.

Tanya Beno stood next to him, her submachine gun still held loosely at her side, "Did you miss me?"

"What's going on?" Myles whispered as he looked at Rory.

Rory had no idea. Why had these two participated in a terrorist hijacking? And why were they now looking at *him*?

Four more black garbed terrorists in ski masks came through the front double-doors, their weapons at the ready. They marched directly across the room to where Valid and Beno were standing.

One of the terrorist pointed at Rory, "You. On your knees, lock your hands on top of your head and slid out to here." He pointed to a spot on the deck, five feet in front of Rory.

Myles moved quickly to get up, "Leave him alone –"

One of the gunmen smoothly swung the butt of his submachine gun around, catching Myles in the jaw.

Myles Kitchener collapsed to the floor, groaning in agony.

The woman behind him cried out and went to his aid.

Salman Valid shook his head as the terrorist motioned again for Rory to comply.

Rory complied, swinging around from his sitting position and onto his knees. Locking his hands over his head, he shuffled forward.

One of the terrorists passed his weapon over to another and then crouched to search Rory.

"I was surprised to see you in here," Valid said as he watched the search closely. "I told the men to keep you separate because of the danger you pose."

"I'm no danger –"

"Of course you are," Valid said firmly.

The terrorist searching Rory stood up and retrieved his weapon from the other one, "He's clean"

Rory detected the masked terrorist had a slight Russian accent, like Valid.

"Take him," Valid instructed with a jerk of his head. "Keep your distance and stay alert. Make no mistake and don't become complacent, he *is* dangerous."

One of the terrorist grabbed Rory's elbow and jerked him to his feet and away from the other hostages.

Two of the terrorists turned and headed for the front doors. One of the terrorists shoved Rory in the back to get him moving and then he fell in behind Rory along with another terrorist, serving as the rear escort.

"I'll go along and make sure everything is done right," Tanya Beno said to Valid.

"Just don't engage in any personal pleasures for the time being," Valid told her.

Tanya Beno laughed as she followed behind the last two terrorists.

RORY WAS POSITIVE HE would be shot and thrown overboard. But instead of taking him to the outer deck, the guard detail marched him to the main staircase. Okay...maybe they were
going to confine him to his suite, like most of the other passengers. That would make sense –

But they marched him *down* the stairs instead of up.

This didn't make any sense. His cabin was up on another
deck. And there was no reason to take him down another deck,
just to throw him overboard. Valid had called him a danger, so
they had something else in mind for him. But what? Rory's mind
raced as he tried to remember what was on the next deck. There
was the main show lounge, the main dining room–

But when they reached the next landing, they simply continued their downward march.

Rory took a deep breath and decided it was no sense worry-
ing. He would know soon enough.

They marched him all the way down to deck 2 and that's
where they escorted him down a familiar passageway.

Rory now knew where they were headed. The brig. They were
going to keep him locked up in a location that had no access to
the outside of the ship, because the brig was below the water line
and had no portholes. They could guard his only way out and up.
And down here, he was segregated from the others and unable to
offer any leadership. Valid knew what he was doing. Or at least he

thought he did, because Rory felt a lot better about this situation than any other that could have happened.

One of the terrorists opened the door to the security office and stepped inside. He moved to stand on the right side of the room and his partner went to the left.

Rory stepped into the doorway and stopped deliberately.

Tanya Beno barked an order in Russian from behind them..

One of the terrorists pushed Rory hard in the back and propelled him forward, "Move!"

"I was going," Rory said as he caught his balance and raised his hands. Then he took the initiative as the two terrorists moved into the room behind him. He walked straight across the rolling floor towards the four cells, opened the door of the first cell and slipped inside, pulling the door closed hard.

All four terrorists were surprised by the bang of the cell door and raised their weapons.

Tanya Beno's face was grim as she crossed the room and stepped up to the bars. She cocked her head slightly, "That's a good boy."

"I know when I'm beat," Rory said as he slumped to sit on the bunk.

Tanya Beno's eyes narrowed and a smile lingered around her lips, "Somehow I don't believe you. But we'll take it at face value for now, Mr. Steele."

Rory pulled his legs up on the bunk and leaned his back against the green wall of the cell. He crossed his arms tightly across his chest as he looked at Tanya, "Can I ask you what your end-game is?"

"You can. But I won't answer," Tanya said with a smirk

Rory shrugged, "Okay. But it doesn't look like things are going too well, whatever you're doing. You've already had to eliminate a number of your own men."

Tanya shrugged in return, "True. But they did their job."

That comment took Rory by surprise and he wondered what she meant by that...they did their job.

Tanya turned and walked away from the cell, setting her weapon down on a desk. Turning around, she looked at Rory for a moment and then said, "Our plan was to stay behind the scenes. But we didn't realize that the two groups we brought in as a front...were from different ethnic tribes in the middle-east. Who knew they would both have the same extremist views...but would have a hate for each other, based on tribal lines," she added with amusement.

Rory thought about what she was saying and then it suddenly dawned on him, "That's why men with Arabic sounding names were disappearing from the ship–"

"They started throwing each other overboard," Tanya said with anger in her voice.

"And that's how Landry Morrissette died," Rory said with a nod of realization. "The poison was meant for one of them."

Tanya nodded, "They wouldn't listen to reason. That little fiasco nearly ruined everything–"

"And the Chief Security Officer was killed because he saw them throwing a man overboard," Rory surmised.

"Exactly," Tanya said. "When they killed the Officer, we figured that would limit the scrutiny and make it harder to figure out what was happening onboard We knew the men under his command were green recruits," She narrowed her eyes and looked at Rory, "And then *you* show up...."

Rory looked into her eyes and saw the answer to another mystery, "And that's why *you* tried to kill me in George Town."

"But you're a survivor," was all she said in answer. "I only missed because I had to use that inaccurate, plastic gun at the last minute. And then...you kept on investigating, because that's who you are...."

"And innocent people like Cassiopeia Lopez kept dying," Rory said as he brushed his hands through his black hair in frustration. They had been one step ahead of him all the way.

"No," Tanya said as she picked up her weapon. "I had to kill her because she saw me talking sternly to that pastry trainee in George Town. He went somewhere where he shouldn't have been. Just to get a plant to make someone suffer and die in agony."

That startled Rory. He hadn't expected that.

Tanya turned and headed for the door out of the security office. The power and athleticism in her body were evident in the tight, black clothing as she walked.

That's when it struck Rory, "*You* were the one who killed the pastry trainee...and escaped up the side of the ship...."

Tanya stopped and looked back, "You were getting too close to finding him. I couldn't let that happen."

Rory shook his head slowly as he looked into Tanya's eyes across the room, "And I thought you were friends with Cassie–"

"I don't have friends. I'm an assassin. You do what you do...I do what I do," Tanya Beno said coldly.

Chapter 40

RORY REMAINED IN HIS POSITION on the cell bunk, leaning back against the green wall as he watched the four terrorists sitting at a table across the room...and did some thinking. Tanya Beno had given him some pieces of the puzzle, but it still left him with a pile of still unanswered questions. From what she had said, Rory gathered the first group of terrorists, the ones who had first taken over the ship, had been hired by Valid, or someone behind him, because of their extremist views. They had been willing to hijack a ship, probably figuring it was going to advance some political or religious viewpoint *they* had. But when they had tribal differences that jeopardized the plan, they had to be eliminated. But the very fact there *was* a second set of terrorists who could eliminate the first, meant there was something much larger at play here. Someone was trying to hide behind well-known extremist viewpoints connected to the Middle-East and Africa. But why? Maybe an opposite political or religious viewpoint was being hidden behind the first one. That was a possibility.

Both Valid and Beno gave him the impression they were professionals. Tanya Beno had said she was an assassin. And the way she said it, Rory believed it. The way the men searched him and escorted him down to the brig, told him the rest were military. Or at least ex-military. And with Russian accents, he presumed Russian military. So who was behind this whole thing? And what exactly was their end-game, one that involved hiring terrorists to hijack a cruise ship?

One of the four terrorists Tanya had left behind stood up and stretched. He said something and one of the sitting terrorists nodded.

They had been playing cards for the last hour and Rory hadn't been able to hear what they said as they talked. But now he recognized the language as one of the northeast Caucasian languages, specifically Chechen. Chechnya and Dagestan had been fighting against the Russian government for years. And the war between Russia and Chechnya had actually been going on for centuries. He was sure Valid's accent was Russian. *Why is a Russian using Chechen terrorists to hijack a cruise ship?*

A second terrorist stood up and also said something as he shouldered his weapon.

The terrorists who were still sitting at the table nodded as they continued to play cards.

Rory watched as the two guards left the security room together. The odds on his escaping had just been cut in half. It was now or never to try his plan. When he had met with Myles and the security team down here, to set up the search for the pastry trainee, Saeed Jan, he had noticed a security flaw in the brig. The lower edges of the bunks in the cells had thin, decorative trim made from thin, wrought-iron metal. A piece of that trim could be used in several ways...and Rory had one in mind.

As casually as possible, Rory swung his feet over the edge of the bunk and set his feet on the floor.

One of the terrorists glanced over, but that was it. He went back to playing cards.

Rory paused for a moment and then slowly slid a hand down to the trim. He bent a piece of the trim back and forth until it broke off. Bringing his hands together slowly, he bent it into an L shape to create a torsion wrench. So far, so good. He palmed the piece and slid a hand back down to the decorative trim. He worked another piece of trim back and forth until it broke off as well. He bent a slight hook into this piece to use as the pick tool. Now he would only need a few seconds...but he needed some way to get those few precious seconds. Palming the two pieces in his left hand, Rory stepped up to the bars, "Could I get a drink of water?"

One of the two terrorists yelled in a loud, heavily accented voice, "Use the toilet bowl."

The other terrorist snickered and made a low remark.

"Please," Rory begged.

One of the terrorists stood up, looking put out, and walked over to a small sink in the far side of the room.

Rory heard a tap running.

The man stepped back across the room, holding a white Styrofoam cup. "Back up," he instructed as he approached the bars.

Rory did as he was told, taking a few steps backwards into the cell.

The man set the cup down on the flat steel bar that ran across the front door of the cell. He gave Rory a hard look and then turned and went back to sit down.

Rory moved forward and picked up the Styrofoam cup, "Thanks." He drank the water and then placed the cup back on the flat steel bar, "Can I have another one –"

"No!"

Rory crumpled the cup and threw it into the corner. Then he leaned with his elbows on the flat bar with his hands through the bars. He blew a breath out and shook his head, as if everything was just too much for him.

The two terrorists watched him hard for a moment and then turned back to playing cards.

Rory discreetly moved one of the pieces from his left to his right. He had positioned himself right over the lock. He kept his head down but his eyes up on the two men, waiting for his moment.

Five minutes passed and the men were engrossed in their cards.

Rory discretely slipped his hands downward and swiftly but quietly went to work on the lock. It was done in seconds. He silently pulled the tools back and slipped them into his right pocket. Then he stood leaning against the door again, careful not to push it open.

One of the men got up and set his cards down. He glanced at Rory and then stepped away from the table. He walked across the room and disappeared into the small washroom.

Rory had his chance. "Hey pal. How about another drink of water?"

The man just turned and looked at Rory for a moment. Then he turned away, ignoring the request.

Rory cursed the man.

The man turned and looked at Rory with a hard stare.

"You wouldn't have the balls without these bars between us," Rory said with a sneer.

The man was up and across the room towards the cell in a heartbeat.

Rory couldn't understand what he was saying but the rage on his face told the story. Rory stayed calm, giving the man a sneer to increase his blind anger.

The man drew his fist back as he rushed forward, intending to strike between the bars at the prisoner.

It was time. Rory pushed the cell door open hard, brutally slamming it against the man's body and face.

The man went down in a heap, blood streaming from his broken nose.

Rory stepped forward and stomped down hard on the man's head, knocking him cold. Then he rushed across the deck towards the washroom.

The washroom door was starting to swing open.

Rory flattened himself against the wall behind the door just in time.

The other man rushed out of the washroom, calling out something to his partner.

Stepping forward, Rory grasped the man's head, twisting violently.

The man fell to the deck - dead.

Voices!

The other terrorists were coming back. Rory sprinted for the table across the room.

The door swung open and a man carrying a plate of sandwiches stepped into the room. His eyes went wide and he dropped the plate when he saw the man on the deck, just outside the open cell.

Rory reached the table, placed his left hand in the middle of it and vaulted over, feet first and turning his body sideways. His feet slammed into the first man at chest height, driving him back into the second man.

The first man's head struck the door jam and he slumped to the deck.

The second man fell backwards onto the deck in the passageway.

Rory landed sideways on the deck and spun around to get his feet under him. He sprang from the deck, jumped the prone body and turned to drive his foot into the second man's head as he rose from the deck.

The man brought his right arm up and deflected Rory's strike.

Rory used the momentum of the deflection to spin around and deliver a round house kick.

The man tried to bring his left up but wasn't fast enough. He yelped and sagged to the deck.

Rory heard a shout from back inside the security room. He saw the first man was struggling to his feet, reaching for his weapon.

The second man was also stirring but groggy as he tried to get his weapon off his shoulder. Fortunately the weapon's sling was wrapped around the man's arm, giving Rory his chance.

Rory turned and ran hard down the passageway. A cross-passageway came up on the right and Rory drove around the corner.

Bullets ripped into the far wall of the passageway.

Rory rolled on the deck and jumped to his feet. And promptly fell hard. He scrambled to his feet and realized he had slipped on partially dried blood.

A number of bloody corpses littered the passageway.

They were members of the crew. Rory could see their bodies had been ripped apart by submachine gun fire. He slipped his shoes off so he wouldn't leave bloody footprints and ran hard in his stocking feet, avoiding the polls of blood and looking for a place to hide. He passed a number of open doors on either side of the passageway. They were all small cabins for crew members and he doubted they offered a safe place to hide in. He came to a junction and recognized where he was. There should be crew stairs outside that far door. He ran for it. Bursting through the doorway, Rory half expected to run into more terrorists.

But the large stairwell was empty.

He started up...and then reconsidered. He thought back to the tour the Captain had taken them on, down to the two lower decks. The storage areas should offer a number of hiding places. The two water filtration compartments, the two air conditioning compartments and the two engine rooms should offer better opportunities to hide until he figured out a plan. But it also meant they could trap him down there once they began a sweep of the ship. He took a deep breath to calm himself...and did the only thing that made sense right now...he started down the stairs.

Chapter 41

RORY SLOWED HIS PACE as he reached the bottom deck. He couldn't afford to blindly run into armed terrorists down here. His breathing was raspy from the run and he felt anyone close by could probably hear it. Pausing for a moment, he closed his eyes and concentrated on trying to get his heart rate down. It wasn't easy. The stress from possibly being shot in the back at any moment kept his heart pounding. He felt the roll of the ship under his feet...and he remembered he was still in his stocking feet. His thoughts went back to those bloody bodies...and the security members hanging from the wire at the bow of the ship. He opened his eyes, clenched his jaw and thought of Valid and Beno. *You two are going to pay for what you did. I don't know how, but I'll make you pay.*

Rory moved on, treading quietly and cautiously down the passageway towards the stern of the ship, listening intently. He looked behind several doors he passed, looking for any possible hiding spot as well as any weapons to defend himself with. He found a room filled with all types of uniforms for the crew and staff but he couldn't find any shoes. He cursed under his breath. He had visions of stubbing his toes when he had to climb through pipes and machinery to hide. Or slipping on the deck in

his socks when he had to move fast. And he still didn't have anything to use to defend himself. This wasn't going well.

He left the room and decided he had to take chances and
move faster to find a hiding spot. It wouldn't pay to have to look
for a hiding spot on the run and he was sure it wouldn't be long
before they started searching down here.

As he hurried past a door on the right, a torn piece of brown
paper on the deck caught his eye. He ignored it as he moved
several more feet down the passageway...and then he froze in his
tracks. He slowly turned his head and looked back at the piece of
paper behind him. Did he read that correctly?

Rory moved back quickly and crouched down to pick up the
paper. There was writing on it. The torn piece read "ethylene-
trinitramine (C_3H_6N." He knew what it was instantly. The full
writing   would   read   cyclotrimethylene-trinitramine
($C_3H_6N_6O_6$). It was the explosive material in C-4, a variety of
plastic explosive! Rory looked at the door, gripped the handle
and slowly pushed it downward. No one jumped out at him
when the door clicked open. Rory slipped through the doorway
and closed the door behind him.

RORY FOUND HIMSELF inside a large cargo storage hold,
the heavy smell of spruce lumber very evident. And no wonder.
Hundreds of wooden crates were piled in eight foot high stacks
on the deck. The stacks had just enough space for a man to walk
in between. Rory was certain these were the crates he saw being
loaded from the pier back in Cozumel. Moving further into the
room, Rory passed several rows of the stacked crates and spotted

something on the deck, beside a stack of crates on the right. It was a large aluminum reel, holding yellow and red cord. Rory stepped over to it and read the label on the top of the reel. PyroCordTex. This was detonator cord. It delivered the charge to a blasting cap that would be embedded in plastic explosives. On the deck next to the reel was a device that looked familiar. He stepped closer and realized it was a remote-controlled, electronic detonator. A label on the side said it worked on a 40 MHz radio frequency. What was going on here?

RORY EXAMINED THE TWO foot high by four foot long wooden crates closer, wondering what they contained. Each crate had a square hole in one side, measuring one foot high and two feet wide. Screw holes on the outside of each square hole told him a board had been screwed in place over the holes in each crate at one time. And someone had removed the covering board. He stepped to a crate that had a hole at eye level and peered inside. He saw thick, brown paper. It was covering whatever was inside the crate. Reaching carefully inside with one hand, he tore a hole in the brown paper, exposing what looked like pink bricks underneath. He detected a faint, oily odor and Rory's heart began beating faster.

They were bricks of C-4 explosive.

Rory scanned down the stack and saw every crate had the same rectangular hole. He looked to the other side of the stack and saw there were similar square holes on that side as well. The next stack of crates was the same. Holes front and back on each crate in the stack. He looked inside several more crates and tore holes in the paper inside. And he found more of the same in each crate...pink bricks of C-4 explosive.

Rory tried to push the top crate up, testing the weight. He estimated this crate alone was two hundred pounds. Rory tried to calm his racing mind to think. If he remembered correctly, the USS Cole had a hole blown in its side in October 2000 by approximately 500 pounds of plastic explosives. He scanned the hold and estimated there must be 200 similar wooden crates in here. That would mean there was a total weight approaching 40,000 pounds of C-4 plastic explosives in this cargo hold.

And that was why Sal Valid had been so anxious to escort him away from the men loading these crates back in Cozumel. The whole thing had been planned like clockwork and he could have easily stumbled into what they were doing and–

Voices!

Someone was outside the door in the passageway.

Rory moved low and fast along the stack of crates, heading for the far side. He heard footsteps as someone entered the cargo hold. Skirting around the corner formed by the crates, he kept moving fast. A low scraping noise sounded back near the door and he stopped quickly, crouching beside a stack of crates.

Men were talking back at the door and he could hear heavy items being dragged along the deck.

Rory slowly crept back to peek around the edge of the crates and towards the door. He saw a number of the black garbed terrorists. But these men weren't wearing their ski masks. They all looked European rather than Middle-Eastern.

Several of the men stood guard, while others began working with the detonator cord. Moments later, more terrorists entered the cargo hold, carrying boxes that they set down before turning and heading back out into the passageway.

One of the men bent over and pulled a bundle of wires out of one of the boxes. Both ends of the wires had a metallic, silver tip. He handed the wires across to another terrorist, standing next to a stack of crates.

Rory knew instantly what they were doing. Those wires with the metallic silver ends were blasting caps.

Inserting them into the C-4 bricks meant the terrorists were going to turn the Caribbean StarLiner into a massive floating bomb!

Chapter 42

NOW WHAT? That's all Rory could think of. Over and over the same thought filled his mind. Now what? He turned and began moving through the row of crates and away from the men, looking for another way out of the hold. It was a good thing he had been forced to take his shoes off earlier. If he made the slightest noise now, it would be over in a heartbeat. Or a hail of bullets. Moving carefully around another stack of crates, he spotted a door at the far end of the cargo hold. Rory crouched low and turned back to make sure the way was clear. It was. Rory sprinted for the door. It was unlocked and he managed to quietly open it just enough to slip through.

Rory found himself in another cargo hold.

It was filled with more wooden crates! The boards were off the ends of the crates in here as well. Rory moved to the first stack of crates, reached inside and tore a hole in the brown paper. More C-4 explosives explosive bricks.

Rory scanned the cargo hold and estimated there were another 300 wooden crates containing plastic explosives in here. That was...100,000 pounds so far in total. He wondered how many other cargo holds–

Rory heard a scraping noise nearby! He held his breath and listened. Someone was in the cargo hold with him. One of the terrorists? If it was, this one didn't have a weapon or Rory would be dead by now. So he was either trying to sneak up to attack...or he was trying to get out of the cargo hold and alert the others. Rory shut his eyes and calmed his breathing, listening intently.

There was movement in the next row over...and it was moving away.

Rory crouched low and moved quietly along the row of crates towards the sound. He estimated he would intercept the other person in the gap between the next two stacks of crates just up ahead. He moved faster and reached the corner–

A figure tried to dash by him.

Rory stuck out a foot.

The figure crashed to the deck.

Rory flipped the figure over and raised a fist.

"No, please. Don't hurt me–"

It was Jaypee Andrada, the Filipino server from the main dining hall.

Jaypee held his hands up and cried again, his eyes closed tight in fear, "Please!"

Rory put his hand over the Filipino's mouth and whispered urgently, "It's okay. It's me, Rory Mack Steele. Remember?"

Jaypee slowly opened his eyes and looked up. It took him a few seconds before he realized who it was.

"Okay?" Rory whispered.

Jaypee nodded but his eyes were still wild with fear.

Rory cautiously took his hand from the Filipinos mouth, "What are you doing down here?"

Jaypee's eyes darted to the left and right, "I was in one of the food storage holds, looking at the mushrooms. The chef trust my judgment...and those men attack...they kill everybody and I run and–"

Rory raised a finger to his lips. He had to get the man to calm down. "It's okay, you're safe right now," he assured him.

Jaypee's body sagged a little in relief, "A-are you sure?"

Rory nodded but jerked a thumb back over his shoulder, "But there are men in the cargo hold back there who could be coming in here soon to work on these crates."

Jaypee looked stricken

"Is there another way out of here?"

Jaypee nodded vigorously.

Rory got off the Filipino and helped him off the deck, "Lead the way."

Jaypee turned and led Rory away from the stacks of crates and began a winding route through a maze of boxes and bags. A door appeared up ahead and Jaypee rushed for it, grabbing the door handle.

Rory quickly jumped to his side and placed a hand on his shoulder and one on the handle, keeping him from pushing it down, "Let me do that. You stand back."

Jaypee stepped back out of the way, his complexion ashen with fear, "S-somebody there?"

"I'm just being cautious, that's all," Rory whispered. He slowly opened the door a crack, ready for an attack.

The passageway was quiet.

"We can go that way, to the hold where they store the fruit," Jaypee said as he indicated to the right. "It cool, but away from men back there."

Rory nodded as he opened the door wider and peeked out. He whispered back to Jaypee, "I can make sure you get there safely, but I need some information. You said before you've been working on ships for a long time."

"Yes, forty year," he whispered proudly. "Three year on this ship since built."

"Okay. The men who took over the ship brought an electronic box to the bridge that jammed all the cell phone signals. No one can call in or out. They've also cut off the signals for the GPS and other systems for navigation. That way we disappear off the face of the earth and a war ship can't be sent to intercept. But they ordered the Captain to steer the ship towards Aruba. I didn't see any charts, so that means they must be using some other type of method or signal to guide the boat. Do you know if there is some other kind of equipment aboard they could use?"

Jaypee lowered his head a bit as he thought, "I think this ship does, yes. I hear some talking about it in crew mess. Ship was built with a backup system they said was old type...they call...low...low-something...."

"LORAN?"

Jaypee's face brightened as he looked up nodded, "Yes, Loran. They could use that?"

Rory nodded, "It stands for LOng RAnge Navigation. It's a radio navigation system, using low frequency radio signals, that goes back to the 1940s. Do you know where it is?"

"In the engine room, I think."

"That would make sense."

Jaypee looked puzzled, "You want to disable? That make it dangerous for ship to not know where it going."

"You're right," Rory admitted. "But I don't want to disable it. I want to try and use it to get a message out, to let people know what's happening."

"But someone will already know when terrorists call them for ransom," Jaypee said, still puzzled.

Rory shook his head, "No. I don't think this whole thing has to do with a ransom of some kind—"

"They hurt everyone on ship?"

"Possibly," Rory admitted, "but I don't have time to explain...and I'm not sure I can...but once we get you safe, you can point me to the engine room—"

"I take you," Jaypee said.

"It's too dangerous—"

"No! This my home and my family. I take you," Jaypee insisted.

Chapter 43

RORY LED THE WAY, as Jaypee Andrada directed their movements bit by bit, through passageways and holds toward the stern and the main engine room. They passed through the main air-conditioning compartment and then the main water filtration compartment, without seeing or hearing anyone. A long, slow hour later, Rory pressed his face against the small reinforced glass window of the door leading into the engine room area on the port side of the ship. He couldn't see any terrorists. But they had to be somewhere in the engine room. He was positive there would be a skeleton crew down here to keep the ship's engines running, like on the bridge, and someone would be watching them.

"Are we going in there?" Jaypee asked him in a hushed voice.

"Yeah, we have to. Just keep your eyes open," Rory whispered. He reached down and gripped the door handle.

Jaypee brushed his hands down his pant legs, nervously getting himself ready.

Rory pushed the handle down slowly, anticipating a guard waiting somewhere on the other side. The door opened a crack and the deep rumbling sound of machinery spilled out, along with the faint odors of grease and industrial oils. Rory paused, waiting for an attack. But nothing happened. He waited a few more seconds, then opened the door wider and slipped through.

Jaypee followed quickly behind him, grabbing the door and slowly closing it, making sure it didn't make excess noise by slamming back into place.

Rory moved cautiously along the walkway, his hands sliding along the green pipe railing on the left.

Followed closely behind, Jaypee looked back every so often, fearing someone was about to attack them from the rear

Rory went down three stairs and followed the green pipe railing to the left. He paused, trying to remember the path the Captain had taken on their tour down here. The problem was, he hadn't really paid that much attention to *where* they had gone. He had been more interested in the *things* he was seeing.

Jaypee took a step ahead and pointed to the left, "I think it that way."

"You're sure?"

Jaypee opened his mouth and then closed it. His eyes blinked a couple of times, "Pretty sure?"

Rory looked back in the direction Jaypee had pointed and grimaced. *Pretty sure?* He shook his head softly, "Okay, I guess a guess is better than what I have." He reminded himself to stay on alert, then began moving in that direction.

Jaypee followed behind again, checking behind every so often. His breathing was short and raspy with fear.

Rory felt some relief when he saw the yellow painted area, where the Captain had taken them through on the tour. The walkway became wider and there was the sound of steel plating underfoot. They *were* getting closer. Of course, that probably meant they were closer to armed terrorists as well–

Voices sounded.

Rory put a hand behind him quickly and stopped Jaypee from moving.

Rory heard several men talking in a foreign language up ahead. It sounded like Russian.

Jaypee's raspy breathing intensified and his hand shook as he pointed, "I think LORAN system just ahead."

Rory turned and put a finger to his lips.

Jaypee swallowed.

"Stay here," Rory whispered. He then slid his hand along the yellow pipe railing, as he moved slowly towards the voices. After a dozen steps, he stopped dead.

Four terrorists, dressed in black, but without the ski masks on, were standing just ahead, leaning against the pipe railing and having a smoke. Their weapons were slung by their straps over their shoulders. But it wouldn't take more than a quick move to unsling them and start firing. There was no way he could find the LORAN system this way. Rory slipped back to Jaypee quickly. "We can't get through, there are terrorists ahead," he whispered.

Looked scared, Jaypee's hands shook.

And Rory didn't blame him. He took Jaypee by an elbow to get him moving and they worked their way back out of the engine room compartment.

Jaypee let out a sharp breath as soon as they were on the other side of the door in the water filtration compartment. It was as if the man holding his breath all the way back.

Rory put a hand on the man's shoulder to reassure him and he said in a low voice, "We're safe here. We can try later, when the way is clear." Then he leaned back against the door, pushing his fingers through his black hair, trying to figure out what else he could do if they *couldn't* reach the LORAN system–

A moment later, Jaypee asked him, "What about other one?"

It took a moment for the question to register with Rory. He looked at Jaypee, "Other one...?"

Jaypee nodded, "Yes, other one. Other engine room. This main one," he said as he pointed at the door. "Other one is back-up."

Rory felt dumb. Why hadn't he remembered that? The Captain had told him about everything having a back-up. "Can you show me the way, Jaypee?"

Jaypee looked around and thought about it for a moment, "It on other side of the ship. But I don't know the way there from this compartment. I only know how from storage areas."

"Okay. Let's work our way back to the storage area and then you can lead us over there," Rory said.

Jaypee nodded and they worked their way back through the air conditioning compartment to the passageway where they had first entered.

"Okay, which way?" Rory asked as he closed the door behind them.

Jaypee pointed along the passageway, "Down there. We can turn right and passageway go right across ship."

"Okay. Stay behind me, like before, and tell me where to go," Rory instructed him. He strode down the passageway, on high alert for any sight or sound of the terrorists.

Following behind, Jaypee glanced back nervously from time to time.

Reaching the corner of the cross-passageway, Rory placed his back against the wall.

Jaypee did the same, nervously looking back.

Rory slid forward and peered around the corner.

The passageway was empty.

Gesturing for the Filipino to follow him, Rory slipped around the corner, treading lightly at first. Then he began moving a little faster. They were too vulnerable out here. Better to be inside one of the compartments with areas to hide–

Voices up ahead.

Rory stopped dead in his tracks and held a hand out to stop Jaypee in his tracks.

The voices sounded just ahead in a cross-passageway.

"We need to hide," he whispered back to Jaypee.

Placing a hand on Rory's arm, Jaypee whispered, "This way."

Now Rory followed the Filipino, glancing back from time to time as they retreated down the passageway as fast as possible.

After forty feet, Jaypee opened a door on the left and ducked inside.

Rory slid inside behind Jaypee and took a quick look at where they were. It was a storage hold, with linen, pillows, bedding, and towels piled high on shelves.

Jaypee started to close the door completely but Rory turned and stopped him.

Rory pulled the Filipino away from the door and held the handle down, keeping the door open a crack. Leaning lightly against the door, he peered down the passageway.

Two terrorists appeared, their weapons held at the ready across their chest. They came this way, down the passageway towards the room.

Did they see us coming in here?

Two more terrorists appeared behind the first two.

Rory could hear one of them call out a name.

The first two turned to look back and said something in Russian, A moment later, they walked back to join the other two terrorists. The four of them began walking and disappeared out of view.

Rory took the chance to open the door a little wider and caught a glimpse of the backs of two terrorists, moving away down the passageway to the right.

"What's happening?" Jaypee whispered from behind him.

Rory thought about it for a few seconds, "It looks like a search team. They're probably sweeping each deck, looking for me."

"What do we do now?" Jaypee asked him. "They are where we have to go."

"I'm going to have to try and sneak by them," Rory said. "You stay here. If they find you, they'll just think you were hiding in here—"

Jaypee shook his head vigorously, "No. I stay with you and help."

"Jaypee—"

"We go back and further down is laundry area," Jaypee explained. "We can work across ship that way too."

"It's too dangerous for you—"

Jaypee gestured to get moving, "Go, go, go."

Rory acquiesced to his wishes and glance down the passageway again. It was clear. Slowly opening the door more, he stepped out and peeked around the door, looking in the other direction. Clear as well. Rory slipped out into the passageway with Jaypee close behind him. They jogged back down the passageway and turned left.

After a few minutes, Jaypee tapped Rory on the shoulder and pointed to a door just up ahead.

Rory nodded. And when he reached it, he placed his ear against the door first. Not hearing anything through the thick door, he opened it slowly–

There was barely enough room but Jaypee slipped past Rory and went inside.

Grimacing, Rory warned the Filipino as he followed him inside, "You have to be more careful."

"But we need to hurry, so don't get caught."

Rory held his tongue as he closed the door and followed the Filipino.

There was a hollow clinking sound from Jaypee's shoes as he went down gray, steel stairs to a yellow path painted along the deck.

Rory detected the heavy smell of laundry soap and he realized where they were. They were inside the ship's immense laundry room. A large stainless-steel barrel, 40 feet long, towered over Rory on the right-hand side. It was an industrial dryer and there was a mountain of bed sheets piled up on a large, low platform at the far end of the dryer. Another pile of sheets was scattered across the floor, the workers obviously abandoning their work when the terrorists had taken over the ship.

Rory followed Jaypee into another section filled with large, industrial laundry washers and dryers. Abandoned carts holding various pieces of clothing were scattered about, other carts were knocked over, probably also abandoned in the frantic bid to flee to safe quarters.

Next came large tables for ironing clothes, industrial pressers for pants and slacks–

"Don't move!"

Chapter 44

JAYPEE'S HEAD JERKED to the right and he stopped dead in his tracks, his eyes wide in fear.

Rory stopped dead as well. Whoever Jaypee was looking at was hidden from his own view by the long line of clothing in plastic bags hanging on a long metal bar to his right. Which meant whoever was there, couldn't see him either. He considered pushing through the garments and attacking whoever was on the other side...but how many were there?

A terrorist in black clothing, minus the ski mask and with his submachine gun at his shoulder, moved closer to Jaypee...and caught a glimpse of Rory. The barrel of his weapon swung around.

Rory dove to the right.

The terrorist opened up, his bullets murdering a long rack of freshly pressed suits.

Rory scrambled to his feet, grabbed the edge of a large laundry hamper on four wheels and propelled it towards the terrorist.

The terrorist was bringing his weapon around in Rory's direction again and squeezed the trigger. The hamper hit him. His bullets tore holes through clothing in plastic garment bags hanging high over the top of his target's head.

Rory pushed his way desperately through another line of hanging garments, looking for some kind of safety. His feet went out from under him. A pile of plastic hangers on the deck went flying in all directions. Bullets ripped through the line of garments behind him and tore into a large industrial, pants pressing machine, ten feet ahead of him.

That was too close.

Once the terrorists came through that line of clothing, it would be all over.

Rory scrambled to his feet and ran hard and low to his left.

The terrorist pushed his way to the line of clothing, spotted his target fleeing and turned his weapon in that direction.

Rory picked up a clothing iron with his left while his right grabbed the end of the electrical cord. Throwing the iron in the air behind him, he caught the momentum with his right hand, brought his left back to grab the end of the cord and whirled the iron around over his head. He let it fly with all his might, falling face down to the deck with the effort.

The terrorist bullets ripped into a huge pressing machine just behind Rory.

The iron smashed into the submachine gun, then ricocheted into the terrorist's face. He screamed in pain. Then he abruptly went silent as a second iron smashed into the back of his head.

Rory watched the terrorist's body fall forward and bounce as it hit the deck.

Jaypee stood rooted to the spot just behind the body, an iron with a bloody edge still held firmly in his hand.

Rory moved quickly to the body and pulled the submachine gun out from underneath him. Then he checked for a pulse in the man's neck.

"He dead?" Jaypee whispered.

"Yeah," Rory said as he quickly rose to his feet and moved to the Filipino. "Are you okay?"

Jaypee nodded but his complexion was pale with shock.

Rory wasn't sure which was worse for the Filipino, killing a man or the near-death experience. "You had no choice. You know that, right?"

He nodded again but Jaypee was obviously still shaken by what had happened.

Rory took a quick look at the submachine gun and grimaced. The magazine had been bent by the blow from the iron he had thrown and the weapon was now unusable.

"Gun not work?" Jaypee whispered.

Rory looked at the Filipino and shook his head no.

Jaypee looked back down at the dead body and licked his lips.

Rory knew they couldn't stand here much longer, "Help me hide the body. These guys were working in pairs and his buddy could be around somewhere."

His eyes went wide and Jaypee looked around in fear.

Rory reached out and took the iron from the Filipinos hand, "Let's get rid of this and the submachine gun as well."

Jaypee nodded, but he stayed rooted to the spot as Roy set the broken submachine gun and the bloody iron on a woman's dress lying on the deck.

Rory flipped the dead terrorist onto his back. Then he wrapped the dress around the iron and the submachine gun. He took the bundle back to the body and stuffed it up under the man's black pullover.

Jaypee just stood there, staring.

Rory took the dead terrorist's feet and began to drag the body across the floor. It was a struggle, but he finally managed to drag the body into the section with all the industrial washers and dryers. He stopped beside the first dryer and opened the huge door. Then he bent to lift the body.

"I help." It was Jaypee. He threw a ball of clothing into the dryer, "I clean up some blood on the floor, so they don't see."

"Good job," Rory said as he lifted the dead man's shoulders.

Jaypee grabbed the dead man's feet and together they stuffed the body inside the industrial dryer and closed the huge door.

"Just point me in the right direction and then find yourself a good place to hide," Rory said.

"No," Jaypee said. "I show you. But we have to go fast, right?"

"Just fast enough not to get caught," Rory said.

Nodding at that, the Filipino took a deep breath to ready himself. Then he turned and headed back to where the attack had taken place.

Rory followed behind him quickly, still unsure of how the man would hold up. And it was understandable. Killing someone was never easy. And especially by cracking a skull with an iron.

Jaypee led Rory quickly past the pressing equipment and the racks of clothes again and into a large storage area for soap, bleach, garment bags, hangars, and other materials for the laundry area. The next passageway was empty and they quickly moved down to a door and into the backup air-conditioning compartment.

As the door closed behind them, Rory reached out to Jaypee to keep him from moving.

Jaypee's eyes were wide in fear. "You hear something?" he whispered.

Chapter 45

RORY SHOOK HIS HEAD NO. "I just don't want to get surprised again," he said in a low voice. He jerked a thumb upwards, "Let's climb to the top of this compartment. That way, we have the high ground and should see someone coming. At least, I hope so."

Jaypee didn't look too encouraged by that last thought but he followed behind as Rory climbed the steel stairs to the next level. It wasn't easy to see through down all of the equipment but it still offered an advantage. Together, they moved cautiously and quietly across the catwalks to the other side of the compartment and into the water filtration area.

This compartment was three decks high and Rory kept an eye out as he moved them over to the next set of stairs and climbed to the top deck. Treading cautiously, they took their time and made their way aft, towards the backup engine room.

Minutes later, Jaypee tapped Rory on the shoulder and pointed to the right.

Rory took a look at where he was pointing. A door was labeled 'Engine Room 2'. Moving quickly to the door, Rory looked through the small, reinforced window. He didn't see anyone in the section painted foam-green on the other side of the door. He tested the door handle. It was unlocked. Cracking the door open, he slipped through.

Jaypee slipped in behind him, making sure the door didn't slam as he shut it behind them.

Cautiously leading the way, Rory kept on guard, listening and watching carefully for any signs of the terrorists.

After twenty minutes of slow, cautious movement, they came to a catwalk. Jaypee tapped Rory on the shoulder again. "Go that way."

Rory led the way across a catwalk.

Jaypee tapped Rory on the shoulder again. "Should be down there," he said as he pointed to a metal stairway.

Rory nodded and they began heading down.

Everything was quiet, with only the deep throbbing of the engines vibrating through the metal stairs.

Slowing his pace as he neared the bottom of the stairs, Rory listened intently for voices through the constant throbbing of the machinery around them.

"Should be over there," Jaypee whispered. He pointed to the right along the metal walkway.

Rory took a brief look to the left and then headed right. Three minutes later, he found what he was looking for, the back-up navigation system. It consisted of a number of panels with an assortment of dials, toggle switches, and digital readouts. He opened three lower panel doors before he found a schematic blueprint of the system.

"How we use this to get message out?" Jaypee asked him in a low voice. He took turns briefly looking at the schematic and his head swiveling back and forth, watching for terrorists.

"It's an earth-based radio system," Rory said as he looked over the schematics. "It uses radio frequencies to determine the ship's position geographically. These terrorists are very well organized and they have the Captain navigating somehow after they cut off the standard navigation system. Since he's not using old-fashioned charts, my bet is they have him using this system. I imagine they have it tied into a land-based system they set up on one of the islands, in preparation for this hijacking."

"So...we steer ship to port?" Jaypee asked him.

"No. Radio frequencies can also be used to communicate with someone." He used his finger to trace a path on the schematic.

"So you call out to send message," Jaypee said.

"No, we can't take that chance," Rory said. He closed the panel and stood up.

Jaypee's scratched his cheek, "No?"

Rory stepped to the left and looked over a number of dials and switches. "More than likely they'd hear or see something like that going through, Jaypee. *But*...amateur radio operators use Morse code to send signals all the time. If I can just figure out how to...."

"How to...what?"

"Here we go," Rory said. He swung the front of another panel open. Behind it were a number of wires on an electrical board. Rory began to trace where each wire went. Rory found the specific wire he wanted and began to work the end soldered to the electrical board back and forth. In a few moments, it broke free.

Jaypee leaned in, trying to figure out what Rory was doing.

"Do you have a pocket knife?" Rory asked.

Jaypee shook his head no.

"Crap," Rory said. Using his fingernails, he tried to pick away the covering from the broken end.

Jaypee dug into a pocket and handed nail clippers to Rory, "This work?"

"Yeah, great," Rory said. He nipped pieces of the wire covering away, exposing the bare wire underneath. Then he gently placed the bare wire against the solder joint where another wire was connected to the electrical board. A small electrical hiss sounded.

Jaypee's eyes went wide in surprise.

"We're in business," Rory said. He gave the bent nail clippers back to Jaypee and said, "Hold this wire away from the board for me."

Putting the nail clippers back in his pocket, Jaypee reached over with a shaking hand.

"You'll be fine," Rory assured him.

Jaypee nodded and finally held the wire in shaky fingers.

Rory moved over to another set of dials and buttons and began pressing and turning them while he monitored several gauges. Finally satisfied he had everything set properly he moved back beside Jaypee and reached for the wire, "I'll take it again,"

Jaypee let go of the wire a let out a breath of relief. "What you do?"

"I've set the LORAN system to a specific frequency used by aircraft for their radio navigation. We can't send a signal around the world...but unless I miss my guess...we may have a friend in the Caribbean Sea who can pick it up." He touched the wire to the board and an electrical hiss sounded again.

Jaypee watched in fascination as Rory used short and long hisses to tap out a Morse code message.

Chapter 46

SANGSTER INTERNATIONAL Airport, Montego Bay, Jamaica

SKYE STEELE STEPPED OFF THE STAIRS of the Gulfstream G650 private jet to the tarmac. There was still no word from Rory or the cruise ship. What was happening out there at sea? A sense of guilt coursed through her veins. *She* had been the one to set up the cruise for her big brother.

The men operating the fueling equipment did a double-take as the stunning, red-haired woman strode panther-like across the tarmac. Skye wore her standard garb of black leather jacket and pants and black, silk blouse. And they did little to hide her sculpted form.

Skye ignored them. She was used to the ogling, although a few cat-calls had resulted over the years in a few quick lessons on manners. No, while the plane was being refueled she was going to —

"Miss Steele?"

Skye turned around. It sounded like Oliver Chatsworth, the pilot, was calling from back inside the plane. Bad news about Rory?

"Miss Steele?" Oliver called out again as he stepped into the planes' doorway.

"What's wrong?" Skye asked. She was back across the tarmac and up the stairs in a heartbeat, fearing the worst.

"Peltier says there's something coming across the radio system you need to hear," Oliver said and he moved back into the plane. Jean-Marc Peltier was the co-pilot and navigator.

Skye moved quickly back inside the luxury jet as well.

Oliver was already back up the aisle and close to the flight cabin.

Fear struck her heart. Oliver usually didn't move that fast. "What is it?" she called out.

"He just said to hurry and get you," Oliver said back over his shoulder. He disappeared into the flight cabin.

Skye hustled up the aisle. Did they find the ship? Was it disabled and floating at sea? Had everyone had to abandon ship and use the lifeboats? So many fears swirled through her mind as she stepped into the flight cabin.

Peltier was sitting in the co-pilot's seat.

Oliver quickly jumped into the pilot's seat, "She's here –"

"Shhhh, listen," Jean-Marc said as he pointed at the radio.

Skye stood perfectly between the two seats and listened intently.

A series of static hisses filled the silence of the cabin.

Jean-Marc looked up at Skye after a moment. "Can you hear it? Or am I crazy?" he whispered.

Skye's eyes lit up, "Morse code. That's Rory."

"Are you sure it's him?" Oliver asked her.

"Positive. Old telegraph operators could recognize each other's handwriting as it were. Rory and I used to practice all the time when we were kids," Skye explained. "*That* has Rory's signature all over it." Get something to write it down. I'll call out what I hear. Speak up if either of you think I have it wrong. It's been a long time...."

Oliver scrambled to get a notebook and pen from his jacket hanging from the back of the cabin door. "Okay," he said as he sat back down.

Skye closed her eyes and listened as the static hisses sounded. A few seconds later she said, "Caribbean."

"StarLiner...."

"Hijacked...."

"Terrorists...."

"N 21° 3' 50.3894"

"W 74° 45' 3.5156"

"That's latitude and longitude," Oliver said as he examined what he had written in his notebook.

Skye nodded in confirmation without opening her eyes.

Jean-Marc looked up at Skye with a surprised look, "Did I hear that right?"

Oliver's eyebrows went up, "That sounded like...C4...?"

Skye nodded and opened her eyes, a solemn look on her face, as she considered the implications.

"FMK-3?" Jean-Marc said. He shook his head, puzzled.

"An Argentine-made submachine gun capable of firing 650 rounds per minute," Skye said. She began chewing on her lip.

"The message is starting over again," Jean-Marc said. He turned his attention to the Gulfstream's navigation system.

"Can you tell where the coordinates are?" Oliver asked him as he leaned over to look at it himself.

Jean-Marc nodded, "It's in the sea, just to the north of Cuba, on the eastern end of the island. Guantanamo Bay would be to the south."

Chapter 47

THE CARIBBEAN SEA, North of Cuba

SAL VALID STOOD ON THE BRIDGE of the Caribbean StarLiner, watching as the massive cruise ship plowed through the sea. He vaguely became aware of something in the back of his mind. He looked around at the members of the ship's crew, to see if someone was doing something. Nothing stood out, yet something nagged at him. He looked back at the sea– suddenly Valid realized what it was. He whirled and shouted, "Turn off the navigation system."

One of the ship's officers, standing at the system, looked up. "Pardon?" he asked innocently.

Sal Valid strode across the bridge and pointed at him, "Turn it off or you're a dead man!"

The officer calmly reached over and switched it off.

The Captain spoke calmly from his seat, "Navigation will be treacherous without–"

"Enough," Valid yelled.

The Captain and the officer exchanged knowing glances.

One of the other terrorists stepped forward and asked something in Chechen.

"Someone was sending a Morse code message," Valid spat in anger. "That's what those hisses were." He grabbed his walkie-talkie and spoke sharply, "Tanya?"

"Yes?"

Valid shouted into the walkie-talkie, "Someone was using the LORAN navigation system to get a message out in Morse code."

"Steele?"

"Probably. The men sweeping the ship haven't found him," Valid admitted in anger. "Take men down directly to the engine compartment *and* the backup compartment and kill *anyone* you find. And then have four men posted specifically at each navigation system. I repeat, in *both* the main engine compartment and the backup compartment."

"On my way–"

Valid shouted into the walkie-talkie, "Kill Steele when you find him. Kill him, do you hear me?"

Chapter 48

ENGINE ROOM 2

RORY STOOD VERY STILL, not moving a muscle as he listened intently.

Jaypee noticed and asked him, "What wrong?"

Rory waited for a moment and then touched the wire back onto the board. There was no hiss. He quickly released the wire and closed the panel, "They know. They've turned the system off on the bridge."

Jaypee looked around the engine room nervously.

"We have to get out of here," Rory said.

Jaypee started for the exit.

Rory reached out and grabbed his arm, 'Let's climb back up to the top first. I'm sure that exit door will be the one they hit for sure."

Jaypee nodded and ran for the stairway.

Rory followed closely behind. He doubted they had much time before a team of machine-gun wielding terrorists were on them.

Reaching the bottom of the stairs after a hard run, Jaypee and Rory began climbing two stairs at a time to a catwalk that would take them over to the next stairway.

The sound of a door slamming back against a wall echoed from somewhere below.

Setting foot on the catwalk, Jaypee ran hard for the next stairway.

Rory took a quick down through the machinery and caught movement. He spun around and ran.

Submachine guns roared from below.

Jaypee threw himself to the metal catwalk as bullets ripped off the metal railings and machinery around them. The ricochets sounded like loud, metal popcorn, exploding all around them.

"No, no! Keep moving," Rory yelled at him. He grabbed the Filipino's arm, pulling him from the catwalk and urging him to run.

A bullet tore across the top of Jaypee's left shoulder. He cried out and stumbled to his knees. Blood stained the ripped material of his white, cotton shirt.

Rory pulled Jaypee to his feet and half-carried the man to the next stairway, "C'mon Jaypee, don't quit on me. Let's climb."

Jaypee struggled to get his feet under him and began climbing the instant his feet hit the metal stairway.

Boots steps echoed loudly off metal stairs below as the terrorists began the climb after their quarry.

Rory took the stairs two at a time, then realized the Filipino was falling behind. He went back the stairway down to help.

Jaypee grabbed the side pipe railing and used it to pull himself upward.

The roar of gunfire filled the air. Bullets ripped into the stairs and the machinery, loud pinging sounds filling the air as they ricocheted in every direction.

Rory put a hand on Jaypee's lower back to assist him - and felt a sharp tug of the material under his arm - a bullet had passed through his shirt material, just missing his side.

Jaypee reached the top deck of the compartment and half ran and half walked awkwardly for the exit door as he held a hand on his wounded shoulder. Blood seeped through his fingers.

"Hurry, Jaypee," Rory urged him. "They're not far behind and they're coming fast."

Jaypee grimaced and nodded, trying to pick up his pace but not succeeding.

Rory looked around for a hiding spot. The exit door wasn't far ahead but he doubted the Filipino could make it before the terrorists had them in their cross-hairs. Then he realized Jaypee wasn't beside him. Rory slid to a stop and looked back. He felt his heart beat hard in his chest.

Jaypee had stopped.

What was he doing?

Jaypee stepped over to a piece of machinery and picked up a length of pipe with his good hand.

Rory saw the terrorists nearing the top step.

Putting the pipe under his left armpit, Jaypee grimaced with pain and began his struggled run again, "Run, Mr. Rory. Run for the door."

Rory hesitated for a moment and then turned and ran hard for the exit. Reaching it, he opened the door, jumped through to the other side and held it open.

A volley of gunfire rang out and bullets rang hard off the wall beyond Jaypee. Rory heard one whiz like an evil wasp over his head and he ducked. But he brought his head back up fast, keeping the door open, waiting on pins and needles as the Filipino struggled to make it before another volley ripped him apart.

A moment later, Jaypee was jumping through the doorway, yelling, "Close, close, close."

Rory put his shoulder against the heavy metal door and pushed with his legs, slamming the door shut.

Bullets smashed into the metal door on the other side, trying to gouge their way through.

Jaypee scrambled around on the floor, yelling and indicating the wheel in the middle of the door, "Turn it, turn it!"

Rory immediately went to work turning the wheel to lock the watertight compartment.

"Okay, okay, okay," Jaypee said urgently as he used one hand to raise the pipe and slip one end through the spokes of the wheel. Pulling down, he worked to slide the pipe through the spokes and down towards the deck.

Rory knelt down, "I got it." Grabbing the end of the pipe, he pulled hard, sliding it down to the deck and anchoring it under the door handle.

Heavy, frantic thumping and pounding began on the other side of the sealed door.

Both men took a step back, turned and ran.

Chapter 49

SKYE STEELE LEANED against the back of Oliver Chatsworth's seat and scanned the ocean through the cockpit windows. They had rented a P-750XSTOL utility aircraft and were nearing the coordinates they had gotten from Rory's Morse code message. Jean-Marc Peltier sat in the co-pilot seat, scanning the ocean as well.

"Are you sure you want to do this?" Chatsworth asked her as he rechecked his heading.

"We don't have much choice," Skye answered him firmly.

"We could wait for the U.S. Navy," Peltier countered.

"And I told you, that's not possible," Skye insisted. "The U. S. Southern Command has all of its vessels participating in a joint exercise with Brazil, Canada, Colombia, the Dominican Republic, Honduras Peru, Chile and the United Kingdom near Panama. The closest ship to the coordinates is a guided-missile frigate out of Charleston, South Carolina. Who knows where the hijacked cruise ship will be by the time they arrive? Unfortunately, *we* are the cavalry."

"I still don't like it. We don't have any experience with this plane," Chatsworth complained. "We don't know its idiosyncrasies, we don't –"

"It'll be fine," Skye assured him with a pat on the shoulder.

Chatsworth wasn't convinced and he grumbled something under his breath.

"But how are you going to find Rory?" Jean-Marc Peltier asked her with genuine concern. "It's the biggest cruise ship in the world. And with armed terrorists onboard, you can't just go wandering around, looking for him."

"I booked his suite for the voyage," Skye said. "He knows that's the only logical spot we can meet."

"And if he doesn't?" Peltier asked her.

Skye didn't answer.

"I don't like this one bit," Chatsworth muttered under his breath.

"There it is," Peltier said as he pointed dead ahead.

The giant cruise ship, The Caribbean StarLiner, was just barely visible on the horizon, a small dark spot against the light of the setting sun.

"Do you want me to start descending now?" Chatsworth asked her grudgingly.

"No. Stay at 12,000 feet," Skye told him. "I'm going to have to jump from here and I'll need the altitude."

Chatsworth looked up at her in alarm, "Are you sure?"

"Flying the plane too close will put them on alert," Skye said. "I'll just be a spec in the sky–"

"Landing on that thing from here is going to extremely difficult, if not impossible," Peltier said as he turned to Skye. "We might not find you if you miss–"

"I'll be okay guys, we have a tail-wind to help," Skye said.

Chatsworth's face was white with fear at the thought about what she was going to do. "Skye—"

She placed her hand reassuringly on Oliver's shoulder and squeezed. He was always worried about her. She did the same thing to Jean-Marc.

"I'm officially telling you I'm against this," Jean-Marc said as he placed his hand on top of her hand and squeezed.

"Officially noted," Skye said. "If I go in, I'll turn the digital beacon on—"

"And *hope* we get to you before the sharks do," Oliver grumbled.

"Jump is in 3 minutes," she said with a smile at his worry.

Oliver looked at his co-pilot for a moment and then said with reluctance, "Mark...3 minutes. On course."

Skye gave another squeeze to his shoulder and then headed to the back of the aircraft.

DONNING HER WINGSUIT, Skye hit the exit button and waited as the jump-door cracked open. The salty fragrance of the ocean washed over her. Stepping into the opening, she felt the wind swirl around her body and felt more than heard the growl of the Pratt + Whitney engines. The adrenaline began to surge through her body. The flight across the sea to the cruise ship would be a difficult one - but she had no choice.

The aircraft banked gently and began a turn to the left.

Skye waited. Her eyes fixed on the darkening horizon. Waiting. The dark speck of the cruise ship came into view and she pushed off. Holding her arms against her body, she cleared the aircraft and rocketed straight down for a moment, gathering speed. Counting down in her head, Skye estimated a drop of 3,000 feet and then spread her legs and arms open. The salt air of the Caribbean caught the webbed wing surface under her arms and between her legs. Leveling out, she began flying at 9,000 feet over the ocean waves.

Skye twisted her arms, hips, and legs, adjusted her heading. Within seconds, she was headed directly for the stern of the cruise ship. So far, so good.

Next...Skye had to maintain height as long as possible. She rolled her shoulders forward, bent her chin down against her neck and put the wingsuit in a head-down position. She adjusted the spread of her legs and then her arms slightly. Keeping her eyes up, she gauged her speed against the cruise ship in the distance. She readjusted a little more. Finally, Skye could see she was slowly gaining on the stern. And she should reach it just as the sun was sinking into the sea. Should. She hated that word right now.

Chapter 50

THE SUN WAS SETTING and she *had* timed it perfectly. Skye kept her eyes scanning up and down the cruise ship for any terrorists as she flew closer. If one spotted her before she could land, she would have to abort into the ocean. *If* she could abort quickly enough, that is. Flying in the open like this would make her target practice for any shooters on board.

Skye made one last scan of all the deck areas she could see, looking for any hint she had been spotted. Once she committed herself it, would be difficult to abort without smashing herself against the ship. From this height, she could see there were a few figures towards the bow. But no one appeared to be on the top deck or on the portions of the lower deck areas she could see in the stern. It was time to land.

Twisting her body and dropping towards the ship, Skye began to look for a landing spot. Her mind ran through all the possibilities and probabilities. She couldn't use the parachute because she would be a slow, descending target if she had missed spotting a lookout. Then again, a fast hard drop would be even harder if she misjudged the rise of the deck from the waves. A landing spot appeared on the third deck down. It was a large, open area between a pool and a line of deck chairs that would work just fine. She adjusted her arms and legs and began her final approach–

A figure dressed in dark clothing emerged from a door and walked out onto the deck area on this side of the pool.

Skye had to adjust quickly. She raised her head, lifted her hips and stretched the wings while pushing down on the salt air to gain lift. Her descent and forward momentum slowed, but any slower and she would drop like a stone into the sea. Her eyes focused on the dark figure as she worked to maintain her height and the forward momentum that matched the speed of the ship. Any miscalculation now would kill any chance to get aboard.

The figure strolled slowly across the deck. A submachine gun was slung over his shoulder.

Skye looked for another spot to land.

The dark figure put his hands to his mouth and a light flared.

There was another landing spot on the top deck further forward. Skye adjusted her wing surface. No. She wouldn't have enough speed to reach the spot. She adjusted her wingsuit another way...but there was no way she could get more height to generate more speed. She was trapped in no man's land.

The dark figure strolled to the railing and leaned on it. He was having a smoke!

The sun was setting fast now. Skye was quickly losing enough light to make a safe land. And the ship was getting farther away! Time to act or take a plunge into the dark ocean.

The dark figure straightened up, turned and leaned back against the railing.

He was near her only landing spot! But Skye had no choice. Without any naval ships to intervene, *she* was the cavalry. Her mind raced and a plan formed. Pulling her arms and legs in, Skye dipped her head and dove straight down to create some speed. She spread her legs and arms to flatten out, turned hard left across the stern and then looped right, taking a heading straight for the ship.

The dark figure brought the cigarette toward his lips and froze, listening. A soft, low flapping and whooshing sound was getting louder. The dark figure turned slowly, still listening–

Skye whipped herself upright at the last moment and spread her arms and legs to cut her speed. The webbing between her legs caught the head of the man.

The man screamed in fright as the massive flying beast from the ocean hit him.

Skye was flipped head over heels and tumbled across the deck. She grunted in pain as her back and hips hit hard repeatedly against the deck as she tumbled. Finally slamming her feet down against the deck, Skye skidded to a stop, sending deck chairs flying in every direction. The breath was knocked from her lungs but Skye ignored it. She had no choice. Death could come in an instant if she didn't. Skye rolled to her knees and looked back at the railing.

The man spun around on his hands and knees, his eyes wild in terror as he looked at the beast on the deck. Slowly he recognized the human features in the low light and snarled. He reached back for his weapon. It wasn't there. The submachine gun lay on the deck, ten feet away from him. Gathering his feet under him, he sprinted for the weapon.

Skye grabbed a wooden deck chair and grunted as he whipped it hard at the man.

The flying object came out of the dim light and the man threw his hands up. But he was slow...the object crashed into his head and he fell to the deck.

Grabbing a second deck chair, Skye sent it skidding across the deck.

The man opened his eyes and lunged for the weapon. Another object smashed into his arm and he uttered a cry of pain as the weapon was knocked away.

Skye rose to her feet and ran at the man...but it was a clumsily run in the wingsuit.

The man shook the pain from his hand - saw the figure running at him and pulled his feet under him to get in a defensive position.

Grabbed another deck chair as she passed it, Skye flipped this one underhanded.

The man brought his hands up. The deck chair slammed into his arms.

Skye threw herself feet first, hitting the man in the chest with a drop-kick. She landed hard on the deck.

The man was knocked backward, arms flailing as he tried to regain his balance.

With a gymnastic kick-up, Skye was one her feet and running again.

The man's backward momentum was stopped by the railing.

Skye hit him with another drop-kick.

The man's eyes shot open wide as he went over the railing backward.

Skye heard the scream for a few moments before it was cut off. Now it was just the sound of the ocean. Skye spun around on the deck, peering into the falling darkness, listening for any movement. There was only the gentle up and down rocking of the deck. Time to move. She quickly peeled off the wingsuit and tossed it over the side of the ship. Moving across the deck, Skye picked up the submachine gun the man had dropped, checking to make sure it was still in working order. It was. Now armed, Skye Steele crept slowly across the deck and into the dark shadows.

Chapter 51

RORY USED JAYPEE'S SHIRT SLEEVES to bandage his wound and make him a sling. "The bullet just grazed you," Rory said as he finished the job. They were hiding in a food storage compartment and only Jaypee's knowledge of the ship had kept them from being caught by the terrorists. The air was crisp and cool in here and smelled of burlap sacks, cardboard containers, and root vegetables.

"Hurts a lot," Jaypee moaned. He sat with his back against a high stack of fifty-pound bags of sugar.

"I don't doubt it," Rory said. He stood up from the sack of potatoes he had been using to sit on and brushed off the back of his jeans.

"Now what we do?" Jaypee asked him. He twisted his neck to look at his wounded shoulder.

"*We* don't do anything," Rory told him. "The odds of us running into the terrorists again is too high. You're staying here safe. I have to—"

"No. I have to help. This is my home, they kill my friends," Jaypee insisted.

"I can move faster—"

"Where you go now?" Jaypee asked him. He struggled to get to his feet, without using his wounded shoulder, and he winced and stopped halfway up.

Rory took the man's arm to help him straighten up, "I have to head up to my cabin–"

"Where your cabin?"

Rory looked at the man for a moment. "It's on the Vista deck."

"Deck nine," Jaypee said as he nodded his head. His brow wrinkled in confusion, "Why you go all the way up there?"

"Let's just say it's a hunch...and maybe a prayer, that I find some help...."

"Okay. We get there faster if go together. We can go to elevators–"

"The terrorists would have disabled them to limit movement to the central stairs," Rory said. "Getting past the men to get up to deck nine will be dangerous. I'm better alone–"

Jaypee shook his head, "No. You need me to go with you. Most people only know main staircase and elevators. But I know this ship well. There are other stairways and passageways for crew and staff–"

"The terrorists may know about them too, Jaypee," Rory reasoned.

"Maybe," Jaypee shrugged. "But cannot guard all. We find safe one...eventually."

Rory didn't have a rebuttal. Or a better plan.

"I help you get there," Jaypee said with finality. He started walking for the cargo hold exit.

LEAVING THE HOLD BEHIND, Jaypee led Rory to the nearest crew stairway. They moved up slowly, climbing two decks, only to hear voices on the next landing. Backtracking down one deck, Jaypee led the way through a back passageway to another stairway only the crew used and they climbed up three decks this time before having to backtrack. For the next half-hour, they threaded their way upwards, deck by deck, back and forth down the back passageways, until they reached the Vista deck. They found the main passageways empty here and it didn't take long for them to reach Rory's penthouse suite.

Rory cautiously inserted his key card into the slot and held his breath as he heard a soft click.

The small light turned green.

Rory gently pushed down on the door handle and opened the door a crack. He was gambling that Sal Valid wouldn't have someone waiting here for him. But if there was...maybe it was Tanya Beno, the assassin, herself. Taking a deep breath, he prepared for a fight, swung the door open and stepped inside his suite.

Jaypee followed close behind, taking cautious steps into the room. He let the door closed softly behind him.

Rory slipped the key card back into his pocket and –

A figure dressed in black, moved cat-like from the small kitchenette area and pointed a submachine gun at Rory.

Chapter 52

JAYPEE GASPED IN FEAR as he watched the woman with the fiery-red hair and sparkling green eyes shift her steady gaze to him. His hands were shaking as he slowly raised them.

"Oidche mhath," Rory said as he raised his hands.

"Good evening yourself," the woman said. "What kept you?"

"Only about one hundred terrorists," Rory said as he dropped his hands.

"Is that all? You must be getting old."

"That's cruel–"

The figure in black lowered the weapon and embraced Rory.

Rory embraced his sister back and then turned and gestured to Jaypee, "Skye, this is a friend who's been helping me, Jaypee Andrada."

The Filipino's eyes were still wide open, looking up at the Amazon-like woman, who was more than half a foot taller than him.

An amused smile on his lips, Rory said, "Everything is fine, Jaypee. This is my sister, Skye."

"It's very nice to meet you, Jaypee."

When the Filipino only gulped, Skye moved forward and embraced him tightly, "Thank you for helping my brother."

Jaypee groaned. "You...you welcome." His eyes bulged in pain as she squeezed him tightly.

"Sorry," Skye said. She released the man and touched the make-shift sling, "I see some blood. What happened?"

Grimacing as he adjusted the sling, Jaypee simply said, "Shot."

"Did you have antiseptic when you bandaged him?" Skye asked Rory.

Rory raised an eyebrow, "How do you know I'm the one who did it?"

"Because your reef knots are sloppy and uncomfortable," Skye teased. "Now...antiseptic or not?"

Rory shook his head, "Nope. We were on the run at the time, Dr. Steele."

Skye handed her submachine gun to Rory, "I found a small first aid kit in the kitchen area. Come and sit here, Jaypee." Skye grabbed the kit and led Jaypee over to one of the plush chairs in the entertainment area.

"Why did you need the first aid kit? We're you hurt," Rory asked her in concern.

"Just a couple of scrapes when I landed," Skye said as she gently undid Jaypee's sling and took a look at the wound.

"You and that wingsuit," Rory said as he shook his head, only half in jest.

"My big brother needed help," Skye protested.

Jaypee looked up at Skye and then over at Rory, "Wing...suit?"

"It's a suit that allowed her to fly over the ocean and land on the ship," Rory explained.

Jaypee looked at Skye in total surprise, "It have motor?"

Skye smiled as she removed the bandage, "No. I jumped from a plane and glided over the ocean. And besides, it wasn't the wingsuit that caused the scrapes, it was the man with the submachine gun, standing guard on the deck."

Jaypee just shook his head in amazement.

"Is that where you got the weapon?" Rory asked her. He set the submachine gun down on one of the other plush chairs, where Skye could reach it.

Skye nodded as she applied a dab of antiseptic to Jaypee's wound.

Rory walked over to the kitchen area and got three glasses, filling them with ice. He opened the mini-bar and used small bottles of whiskey to make three drinks. He walked back and passed one to Jaypee, then set one down on the coffee table for Skye.

Rory sat heavily in one of the plush chairs and watched Skye work on Jaypee.

"Any idea how many terrorists there are?" Skye asked.

"A lot less than there were at the start," he answered. "The first set of terrorists was eliminated by a second set of terrorists."

"Really?" Skye narrowed her eyes as she bandaged Jaypee's shoulder, "That doesn't make any sense."

"Apparently, the leader of the second set of terrorists hired the first set as some kind of diversion. The first group had a middle-eastern background. But they were apparently from different ethnic tribes and began killing each other off. I'm guessing that was jeopardizing whatever the main purpose is for hijacking this ship and the second set had to act."

"Any idea what that purpose is?" Skye asked him as she placed a square gauze pad over Jaypee's wound.

"No."

"The cruise owners said they were in the dark as to why their ship disappeared off the face of the earth as well," Skye said. "They claim there's been no ransom demand." Skye put Jaypee's sling back on, tying a proper reef knot to finish it off.

"Unless they're lying," Rory said.

"Could be," Skye conceded as she adjusted Jaypee's sling.

"Was Avis able to find anything from the information I sent?"

Skye reached into a square pocket on her black tactical pants and pulled out two small pictures. She handed them across to Rory, "This was the only thing she had found before I left on the Gulfstream."

Rory took a look at them. "That's Valid!" Rory said in surprise.

Skye's eyebrows went up, "You know him?"

"He was one of the passengers at the Captain's table the first night out," Rory said. He looked at the other picture, "And that's Tanya!"

Skye cocked her head, "*She* is onboard as well?"

"Yeah. She was also at the Captain's table," Rory said. "What's going on here, Skye? How did Avis come up with these two?"

Chapter 53

"**WE GOT AN UNEXPECTED HIT** on a fingerprint that was in the cabin of the second set of missing men," Skye explained. "It led us to the man in the picture. His name is actually Igor Arkady Koreshevko. He works for the Russian billionaire, Alexei Vinokurov," Skye said. She began putting the items back in the first aid kit.

"Where have I heard that name before?" Rory said, more to himself.

"After the collapse of the Soviet Union in the 1990s, a number of government officials and their relatives or close associates gained a massive amount of wealth by acquiring state assets very cheaply. Some were even given them for free during the privatization process," Skye explained. She moved over to one of the other plush chairs and sat down.

"I remember reading about that," Rory said. "A lot of instant billionaires were created."

"Right. And Alexei Vinokurov was one of those associates of the people in power who benefited," Skye said. "But some of these billionaires eventually wanted more than just money. They wanted power as well. And they tried to use their ill-gotten gains to oppose the Russian President politically."

Rory nodded, "I remember the firestorm it started politically and the resulting push back. A number of those billionaires had to move their fortunes into offshore accounts when the Russian president threatened to confiscate everything they had."

"Right. And Vinokurov was the latest political opponent who was threatened by the Russian president," Skye said. "He nearly had all of his wealth confiscated. Until he backed off."

Rory tried to make sense of it all, "And Valid...or this Koreshevko...whatever his name is...he works for this Vinokurov?"

Skye nodded, "Vinokurov is the real power behind the Head of the Chechen Republic, which is a federal subject of Russia. This Igor Arkady Koreshevko is an ex-KGB Colonel and Vinokurov's right-hand man. The picture of the woman popped up because she was reportedly Koreshevko's top agent in the KGB and is still with him. I didn't expect she would be onboard, though."

"Both are ex-KGB? So Tanya was probably telling the truth...she *is* an assassin," Rory mused.

"She told you that? When?" Skye asked him.

Rory didn't answer...he was deep in thought.

Skye watched her brother piecing together the information.

Rory looked at Skye after a few moments of thought, "But why would two ex-KGB members hijack a cruise ship, using middle-eastern terrorists as a front? It doesn't make any sense. What would they get out of it? What would their boss...Vinokurov...get out of it?"

Skye's eyes blinked several times in surprise. Then she cursed under breath. closing her eyes tightly.

Rory shifted in his chair, "Skye? What is it?"

Silent for a moment, Skye opened her eyes and said, "I just realized what's happening. This isn't just a standard terrorist hijacking like we thought. When this KGB guy popped up because of his fingerprints, we didn't know he had taken over the ship."

"How does that change things?" Rory asked her.

Skye looked firmly into Rory's silver-blue eyes, "Right now this ship is north of Cuba and on a heading for the United States - specifically Key West, Florida."

Rory nodded, "I assumed as much. They have a cruise ship loaded with C-4. The U.S. would make the logical target for terrorists. An attack against US soil would cause the most impact on the world stage. But how does *faking* a terrorist attack on the United States, by men associated with the middle-east, help a Russian billionaire? Or an ex-KGB Colonel, if he's acting on his own? It doesn't make any sense."

Skye took a deep breath and continued, "When we got that hit on the fingerprints, Uncle Murdock talked to the State Department, to see if they could get some deeper information on Koreshevko from the Russian government. The Russians said they were willing to cooperate, but before they could give us any information on a former member of the KGB, they needed to get their President to sign off. And that would have to wait - until he returned."

"Returned from where?"

"He's secretly on a yacht anchored near Key West," Skye revealed.

"He's in Key West, Florida?"

Skye nodded, "Near the Key West Naval Station. It's a state-of-the-art training facility for air-to-air combat fighter aircraft and normally offers a lot of security–"

"Then the Navy may see the ship coming and take action–"

Skye shook her head, "No, they won't. The problem is the U.S. Southern Command has everything off on a training exercise with some other countries. The closest ship is a guided-missile frigate out of Charleston, South Carolina. The Navy has the frigate heading this way, to try and intercept the cruise ship, but it has to travel through the storm and could take another eight hours to get here. I would estimate this cruise ship is about one hundred and twenty five miles from Key West–"

"Ship traveling fast now," Jaypee said, "we make there in five...six hour." He swallowed

Skye shook her head, "Even if they knew where we were headed, they won't make it in time."

Rory ran a hand through his black hair as he mulled over the new information "I estimate I saw 100,000 pounds of C-4. That's fifty tons. C-4 is 1.34 times more explosive than TNT so it's more like nearly seventy tons...and there's no telling how much I didn't see." He ran his hand over the stubble on his cheek, thinking, "The way I see it...these guys plan to sail the cruise ship, loaded with 70 tons of C-4 explosive, next to the Russian President's yacht and detonate it. All of the Keys are basically flat and won't offer any hindrance to a blast of this magnitude. The devastation to the surrounding area would be enormous."

Skye nodded her head slowly, "And killing the Russian President, the political rival of Vinokurov, as well as anyone else in Key West."

"I would say this raises the stakes in dirty politics," Rory said. He shook his head in amazement at the plan.

"And the investigation will probably lead everyone to put the blame squarely on terrorists like Al-Qaeda or some other middle-eastern group," Skye added.

Rory frowned and shook his head, "No. It might look that way at first. But once everyone realizes the Russian President was the most likely target, it makes it look like Chechen terrorists instead. And possibly putting a spotlight on opponents like this Vinokurov, which is what he *wouldn't* want. I'm sure an ex-KGB Colonel would have thought of that as well. No, there has to be another reason for the hijacking."

Now it was Skye's turn to shake her head no.

"Why not?" Rory asked her. "It only makes sense–"

"Because the Russian President is actually in the United States on a working holiday. And there will another target for the investigation to consider," Skye explained. "Anchored right next to him...in another yacht...is the President of the United States."

Chapter 54

SKYE WATCHED HER BROTHER ABSORB THE NEWS. News that added a whole new dimension to an already overwhelming and dangerous situation. "So what do we do?" Skye asked him finally.

Rory sat still, looking inwards for a moment and then said, "I'm not sure. But...."

Skye looked at her brother, sentence unfinished, and waited. Then she prompted him, "But what?"

Breaking out of his thoughts, Rory looked at Skye, "But we may have lucked out a bit. Valid - or whatever his name is - was upset and came storming onto the bridge when we started turning back, rather than go on to Aruba. I suspect he was going to load the detonator cord there."

"Why would you think that?"

"Because I only saw *one* reel of detonator cord down in the hold, so they don't have enough to link much more than a few dozen crates of C-4 together."

"What does this cord look like?" Jaypee asked.

Both Rory and Skye turned to look at the Filipino. They had almost forgotten he was there, he had been so quiet.

"It's yellow and red and the cord is a little smaller than my baby finger," Rory explained. He made a round shape with his hands, "It's wrapped around metal or wood reels."

Jaypee nodded and looked scared, "That's what I see them bring aboard when the ship stopped in the ocean."

"Are you sure?"

"Yes," the Filipino affirmed. "I was hiding and saw. They transfer from another boat when we stopped. They bring onboard those guns they carry and large number of round metal with red and yellow wire on it. I see."

"So I was right. At least about the submachine guns," Rory said in a hushed tone. He looked at Skye. "The C-4 I saw was in crates, with a board taken off each end, to allow access to the plastic explosive inside. They had plenty of blasting caps down there, so they're all set. They'll put a blasting cap in each crate and use the detonator cord to run from one crate to the next."

"They'll daisy chain them together," Skye said.

"Exactly."

"They blow themselves and all of us up?" Jaypee asked. He visibly shuddered at the thought.

Rory's eyes narrowed as he considered the possibility. Then he shook his head slowly, "No. I don't think so. They'll blow the ship up, but not themselves. These guys are professionals, not crazy terrorists. I'll bet that's why the first group of terrorists was hired, to do just that. They probably would have contacted someone like CNN or Al Jazeera television to let the world know what was happening. They would have set up one of those terrorist scenes with a black flag in the background and delivered a speech. And then - boom."

"But how will the second group, who took over, get off the ship?" Skye asked him. "They'd have to guide the ship to those two yachts in Key West and get close enough to make sure they blow up the Russian President. I don't imagine the Secret Service, and whoever is guarding the Russian President, will allow a cruise ship to simply park beside them."

"You're right. But there are cruise ships that use Key West and it won't look out of place. And Key West is not like having to maneuver into a harbor," Rory explained. "It's at the end of the string of Keys and once they sail around the tip, it's a lot of ocean and a clear run at those yachts. Once they get running at full speed, the forces guarding both Presidents wouldn't be able to stop a cruise ship this size, before it's right on top of them. But Valid won't sacrifice himself in a suicide run. He'll get off... and I think I know how he'll guide the cruise ship to its target once he does."

"Okay, I bite. How?" Skye asked him.

"First things first," Rory said. He looked at Jaypee, "Do you know if we can get our hands on a portable radio? One that uses batteries? And maybe a flashlight? A small hand one would do –"

Jaypee nodded vigorously. He got up and walked into the kitchenette area, where he pulled open a drawer. Pulling out a small hand-held flashlight, he held it out to Rory, "This do?"

"That's great," Rory said as he got up and took the flashlight. "Now all –"

Jaypee was off quickly and moved down into the bedroom.

Rory opened up another drawer and pulled out several knives.

Skye got up and joined Rory, "Anything I can do to help?"

Rory looked over at the large, flat screen television and handed Skye a small knife, "Can you take that thing down, unplug it and take it apart, so I can access the electronics inside?"

"You want me to take it apart?" Skye said.

"I know my little sister is better at breaking things than fixing them," Rory said.

"Very funny, big brother."

Jaypee was back and held out something to Rory, "This a portable satellite radio many of the suites have for guests. It uses batteries."

"Perfect, thanks Jaypee," Rory said. He flipped the portable satellite radio over, set it down on the counter and began to work getting the back off.

Skye watched her brother work, "If you're putting some electronic thingy together, you'll need solder and a soldering iron for the wires, right? Where do I get that for you?"

Rory glanced at Jaypee.

The Filipino shrugged, "Electric crew part of Engine department."

Rory clenched his jaw, "That's all the way down on deck one."

Skye looked at Jaypee, "Tell me how to get there—"

Shaking his head, Rory said, "No. We don't have the time to go looking." He bit his lip for a moment, thinking, "I'll use the tape from the first-aid kit."

"I get," Jaypee said as he made a bee-line for the kit.

"Are you sure that will work? *And* stay together if we have to move fast?" Skye asked him.

"No, but we don't have much choice," Rory admitted.

Skye took a deep breath and headed for the television, "You do recognize I'm not going to pay the bill for this when it comes in the mail."

"That's okay, I'll blame it on Jaypee," Rory said as he removed the last of the tiny screws from the back of the satellite radio.

"Everyone blame Jaypee," the Filipino shrugged as he returned. He set the first-aid kit down on the counter, "Can you tell Jaypee what he being blamed for?"

Rory nodded, "I'm making a homemade electronic detonator."

"Detonator?" Jaypee looked at him in concern, "You mean...?" He made an exploding gesture, accompanied by an exploding sound.

"Something like that," Rory said. He removed the 8 AA batteries from the cradle inside the radio and placed them on the counter. Then he set to work to remove the cradle itself, "Are there any remote controlled toys on board the ship?"

Jaypee shook his head slowly as he did some thinking, "No. Nothing that I know of. Why?"

"I just need an electronic toy or device that uses a 40 MHz radio frequency," Rory explained to him.

"How about the TV remote control?" Skye asked as she pulled the back of the television off.

Jaypee was off like a shot to the coffee table. He picked up the remote and hustled it back to Rory.

Rory quickly pried the back off with his knife. "Crap!"

"No good?" Skye asked him as she worked on the television.

Rory shook his head as he tossed the remote on the counter, "No. No good. It's 36 MHz."

"How about internet things?" Jaypee asked him.

"The ship has an internet connection?" Skye asked n amazement.

Jaypee nodded and hustled over to a small desk and pointed at a router, "Yes. From satellite. Cost lots of money, but some people use."

Rory quickly stepped over to where the Filipino was standing and picked up the device, examining it front and back. "Yeah, this will work. It has 20/40 MHz channel operation. I could kiss you Jaypee."

"That okay," Jaypee said with a wave of the hand and a frown. Then he smiled and pointed at the beautiful redhead taking the television apart, "But she can do."

Chapter 55

RORY ASSEMBLED THE PIECES of his homemade electronic detonator, using the white tape from the first-aid kit to hold them together, and then placed the makeshift unit inside a small candy tin that measured 6" x 4". Using a knife, he punched a hole in the lid for the on-off switch and a second small hole. Then he threaded a wire through the second hole. The end of the wire outside the candy tin had a half-inch of cover stripped away.

Jaypee leaned closer, his brow knit together as he looked at Rory's creation, "Will it work?"

As Rory wrapped a piece of white tape around the tin, to hold the lid in place, he feigned hurt, "You doubt my handiwork?"

"Not look handy to me," Jaypee whispered.

"I have a tendency to agree," Skye said. "But I doubt we have much choice at this point."

"True," Rory admitted as he slipped the device carefully into the back pocket of his jeans. "As long as I don't fall on my ass...."

"Just don't start dancing," Skye said. "You're okay walking, but dancing..." She wiggled her hand back and forth.

"Good thing we're not on Dancing with the Stars then," Rory said.

"So what's the next part of your plan? I presume you have one?" Skye asked her brother as she turned serious.

Rory nodded, "I do. Right now, I have to go back down to the storage holds, where they have the C-4."

"I go with you," Jaypee said quickly.

Skye got up and reached for the submachine gun, "I'm ready too."

"Actually...for my plan to work, we need to split up at this point," Rory said to Skye.

"Are you sure that's a good idea?" Skye asked him in concern.

"Yes. For my plan to work, I need you to do two things for me. First... once I get down there...I need you to create a temporary diversion on the upper decks towards the front of the ship."

"Okay," Skye said slowly.

"And then I need you to go to Deck 8 and keep an eye on the bridge. Right now the Russian has the Captain and a few of his crew running the ship. But if they get off the ship, like I think they will, they'll lock up the Captain and his men and run the ship remotely. You'll have to free them, so they can take control off the ship if my plan works–"

"And if they kill them? What do I do then?"

"Then I guess you'll have to learn to steer this baby real quick."

Skye nodded and then shrugged as she looked at Jaypee, "How hard could it be? Right?"

Jaypee swallowed hard.

Skye took a breath, thinking, and then let it out, "Okay. For the diversion, I'm going to need a few things...like tin foil. She went over to the kitchenette, pulled open a drawer and looked inside.

Jaypee went over to her, shaking his head, "No. Won't be in cabin. But I can get you some."

Skye closed the drawer, "Okay. How about toilet bowl cleaner? Can you get me that as well? I need something with hydrochloric acid."

Jaypee shrugged, "I not sure if we have acid but we do have the cleaner. We have room with supplies for taking care of cabins." Jaypee headed for the door.

Skye moved quickly, taking his elbow and stopping him near the door, "Let me check first."

Nodded, Jaypee stepped back. He watched as the tall, beautiful redhead held the submachine gun in one hand and cracked the door open.

Skye checked both directions of the passageway. "Okay, which way?"

Jaypee stuck his head out the door, checking the passageway himself. "This way," he whispered, pointing to the right.

"Okay," Skye said, "lead the way."

As they moved out of the cabin, Rory followed right behind them, pulling the door shut and keeping watch to the rear as they moved down the passageway.

Jaypee stopped at a door labeled *Housekeeping* and went inside.

Skye followed him inside.

Rory checked the passageway in both directions and then slipped into the room as well, closing the door lightly.

The room was filled with towels, blankets, bedspreads, pillows, and various cleaning supplies. Jaypee walked over to a shelf on the far side, reached up to an upper shelf and took down a plastic bottle of toilet bowl cleaner, handing it to Skye.

Skye gave Rory the weapon, took the bottle and flipped it over to read the ingredients.

Jaypee wandered off to another shelf.

Skye nodded, "Hydrochloric acid. This will work perfectly."

"And this," Jaypee said as he handed her a red and white box containing a roll of tinfoil.

"Perfect," Skye said. "I noticed there was a large, plastic bottle of water in Rory's suite. Do you have more–?"

Jaypee was already on the move and went to a box that contained two dozen large bottles of water.

Skye went over to a shelf holding pillows. She stripped the pillowcase off one and tossed it to Jaypee, "I need half a dozen empty bottles. Pour the water out and put them in there."

Jaypee caught the pillowcase and looked around, "No sink."

"We can empty them back in the suite," Rory said.

Skye stripped the pillowcase from another pillow and stuffed several more bottles of toilet bowl cleaner inside. Throwing the tinfoil inside, she threw the sack over her shoulder.

Jaypee did the same with his and a few minutes later they were all back in Rory's suite, putting all the items from the pillow cases on the small kitchenette's counter.

Skye explained what she needed Rory and Jaypee to do and everyone set to work

Rory used the scissors from the first aid kit to cut strips off the roll of tinfoil.

Jaypee crumpled the strips into loose balls, dropping each one into one of the pillowcases.

Skye emptied the water out of the bottles. Then she poured enough toilet bowl cleaner liquid in each plastic bottle to fill it halfway and then put the cap on, putting the bottles into the other pillowcase. Then she took the pillowcase from Jaypee - now filled with dozens of loose balls of tinfoil - and put it next to the other one, "Okay, I'm all set. But how am I going to know when you me to start the diversion?"

Rory looked over at Jaypee, "How long did it take us to get up here, half an hour?"

Jaypee nodded.

"Give me an hour, just in case we get delayed. Then do your thing," Rory said as he picked up a butter knife and slipped it into his pocket. Hugging his sister, Rory headed for the door, "Let's go Jaypee."

"Okay." But as the Filipino moved towards the door, he was surprised when Skye gave him a hug as well, telling him to 'stay safe'. The man had a goofy, lopsided grin on his face as he joined Rory at the door and they slipped into the passageway.

The Filipino led Rory back down, threading their way from passageway to passageway, stairwell to stairwell, deck by deck. It was slower going than the climb up as they encountered teams still sweeping the ship for them. Finally reaching the passageway leading to the compartments with the C-4, Rory saw only two gunmen standing guard at the far end. Now all they could do was wait for Skye's diversion and see if it worked. If not, he had to come up with another viable plan. And without weapons to force their way into the compartments, there really wasn't a single alternative he could come up with at this point. It was all up to Skye.

Chapter 56

SKYE STEELE SLIPPED OUT of Rory's suite, both pillow-cases slung over her shoulder and the FKM-3 submachine gun firmly held in hand. Jaypee had explained how to get to the crew and staff staircase and she found it quickly. She climbed the stairs cautiously, deck by deck, watching for any sign of terrorists.

Reaching the top deck without seeing anyone, Skye set the pillowcases down and peered out into the passageway. It was empty and quiet. She took a deep breath to prepare herself. Her goal was to find a few terrorists on watch. And hopefully, they wouldn't see her in the process. But with the sun starting to come up, she wouldn't have any shadows to hide in if they did. She set the selector switch on the submachine gun to limit each burst of fire to three bullets. She couldn't afford to run out of ammo too quickly if it came to a firefight. Picking up the pillowcases again, Skye threw them over her shoulder and slipped into the passage-way.

The quiet of the cruise ship was eerie. There should have been laughing passengers and children screaming in delight. Instead it was like a morgue - deadly quiet.

Skye reached a cross passageway and saw a door at the far end. According to the signage it would lead to the outside deck.

She headed for the door. Edging closer to the large porthole in the door, she spotted two black-garbed men through the glass. They were standing at the stern of the cruise ship, submachine guns slung over their shoulders as they shared a cigarette. No doubt the guards were now working in pairs, probably because one of them had disappeared when Skye came onboard. Darting to the other side of the door, Skye checked in the other direction through the porthole. She spotted two more guards. They were walking along the far side of the deck, heading towards the bow of the ship. Time to attract some attention.

Skye set the pillowcases down and then her weapon. She removed one of the water bottles from a pillowcase and took off the cap. Taking several of the tinfoil balls from the other pillowcase, she dropped them into the water bottle, watching them sink to the bottom of the hydrochloric acid. She added more tinfoil balls until she was sure she would get the desired effect. She replaced the cap tightly and shook the bottle vigorously. Then she cracked the door open, just enough to pass the bottle through and set it on the deck. Closing the door, she then picked up her weapon, slung the pillowcases over her shoulder and took off at a run.

Within a minute, white smoke began to form inside the large water bottle Skye had left on the deck. Within another fifteen seconds, the water bottle expanded grotesquely and then....

Bang!

The combination of tinfoil and hydrochloric acid exploded, creating a deafening noise.

All four terrorists turned quickly, crouching and looking for the enemy. One yelled and pointed to a wisp of white smoke hanging in the air across the deck.

The other three terrorist pulled the triggers on their submachine guns, bullets ripping through the white smoke, through the door and into the passageway behind it.

Skye ran back to the cross passageway and stopped just around the corner, with her back against the wall.

The gunfire stopped.

Waiting a few moments, Skye then peered around the corner.

No one had come inside yet.

Skye quickly pulled out another bottle, uncapped it and dropped balls of tinfoil inside. Capping it tightly again, Skye shook it vigorously, lay it on the deck and rolled it hard down the passageway, towards the bullet-ridden door at the far end. Picking up the pillowcases again, she ran hard down the passageway. Her next stop would make the most noise and hopefully pull some of the terrorist up from the lower decks.

Behind her, another loud bang filled the passageway.

More submachine gun fire reached her ears.

Skye Steele hit the crew staircase at a run, watching below to make sure she wasn't caught unawares as she descended.

Chapter 57

RORY WATCHED AS one the gunmen answered his walkie-talkie. But rather than leave, both men stayed put.

Fifteen minutes passed.

Rory began to worry they weren't going to be able to get into the storage area. He was going to have to come up with an alternative plan, after all.

"They not leave?" Jaypee whispered from behind Rory.

Rory just shook his head in frustration.

"How we get in now?" Jaypee whispered

"Good question."

"How long you have to be in hold?"

"It shouldn't take longer than a few minutes. I just have to cut into the C-4 and take some out," Rory explained.

"It not blow up?"

"Not as long as I'm careful," Rory said.

Jaypee leaned over Rory, looking at the gunmen

"Careful," Rory said.

But seeing the gunmen had their backs turned, Jaypee said, "I distract. You hurry."

Before Rory could say no, the Filipino stepped out into the passageway and moved quickly but quietly down a few doors, in the direction of the gunmen. Pulling open a big door for a large storage cooler, Jaypee disappeared inside and then pulled the door closed with a bang. The door bounced back and stayed open half-way.

The gunmen were startled and they turned quickly, their weapons up and ready. Positioning themselves on each side of the passageway, they made their way quickly down to the open cooler door. One man pulled it open fully while the other one darted inside, weapon at the ready.

As soon as the second man followed the first inside, Rory was on the move. Racing for the nearest door into the second storage hold, he glanced over at the open doorway for the storage cooler as he passed – *Please stay safe my friend.*

Rory pulled open the hold door open a crack – and slipped inside, gambling no one was on the other side.

There wasn't.

Softly pulling the door closed, Rory headed across the floor for the crates at the far end of the compartment. As he moved closer to the stacked crates, Rory's heart sank. He was hoping Jaypee had been wrong. He wasn't. Yellow and red detonator cord snaked in and out of each crate. With the crates daisy-chained together like this, everything was now set to blow up the cruise ship, killing everyone onboard, along with two presidents.

Chapter 58

RORY PULLED THE BUTTER KNIFE from his pocket and carefully reached for the square hole in the side of the closest crate. He had to avoid contact with the detonator cord - or detonate the whole thing. He could feel beads of sweat form on his lip as he slowly squeezed his hand between the cord and the edge of the wood.

Rory carefully pushed the knife into the C-4 and through the brown paper. He paused...and then slowly worked to carve a rectangular cut in the putty-like material. Then he used the knife like a lever to carefully work around the cut and peel the section of C-4 away from the larger brick. *Just a little longer Jaypee.*

Palming the knife, Rory now used his fingers to carefully pull the chunk of C-4 through the hole in the crate.

The knife dropped against the detonator cord!

Rory froze. The butter knife was wedged between the edge of his hand and the cord. Rory cursed under his breath.

Reaching up with his other hand, he gripped the handle of the knife and carefully slid it out from between his hand and the cord. His heart was beating wildly as he slowly pulled both hands away from the crate. That done, he backed away from the crate.

His hand was actually shaking as he pulled the homemade detonator from the back pocket of his jeans. *That was a little too close.*

He then knelt on the deck, beside the stack of crates, and went to work. Stretching the chunk of C-4, he wrapped it around the homemade detonator and molded it to stay in place–

A door banged out in the passageway.

Rory froze in place. That sounded like the cooler door again, where Jaypee had lured the men. He listened carefully. If they came in now it would be all over. Rory began moving back to the exit door as fast as possible. He had to get behind the door where he could catch the men off-guard–

The door into the compartment swung open and Rory was caught–

It was Jaypee. He peered into the storage compartment, his eyebrows frosted white.

Rory exhaled, "Where are the men?"

"I lock them inside, but they figure out how to unlock from inside fast. You finished?"

Rory nodded and gestured to the Filipino that they had to get moving, "Back to the stairs."

Jaypee rushed back down the passageway, pushing his legs as hard as he could.

Following the Filipino closely, Rory firmly held onto his homemade detonator.

Jaypee ducked into the crew stairway, "Now what?"

"We need to go to the lifeboats on deck five, the ones that are on the starboard side, closest to the central staircase," Rory told him.

"Okay," the Filipino said, "but that means we have to be in the open."

"And in danger of being spotted. I know," Rory said. "But if I'm correct, that's where we need to go."

"And if you not correct?"

Rory didn't reply.

And Jaypee didn't ask any more.

Chapter 59

REACHING DECK 5, Jaypee led Rory down a short passage-way that entered into the large, opulent promenade. Trying to use the outer deck to reach the lifeboat he needed would leave them too exposed. The plan was to try and use the various shops, stores, and restaurants on the inside as hiding spots if they came across terrorists. Provided they spotted the terrorists first and not the other way around.

Reaching the entrance door to the promenade, Rory checked through the large porthole in the door. He couldn't see anyone but the view was limited. He cracked the door and listened. No voices or footsteps. Rory slipped through to the other side of the door and knelt close to the wall.

Jaypee followed closely behind him.

The promenade was eerily empty, compared to the crowded, boisterous avenue it had been before the hijacking.

Jaypee pointed over Rory's shoulder and whispered, "That way to central stairs."

Rory nodded and then gestured for Jaypee to follow in a low run. Ten feet ahead, Rory knelt inside the doorway of a gift shop to survey the way ahead.

"No see anyone," Jaypee whispered.

He was right. Rory had been afraid they would have a difficult time getting past the main dance floor up ahead, where he had been held. Instead, he was surprised there wasn't a single terrorist standing anywhere near the double-doors. *Maybe something happened to the people...including Myles? No. All the guards had been inside. That had to be it.*

Jaypee tapped Rory urgently on the shoulder and pointed up.

It was a terrorist one deck up, on the port side of the promenade.

Rory watched him closely. No doubt he was supposed to be a lookout for any passengers or crew daring to leave their rooms. But boredom must have kicked in. He was leaning back against the railing, his weapon slung over his shoulder, and enjoying a cigarette.

Rory placed a hand on Jaypee's knee, pointed to the terrorist and whispered, "We're going to have to make a move for the main stairs before he turns back around. Head for the closest door to the stairs that leads to the outer deck. Try to move as quietly as possible. Okay?"

Jaypee looked up at the terrorist, and nodded, his head shaking in fear.

Rory felt for the man, "Tell you what, wait here and–"

Shaking his head no, Jaypee got into a crouch, getting ready to run.

Rory was afraid the Filipino was shaking so badly he might stumble and give them away. He put a hand lightly on his shoulder, "Are you sure? You don't have to do this."

Licking his lips, Jaypee nodded yes.

Giving his shoulder a reassuring squeeze, Rory said, "Okay, then. Let's go."

Jaypee took off at a low run and Rory followed closely behind. Both men tried to run as fast as possible, without making any noise in the empty promenade, but there was a light echo.

As they neared the halfway point across the floor, the terrorist moved away from the railing and tossed his cigarette down, stepping on it to put it out.

Rory watched the terrorist as he ran. *We're in trouble if he turns and looks down now.* He reached out and took Jaypee's elbow.

Jaypee was startled and nearly stopped running.

Rory kept a grip on the Filipino's elbow, urging him to keep running and then steered him into a clothing shop for women. Rory had Jaypee stand and hide behind a mannequin on the right while he stood behind a clothing rack on the left.

The terrorist turned and looked down over the promenade while adjusting the weapon slung over his shoulder.

Had he heard the echo when they were running?

The terrorist's steady gaze swept up and down the promenade deck below. After a few moments, his gaze shifted to the deck he was on and the restaurants and small cafe areas that were empty and quiet, like the deck below.

Rory felt some relief. It didn't look like he had heard them. But would he just stand there now? How were they going to get the rest of the way to where they need to go? Rory turned his head to look for a rear exit from the small store. Nothing he could see. The front doorway was the only way in and out of here. Rory cursed under his breath.

Jaypee stood behind the mannequin, his eyes closed and his body shaking.

The terrorist stretched and then rolled his shoulders. His gaze swept over the promenade area below again. Turning to his left, the terrorist began walking, his hand sliding along the railing.

Rory waited for a few heartbeats and decided it was now or never. He called softly to Jaypee and got his attention.

The Filipino looked like he was going to have a heart attack.

Rory gestured to the terrorist walking the other way and then waved for Jaypee to start moving again.

Taking a deep breath to steel himself, Jaypee slipped through the doorway into the promenade and ran low across the deck.

Rory was right behind him, running low with an eye on the terrorist one deck up in case he turned back again.

Jaypee reached a short passageway between a cosmetic shop and a shoe store and crouched against the wall. The central stairway was off to the right across the deck.

Rory knelt beside Jaypee and glanced back.

The terrorist was still walking the other way.

"That passageway is one you want," Jaypee whispered. "It go to the outside."

Rory nodded, slipping past Jaypee to the edge of the passageway, "Keep an eye on that terrorist up there, while I check the door."

Jaypee nodded, turned slightly on his heels and kept watch.

Slipping around the corner, Rory crept low down the ten-foot long passageway. The door that led to the outer deck was just ahead. Halfway there, he froze on the spot. He could see the back of a terrorist's head through the porthole in the door. He raised himself out of the crouch and moved closer.

The terrorist was standing with his back to him, his weapon slung over his shoulder.

Creeping a little closer, Rory spotted three more terrorists. They were all standing guard near of the lifeboat Tanya had used to tie-off her climbing rope when she had killed the pastry training. It had offered her the perfect escape route after the kill. He glanced back. There was no doubt this lifeboat had the quickest access from the central staircase. And the fact it was being guarded confirmed Rory's theory on what they were planning to do. This was no doubt the route the terrorists would use to abandon the cruise ship when they were ready to blow it up.

But the fact the guards were still here also told him Skye's diversion wasn't working. Rory was sure they would have been drawn away. Now he had to try and figure out another way to get on board this specific lifeboat.

Chapter 60

AS SKYE MOVED DOWN THE CREW STAIRCASE, she heard running footsteps several times and had to stop. She couldn't afford to run into terrorists and be sidetracked into a firefight. But that also meant it took longer to get down to the next spot she had planned for the diversion than she expected. She finally reached Deck 11 and checked through the porthole in the door leading out to the open atrium. There was no one in sight. Time for the big ruse. Skye stepped outside and quickly set up her last four bottles. She shook each one vigorously and rolled them hard, one by one, out into the open deck.

Slipping back inside, Skye took off at a run heading for Deck 8 and the bridge area. Now all she had to do was hope the terrorists didn't simply kill the bridge crew. That would create a whole new problem. One she wasn't sure she could solve if it came to that.

The four bottles she left behind filled with smoke in a minute...the plastic bottles ballooned grotesquely...and exploded in a loud cacophony of sound that echoed loudly off the sides of the atrium.

DECK 5

Rory heard a squawk.

One of the terrorists next to the lifeboat quickly reached for his walkie-talkie and said something into it.

A voice said something urgently in a foreign language.

Three of the terrorists turned and ran for the door into the ship.

They were headed right for him. Rory turned and had to move fast. He reached the end of the short passageway and startled Jaypee as he darted around the corner. In one motion he grabbed the Filipino and pulled him into the cosmetics shop, where he whispered urgently, "Down, down,"

Jaypee sunk to the floor, just behind the open glass window filled with small bottles and boxes, while Rory stayed low just inside the doorway, watching.

Three of the terrorists burst from the short passageway and quickly headed to the central stairway, their submachine guns now held at the ready. The echo of running boots sounded on the next deck up in the promenade as well. It was the terrorist on guard duty and he was also running hard for the central staircase.

Rory realized the diversion was finally working. That was perfect. Now all he had to do was run back and take out the last terrorist. He rose to his feet and then froze with one foot outside the cosmetics shop doorway as pounding footsteps sounded from the short passageway. His heart jumped when he saw the fourth terrorist emerge into the open. Then he let a sharp breath out as the terrorist headed for the stairs. *That was close.* He didn't move a muscle as he waited for the sounds of running footsteps to disappear. He turned and whispered, "Jaypee, let's go." As soon as the saw the Filipino rise to his feet, he took off at a run. A moment later, he was headed down the short passageway, making a bee-line for the lifeboat directly outside the door. He could hear Jaypee close behind him. As soon as they were on the deck outside, Rory turned to the Filipino, "Stay here and keep watch while I go inside the lifeboat. Knock on the window if you hear or see someone coming, and then hide."

Jaypee nodded but he looked scared.

Rory clambered up the steel stairs at the stern of the lifeboat and descended into the passenger compartment. Stepping between the gray bench seats, Rory headed to a spot directly over the fuel tanks. Using the butter knife and his hands, he worked to shape the C-4 charge around his electronic detonator. Satisfied he had the shape he needed, he got on his knees and carefully slipped the detonator under the nearest bench seat, pressing it into the triangular meal corner to keep it in place. Getting up, he looked at the bench seat from all angles. No one coming into the lifeboat would see the detonator. Confident everything was in place, Rory headed for the stairs back out of the lifeboat...and froze when he turned to step down to the deck.

Jaypee was just in front of him.

And behind him was one of the terrorists, standing firm on the deck with one arm around the Filipino's neck and the other resting a gun across Jaypee's right shoulder and aimed directly at Rory.

The terrorist's eyes stared directly into Rory's, emphasizing his willingness to kill.

Rory wondered if he would hear the sounds when the bullets ripped through his body.

The terrorist gestured with his head for Rory to step down to the deck.

Jaypee's eye looked from the barrel of the submachine gun resting on his shoulder to Rory's eyes. Jaypee shook too much to say anything, but his eyes showed just how scared he was right now.

The terrorist said something to Rory that sounded Russian. His eyes sent a menacing message to Rory to move down to the deck or else.

Rory knew he had to act quickly but he only had one chance. He shuffled his feet forward to show he was complying while he looked intently into Jaypee's eyes.

Jaypee's brows raised and pulled together. He licked his lips as Rory's eyes bored into his.

Now Rory flicked his eyes down to look at the deck. He did it three times in a row, hoping Jaypee would understand.

The Russian said something in warning, "Тепер–"

Closing his eyes tightly, Jaypee let himself go, slumping and sliding down the terrorist's body.

The terrorist grunted and tried to maintain his hold - he realized his mistake when his weapon shifted away from Rory.

Rory still had the butter knife in his hand and smoothly threw it underhanded.

The knife sliced through the terrorist's left eye into his brain. His body dropped to the deck.

Rory jumped down to the deck, grabbing the submachine gun with one hand before it hit the deck while urging Jaypee to his feet with the other, "Sorry, but we have to get rid of this body before someone shows up."

Jaypee was shaking as he got up from the deck but he managed to help drag the dead body to the gap between two of the lifeboats.

"I wasn't sure you would understand what I wanted you to do," Rory said as they lifted the body to the railing.

"Not sure if I guessed right or legs just give out," Jaypee admitted with a shaky smile as he and Rory pushed the body.

The body dropped swiftly overboard to the sea below.

"Rory!" Jaypee whispered.

Rory looked at where the Filipino was pointing. What he saw not far off in the distance was disconcerting and he cursed. "Let's go before someone else comes," he said urgently.

The two men headed back inside the cruise ship.

Chapter 61

TANYA BENO ENTERED THE BRIDGE, followed closely by a number of men. Sal Valid was standing in front of the large front windows, hands behind his back.

"Did you find out what was happening?" Valid asked her as he turned.

Tanya tossed a grotesquely enlarged and deformed water bottle, with a blown-out hole in it, across to him, "Some kind of kid's toy. Someone was trying to attract our attention."

Valid caught the deformed plastic and looked at it with a sneer, "It has to be Steele."

Tanya stepped up beside Valid and lowered her voice "But why?"

Frowning, Valid shook his head slowly as he admitted quietly, "I have no idea what he's up to."

Tanya chewed on her lip for a moment, "He drew us upwards for some reason."

Valid raised an eyebrow, "Which means he wanted us away from the lower decks."

Tanya adjusted the weapon over her shoulder and took hold of her walkie-talkie, "I'll take half the men back down to the cargo holds with the crates and make sure everything is still ready to put our plan in motion."

Valid tossed the deformed water bottle to the deck, "And keep them down there and on high alert until we're ready to go. We have *no* idea what Steele is planning."

Tanya nodded and looked out the large front window, "How much longer?"

Valid looked out the window himself. Not far off to the right was a low line of buildings, behind a long pier. "That pier is called The Mole. It's in front of the Truman waterfront. Tank Island is just up ahead on the left, which means we'll be able to make a direct run at our target before long."

"No one has tried to stop us or hail us?" Tanya asked.

Valid shook his head and smiled, "We just look like any other cruise ship in the area. I have the Captain running the ship at quarter speed, so we don't attract attention until everything is ready."

Tanya nodded, "Good. If I can find the right items fast enough, I have an idea on how to keep Steele from interfering any further. I'll contact you when we're done."

SKYE STEELE WAITED inside a housekeeping room. From here, with the door cracked open like this, she could see the passageway leading to the bridge. She had no idea how many guards would be inside–

A dark-haired woman in black garb - a submachine gun slung over her shoulder - exited the passageway to the bridge. She was issuing instructions into a walkie-talkie as she walked with a purpose in Skye's direction.

Skye instantly knew the woman had to be the Russian assassin Rory had talked about. The way she moved said she would be a difficult opponent in any type of fight.

Behind the woman walked a number of black-garbed men, also armed with submachine guns, and their demeanor was deadly and serious.

Skye wondered how many guards were left back inside the bridge area. If these men were any indication, anyone left behind to guard the bridge would be very well-trained and difficult to overcome. Storming the bridge to free the crew wouldn't be easy. Then again, if she heard gunfire on the bridge now, she knew she would be driving the ship all by herself. Skye hoped crashing a giant cruise liner into land wasn't going to be the last thing she did. She closed the door silently as the terrorists approached.

RORY AND JAYPEE REACHED the end of the short passageway.

Heavy boot steps. Lots of them! Someone was coming down the central staircase.

Jaypee froze on the spot.

Rory grabbed the Filipino roughly by the arm and pulled him over into one of the stores on the promenade.

Just in time.

Through the front window of the store, Rory caught sight of Tanya coming down the stairs. Behind her were a number of the terrorists carrying submachine guns. *Are they headed for the lifeboat right now?* That meant things were about to go down–

Tanya turned at the landing and continued to walk down the stairs to the next deck below. Her black-garbed entourage followed her.

That surprised Rory. *She's going below? Why?*

More boot steps sounded on the stairs. A few moments later, more black garbed terrorists with submachine guns hustled down the stairs. They didn't head for the lifeboats either. They took the stairs for the decks below.

Rory shook his head. *What are they doing? Did I guess wrong?*

More terrorists came down the stairs, heading for the decks below.

Are they going to do another sweep for me below decks? No, it's too late for that.

More boot steps…six more men garbed in black descended the opulent staircase. But these ones *didn't* continue on below decks. Instead, they crossed over to the short passageway, headed for the lifeboats outside.

"What we do now?" Jaypee whispered.

"I'm not sure right now," Rory admitted. *What was Tanya doing? And where was Valid? Do I have their plans all wrong?*

Chapter 62

SAL VALID STOOD PATIENTLY on the bridge, looking through a set of powerful binoculars. The cruise ship had passed Wisteria Island at full speed, carved an arc over top of Fleming Key and now had Dredgers Key off to the right. Several sailboats dotted the waters in the distance, making everything look like a normal day at the beach for the Americans. He spotted the Russian President's large yacht docked at Key West Naval Station dead ahead. And right beside it was another large, expensive yacht. Then he looked at the six speedboats in front of the yachts. They were the floating guard details for both Presidents. Valid pointed in their direction, "The targets are there. And we have a guard of six."

One of the terrorists, standing back at the navigation table, picked up his binoculars, equipped with an integrated GPS unit, and looked at where his boss was pointing. A moment later he said, "All right, I have the coordinates."

Valid's walkie-talkie came to life. He lowered his binoculars and took the walkie-talkie from his belt, "Go ahead."

"All set. And I made sure no one can get into the cargo holds," Tanya Beno said.

"Good. Head for the lifeboat and contact all the men to do the same. I'll finish with everything up here on the bridge," Valid said.

"Confirmed. Meet you there."

Valid turned to his men, "Take the Captain and his crew and out into the passageway and wait for me there. And take the jamming equipment as well."

The Captain and his crew were urged to move to the bridge exit by the terrorists waving their guns. Two of the terrorists shouldered their weapons and picked up the electronic jamming box between them and carried it to the passageway, following behind the other men escorting the crew members.

Valid raised his binoculars again and looked at the two yachts, savoring what was about to happen.

SKYE STEELE WATCHED as two terrorists, carrying submachine guns, marched three men in white uniforms out of the bridge and into the passageway. Two terrorists emerged behind the first group, carrying a large electronic box between them. Sky expected them to move down the passageway in her direction but they all stopped instead. The three men in white were made to stand against the wall and Skye was positive they were about to be executed. And she couldn't do anything about it. It looked like she was going to have to drive the ship all by herself, after all.

But nothing happened. Instead, the entire group just stood there.

LOWERING HIS BINOCULARS, Valid turned to see that everyone, except the man standing at the ship's navigation table, had left the bridge. "They're all gone, Anatoly," Valid said, "time to set up the control."

Anatoly set his binoculars down on the navigation table. Bending down, he grabbed a large backpack that was on the deck and unzipped it. Next, he removed a side panel from the navigation table, exposing the inner electronics. Turning his attention to the backpack again, Anatoly pulled out a small electronic device and carefully placed it next to the electronics inside the navigation table. Pulling a set of tools from his pocket, he began hooking it into the navigation control system of the cruise ship.

"How long?" Valid asked.

"About ten minutes, maybe less," Anatoly answered. He pulled several clip-on wires from a pocket.

Valid nodded and turned back to look through his binoculars, examining the defense perimeter of the two yachts.

SKYE COULDN'T FIGURE it out. Time dragged on. The terrorists just waited in the passageway, watching the three ship's officers. The two men carrying the box had set it on the deck and just stood there as well. *What are they waiting for? Orders to kill these crew members?* Skye carefully moved her hand to the selector mechanism on her submachine gun. *Semi or full automatic?*

"WE HAVE CONTROL," ANATOLY said finally as he replaced the side panel on the navigation table. No one coming onto the bridge would ever know the small electronic device was inside the ship's navigation controls.

Valid turned, "Good. Time to go then." He headed for the exit, dropping his binoculars on the navigation table as he passed.

Anatoly retrieved his submachine gun that was leaning against the navigation table and followed Valid.

SKYE MOVED HER HAND away from the selector mechanism when she saw two more terrorist step out of the bridge area.

The older one issued instructions and the terrorists began escorting the three men in white uniforms down the passageway again.

Skye closed the door softly to let them pass by. She assumed the man who had issued the instructions was Igor Arkady Koreshevko, Vinokurov's right-hand man. Since this man - and the woman who had to be the assassin - had left the bridge, Skye was positive that their final plans were being put into play. Her task now was to rescue those three ship's officers and get them back to the bridge.

The group in the passageway passed by and their footsteps kept moving down the passageway and away from Skye's position.

Skye cracked the door open.

She didn't see anyone back by the bridge. She took the chance and stuck her head out and peered around the door. She could see the backs of the terrorists as they moved down the passageway. Slipping out into the passageway, Skye began to follow them at a distance, gambling that no one would turn around to look behind them. If anyone *did*, she would probably be spotted. But she had no choice. She had to keep them in sight and hope they locked the crew up somewhere. She didn't relish the alternative if they shot the crew or threw them overboard.

Skye maintained her distance as she trailed the group of terrorists to a large stairway. She pressed her body against the wall as she watched them descend the stairs to the next deck, keeping her weapon in both hands and ready. When they disappeared below the top step, she counted slowly to ten. Then she took off at a sprint, only slowing her pace as she reached the top of the stairs. Peering over the railing, Skye didn't see anyone. Quickly slipping down several of the stairs, she finally caught a glimpse of the black-garbed terrorists at the landing on Deck 7. She waited as they continued their march down the stairs and then as quietly as possible, moved down after them. She was able to see them reach Deck 6. But instead of continuing down the stairs, they disappeared off to the left. Skye waited for a few seconds and then carefully descended the stairs, looking to see where the group had gone

When she reached the wide landing, Skye spotted the men in white, surrounded by the black-garbed guard terrorists, being herded along the deck to the left in an immense, fancy area. The sign on the wall designated it as The Boardwalk. Skye moved to the left and headed for the outside patio of a small restaurant. Squatting behind several chairs, she watched to see where the terrorists were taking the crew. But there was no sign of them. *Where did they go?*

Skye could see a number of stores lining both sides of the open space, but she couldn't see the group anywhere.

The light echo of voices reached her ears.

An ice cream booth up ahead jutted out and she couldn't see beyond it. Skye was torn between moving down to see what was happening and staying put to avoid being spotted. It wouldn't do her any good to get caught, but –

The sound of boot steps reached her ears. Someone was coming in this direction!

Skye hesitated for just a moment and then realized the terrorists was heading back this way towards the stairs. She ran for the stairs, staying on her toes to prevent any running noises on her part. Reaching the stairs she bounded upwards. Stopping at the next landing, Skye peered over the railing, watching and listening.

The group of black-garbed terrorists appeared below on the stairs….they headed downward.

Skye quickly moved down the stairs to the landing and peered over the railing. She could hear the echo of boot steps tramping down the stairs. Then they faded off into the distance. Skye licked her lips. She had no idea if the men in the white uniforms were still with the terrorists. *Should I follow them?* She turned and looked down the Boardwalk, lined with stores and shops on both sides. *Why did they take a detour down there?* She turned to look back down the stairs. *I can't afford to be wrong.*

Making a decision, Skye slung her weapon over her shoulder, turned and jogged along the deck towards the shops and stores. *Why did the terrorists stop somewhere down here? What were they doing?* She passed the outside patio of the small restaurant and skirted the ice cream booth. Beyond it was a candy store. Nothing stood out.

Next was a photography shop. The next shop sold stuffed toys for kids. Next was a music store.

Skye clenched her jaw. Each store had windows that allowed her to see inside…and there wasn't a sign of the bridge crew anywhere. Had she made a mistake not following when they went down the stairs?

She continued jogging, passing a toys and games store. Again – nothing. *Sorry, Rory. I guess I screwed up.*

Skye considered turning around and running hard for the stairs. *Maybe I can catch up with them.* She passed a movie theater. The next shop was a computer store - Skye stopped in her tracks. She blinked her eyes several times, thinking. Then she turned and jogged quickly back to the movie theater. The handles to the double doors were tied together with wire. And hanging from the wire was a shaped-charge of C-4 explosives.

Chapter 63

RORY AND JAYPEE WATCHED as large number of terrorists, marching down the staircase, met a large group of others coming up from the decks below. All of them headed directly to the passageway that led to the lifeboats outside.

Rory spotted Tanya Beno coming up the stairs with the group of men coming up from the lower decks. She went with the others down the passageway to the outer decks and the lifeboats.

"What we do now?" Jaypee whispered.

"We still have to wait," Rory whispered back. The problem was, he hadn't seen Sal Valid come down the stairs...or come from the decks below either. *Where is he? Did we miss him going by?* A few more terrorists came down the stairs and headed towards the outer decks. But still no sign of Valid. Rory couldn't make a move until he knew *all* the terrorists were leaving the ship. He couldn't afford to get caught, not now. Rory cursed inside. *Where is Valid?*

SKYE STEELE LICKED her lips as she slipped the weapon's sling off her shoulder. Were the men in the white uniforms from the bridge locked in behind this door? She looked to the left and the right. She didn't see anyone. She lifted her hand to pound against the door and then thought better of it. She looked down at the C-4 explosive. No way of telling if the vibrations would set it off. She looked to the left and the right again. Then Skye made a decision. Hopefully, no one was in earshot. "Hello," she called out, trying not to be too loud. "Anyone inside the theater?"

A moment later a muffled voice in a Norwegian accent came from the other side of the door, "Yes. Yes. This is Captain Tor Amundson. Who is this?"

"My name is Skye Steele. I came here to help my brother–"

"Mr. Steele? Is he with you?"

"No–"

"Where is he? We need his help to get out of here," Amundson said. "The terrorists put me in here with Karlsson and Breckenridge and said they had rigged this door to explode."

"Yes. There's a charge of C-4 explosives wired around the door handles," Skye told him.

The Captain swore a blue streak on the other side of the door. Two other voices joined in with a few colorful curses.

"Is there another way out of there? An exit?" Skye asked the Captain.

"There is, but they said they rigged that with explosives as well," Amundson answered. "We can't tell from in here, but...."

Skye understood. She doubted the terrorists were able to rig the other door. They weren't here that long. But it was also possible they had set it up beforehand. The problem was, there was no time to try and figure out where the exit was. And if she told them to use the exit and they blew up....

Skye looked to either side of the door. There were tall glass windows, revealing movie posters, on both sides. Peering into the glass she couldn't see any door...it looked like the posters were placed inside by opening the glass from this side. Stepping back, Skye looked closely at the overall structure of the theater. She couldn't see any other way inside. Which meant she only had one choice...try to disarm the C-4 explosives molded around the door handles.

SAL VALID MARCHED WITH his man down the stairs to Deck 6. He picked up his walkie-talkie and spoke into it, "I'm headed your way now."

"Good. Everyone else is aboard the lifeboat," Tanya Beno said.

Valid return the walkie-talkie to his belt as he reached the landing and marched with his men across the deck towards the short passageway to the lifeboat.

RORY FINALLY FELT SOME relief when he saw Valid. He watched him disappear down the passageway towards the lifeboat. Counting to ten, he rose to his feet and whispered to Jaypee, "Follow me."

Leading the way to the short passageway, Rory peered around the corner. Everyone had gone through the doors to the outer deck. There was no more time to waste. "Okay, time to head back down. We need to disable the explosives," he said urgently to Jaypee. Rory and Jaypee took off at a run and they hustled across the deck towards the central staircase and down the stairs. Next stop was the two cargo holds, containing the thousands of pounds of C-4 explosive.

SKYE STEELE KNELT IN front of the double doors to the theater, placed her weapon on the floor and began examining the C-4 explosive. There was no timer and that made sense. The way it *was* set up was simple...if someone from the inside tried to push their way out, it would simply trigger an explosion. There were two wires that she could see. They came from a small electrical trigger that would supply the juice to trigger the blasting cap. That would be embedded in the C-4 at the end of one of the wires. The problem was; two-thirds of the electrical trigger was buried underneath the shaped charge, so she couldn't access that to disarm it. And both wires were the same color, red. Bomb-makers usually color-coded the wires, so they knew which wire was the trigger as they built the device, but not *this* terrorist. Skye cursed under her breath. She had no way of knowing which one to pull out and defuse the bomb. If she pulled out the wrong wire, the one attached to the cap, she would be blown to bits. *Now what?*

SKYE STEELE WIPED HER hands on her thighs several times, preparing herself. World statistics said that only 10% of the world's population was left-handed. That meant there was a 90% probability that the person who had prepared this C-4 explosive package was right-handed. Which meant he would use his dominant hand to carefully insert the wire with the blasting cap into the C-4 material...and on the right side of the charge. Of course, if she was wrong, there was 100% chance she was dead.

"I want everyone inside the theater to get away from the door," said Skye in a loud voice.

After a few moments to give them time to get back, Skye held her breath.

Then she reached out, gripped the wire on the right side...and pulled.

Chapter 64

DECK 0 - THE CARGO Holds

RORY AND JAYPEE REACHED THE LOWEST DECK and ran hard for the storage cargo holds that contained the crates of C-4. Rory reached the first cargo hold door and pushed on the handle to get inside–

Jaypee bumped into him from behind and bounced back, staggering. He regained his balance and looked at Rory, "What wrong?"

Rory shook his head as he jiggled the handle several times. He stepped back and looked at the door, "I'm not sure–"

"It won't open?" Jaypee asked in concern.

Rory shook his head no, trying to figure out what the problem was.

Jaypee reached past Rory and tried the handle himself, "It locked?"

Rory didn't reply...he had spotted something...and realized what had happened. He ran his hand along the edges of the door, feeling the dread build inside himself. His fingers traced beads of metal that filled the tiny crack of space that *should* be there, between the door and the door frame...but it *wasn't* there. His blood ran cold, "They've welded the door shut!"

"What?" Jaypee jiggled the handle hard. Then he pushed in front of Rory and applied his full weight to the handle, trying desperately to get the door open somehow.

Rory knew it was useless. He took off at a run down the passageway.

Jaypee pushed down on the handle and banged his shoulder against the door...over and over he slammed his body against the door, desperate to get it open.

Reaching the next door for the cargo hold, Rory grabbed the handle and then realized...this door was welded shut as well. He cursed

Jaypee stepped back and tried to kick the door in. Over and over he slammed his foot against the door, to no avail.

Rory ran for the next door – welded shut. *All* entrances into the areas that held the C-4 plastic explosives were welded shut!

Jaypee returned to slamming his shoulder against the door, desperately trying to get inside the cargo.

Rory was at a loss. He chastised himself, *Think, Steele, think.*

"What we do?" Jaypee yelled.

Rory ran his hands slowly through his black hair, *Good question.*

"We all die," Jaypee yelled.

He was right.

DECK 6 - THE THEATER

Skye Steele carefully peeled the C-4 explosive package away from the door handles and placed it on the floor to her right. She reached for her weapon and then stood up, ready for anything.

Pushing down on the door handle, Skye swung the right door open and stepped inside.

The tops of several heads, eyes wide open, appeared slowly over a row of theater seats.

"Captain Amundson?" Skye called out.

A tall, regal man with a full, white sailor's beard stood up, "That would be me."

Karlsson and Breckenridge stood up slowly on either side of their Captain, eyes wide as they considered the beautiful, Amazon-like woman standing in the doorway, weapon held at the ready across her shapely body.

"We need to get to the bridge. Now!" Skye said. "The terrorists plan to run this ship into two yachts—"

The Captain headed for the end of the row of seats with considerable urgency, "Where is Mr. Steele?"

"He's off somewhere trying to stop the terrorists from blowing up your ship," Skye told him.

Amundson stopped dead in his tracks, his eyes wide in fear, "We have to abandon ship. We have to get the passengers off—"

Karlsson and Breckenridge plowed into the back of the Captain, nearly knocking him over.

"We won't have time," Skye said firmly. "Rory wants us to steer the ship away from those two yachts. He's working to disable the explosives and we have to trust him to do his part. Let's go."

Captain Amundson hesitated for a moment, "But—"

"Now!" Skye commanded.

Amundson reacted with a start. Then he ran for the door. "Let's go, gentlemen," he urged the others.

Skye took off running, back through the theater entrance, and heading for the central staircase.

"The elevator will be faster," Amundson yelled as he emerged from the theater behind her.

Skye stopped and looked back, "The elevators aren't running. The terrorists disabled them to better control the situation by limiting movement to the stairways."

"In that case, why don't we use the crew stairway at the bow of the ship," Karlsson said. He was pointing in the opposite direction away from Skye.

"He's right. It will be faster," Amundson agreed. "And it's less likely we would run into any terrorists."

"All right," said Skye as she ran back to the men, "but let's hurry."

DECK 0 - THE CARGO Holds

Rory calmed himself, trying to think. *Either the terrorists brought welding equipment aboard or they used something they found, probably in the engine room. Would they put it back in there? Or would they throw it overboard? No, I doubt they would take the time to carry it all the way to the stern or up the stairway. So if they didn't take it to the engine room or up the stairs–* Rory yelled down the passageway to the Filipino, "Jaypee. Check in the rooms around here for welding equipment."

"What?"

"Welding equipment," he yelled again as he headed for the storage cooler door where Jaypee had hidden earlier. "You know, welding tanks, goggles...."

Jaypee turned and looked around him. He headed quickly for the first door down the passageway.

Rory opened the cooler door and moved inside fast, looking for anything that looked like welding equipment. He looked inside boxes as well as behind them. He looked in every nook, cranny, and corner - nothing. He ran for the doorway. *Time is running out.* Out in the passageway, he headed for the next door. He pulled it open and ran inside another storage unit...and skidded to a stop.

He thought he heard yelling. He listened. *That sounds like Jaypee.* He ran back through the doorway.

Jaypee emerged from a doorway and ran down the passageway, yelling and gesturing.

Rory started running towards the man, "What is it?"

The Filipino skidded to a stop, halfway to Rory and motioned with his hand, "Come. I find...something...." He turned and ran back down the passageway, disappearing through an open doorway on the right.

Rory ran hard down the passageway. *Please, please be what we need. We're running out of time.*

"This it? This it?" Jaypee yelled anxiously as Rory burst into the room. He pointed down at some items piled one on top of another in a corner.

Rory wasn't sure. He skidded to a stop next to the pile and knelt down. There were welding gloves, a welding helmet, some electrical cord and other items he recognized. But he didn't see a portable generator/welder unit. He picked up a small cylinder. A label on the side read: Porta-Welder, Made in Philippines. Rory shook his head in frustration and looked around. Then he looked back at the cylinder. Porta-Welder? This *had* to be what the terrorists had used. But it wasn't like any piece of equipment he was familiar with from his days in the Canadian Army. It was more like a toy.

Jaypee was talking anxiously beside him, words tumbling out in a torrent of questions.

Rory tuned him out. He had to. Doing his best to concentrate in the midst of looming death, he knelt down and picked through each item, slowly figuring out how to attach the electrical cord to the cylinder and where the welding rod went. He wasn't sure how the ground wire would work, but time was running out. He would either electrocuted himself or die in an explosion of C-4. He told Jaypee to grab the welding mask and gloves and he carried everything out into the passageway and set it down in front of the first welded door to a storage hold.

Jaypee followed Rory's instructions, finding an electrical outlet back inside the doorway down the passageway.

The electrical cord was just long enough. That meant this *had* to be the way they welded the doors shut. *But they knew how to use this stuff.*

Rory had Jaypee attach the ground wire to the handle on the door down the passageway as well. It would either work or he was dead. But it was the only way the terrorists could've done it as well. *At least that's the theory.*

Rory put on the gloves and the welding mask - held his breath - and flipped the switch to start up the portable welder.

Chapter 65

THE LIFEBOAT

FOUR OF THE GUNMEN on the outer deck swung the lifeboat out from the ship, set the winches on each end in motion, and then clambered up the stairway and into the lifeboat as it began swiftly lowering to the sea below.

Valid and Tanya Beno settled into the wheelhouse, along with the terrorist who would act as the pilot. When the lifeboat was thirty feet above the sea and still dropping, the pilot started the engines. He cranked the wheel hard away from the ship and then waved his arm to signal the men at the front winch. Working in coordination with the men at the rear winch, at ten feet above the sea they simultaneously released the cables and held on. The lifeboat landed in the sea with a jolt. The pilot applied full power and the twin 70 HP diesel engines growled. The catamaran-hulled lifeboat moved deftly away from the cruise ship and they were moving at 6 knots within moments.

The massive Caribbean StarLiner continued sailing on its set heading, north of Fleming Key.

Valid pointed to the northeast, "Head for that island and take us around the back to shield us."

The lifeboat pilot acknowledged the command and set the proper heading for Cayo Agua Island.

Valid pulled a handheld, remote radio-control used for model ships from a backpack and then walked calmly to the back of the lifeboat. Setting his legs apart, he braced himself against the roll of the sea, lifted the remote control and pressed the 'on' button. Green lights lit up on the control. Pressing a red button, the Russian took full control of the massive Caribbean StarLiner cruise ship and its diesel-electric propulsion system. Grasping a small joystick on the remote radio-control, Valid tilted it slightly.

The Caribbean StarLiner carved a turn to starboard in the blue-green water and took a heading to the southeast.

Valid tilted the joystick back a quarter inch.

The Caribbean StarLiner responded by adjusting its heading to port side....and within moments it was driving directly for Key West Naval Station and the yachts holding the President of the United States and the President of Russia.

Valid next twisted a dial on the remote radio-control to its maximum setting.

Deep in the engine room of the Caribbean StarLiner, the diesel-electric propulsion system roared and began pushing the massive cruise ship to top speed.

THE BRIDGE

Skye Steele led the way inside the bridge, weapon at her shoulder and ready, in case someone had stayed behind for a suicide mission. The bridge was empty and she called out, "It's clear."

Captain Tor Amundson, Karlsson and Breckenridge darted inside behind Skye. Captain Amundson immediately barked out instructions and all three crewmen set to work to gain control of the massive cruise ship.

Skye lowered her weapon and stepped to the front window of the bridge. "I see two large yachts dead ahead. We're almost on top of them!"

Captain Amundson stepped across the deck to see for himself and gasped. His voice rose in pitch, "Mr. Karlsson? Do you have control of the ship yet? We're almost out of time–"

"No sir," Karlsson yelled. "It's...it's being controlled from the outside–"

"Nonsense," the Captain yelled, "they can't–"

"He's right," Breckenridge yelled. "And we can't override it, Captain."

Captain Amundson ran back across the deck to help.

Karlsson banged at buttons and twisted knobs, trying to regain control, "We're at full speed now!"

Skye watched it all unfold in front of her. There wasn't a single thing she could do. It was all up to these men. And Rory.

In front of the two yachts, the half a dozen speedboats, acting as the guard, immediately went into action. They smoothly converged into an attack group, heading directly towards the cruise ship.

"The guards of both presidents are headed our way," Skye said.

Captain Amundson turned on his heels, eyes wide in alarm. "What do you mean both presidents?"

"The President of the United States and the President of Russia are supposed to be on those two yachts...and we're the bomb," Skye told him without looking back.

Amundson swore a blue streak.

"You sound just like a sailor," Skye said as she watched the men on the speedboats shoulder automatic weapons. "And those men will be shooting at us in a few moments."

"We can't get a message out either," Karlsson yelled. He banged his fist in frustration against a panel.

Amundson looked around the bridge quickly, "They had some type of jamming equipment in here–"

Skye turned, "Was it a large electronic box?"

"Yes. Do you see it?"

"I saw them carrying it out of here when they marched you down the passageway," Skye told him.

Amundson cursed a blue streak again.

Automatic weapons fire erupted from each speedboat as they approached the massive cruise ship at full throttle.

Bullets bounced off the thick glass window of the bridge.

Skye dove for the deck.

More automatic weapons fire - bullets penetrated the thick window glass this time and ricocheted across the bridge.

Amundson, Karlsson, and Breckenridge all dove for cover.

Captain Amundson swore another blue streak as he and his men scrambled to their knees and tried to work from behind cover to get control of the massive cruise ship.

Skye got to her feet against the right wall and peered around through the shattered glass.

Four of the speedboats misjudged the speed of the cruise ship and were too close.

The massive Caribbean StarLiner plowed right through them without the least shudder.

The speedboats exploded in orange fireballs and fiberglass splinters, sending bodies in all directions.

The other two speedboats managed to veer away.

DECK 0 - THE CARGO Holds

Rory threw off the welding mask as he cut through the last bit of welding holding the door in place. He stepped back and kicked the door in as he shrugged off the welding gloves. He moved inside the cargo hold quickly and headed for the nearest stack of wooden crates. Detonating cord snaked in and out of every single crate and down through every single stack of crates. The door at the far end was open and the detonator cord snaked through the doorway to the other crates as well. Everything was set for one massive explosion.

Jaypee moved in behind Rory, willing to do anything Rory needed from him.

Moving to the first set of stacked, wooden crates, Rory looked frantically inside the square hole, in the side of each crate.

"What we look for?" Jaypee asked as he stepped up beside Rory.

"A detonator. Just like the one I built in my suite," Rory explained as he looked through another hole in a crate.

"I look too," Jaypee said as he moved to the next stack of crates.

"Don't move any of the wires," Rory yelled to Jaypee as he stepped to the side of the stack. He cringed as he watched the Filipino step through the wires snaking between the stacks of crates.

The two men looked frantically for the detonator...it could go off at any moment.

THE LIFEBOAT

Onboard the lifeboat, Salman Valid calmly watched as the massive cruise ship, loaded with the crates of plastic explosives, reached full speed, heading directly for the two yachts. He passed the remote radio-control over to Tanya Beno, "Time to complete our mission."

Tanya Beno simply nodded, a look of superiority on he face.The victory and celebrations were about to take place.

Valid calmly walked back to the backpack and pulled out another remote control. This one controlled the electronic detonator onboard the Caribbean StarLiner. Walking back to stand beside Tanya, Valid looked across at the Caribbean StarLiner again, gauging the speed and distance. He waited a few more moments to make sure the two yachts would definitely be evaporated inside the blast zone. Then he smiled and tripped a switch on the remote control.

The shaped charge Rory had left under the seat in the lifeboat contained an *identical* homemade electronic detonator as the one left onboard the Caribbean StarLiner by the terrorists.

Valid's smile - and Beno's look of superiority - were frozen into eternity as the charge detonated straight down and into the fuel tanks. A second later, the yellow lifeboat exploded in a massive fireball, incinerating everyone onboard.

DECK 0 - THE CARGO Holds

Inside the cargo hold on the Caribbean StarLiner, filled with thousands of pounds of C-4 explosive, Rory sat on the deck. His hand was shaking as he held the electronic detonator the terrorists had embedded in the C-4 in the bottom crate. Rory had pulled it free just before a tremendous explosion could be heard in the distance.

Jaypee knelt shakily in front of Rory, whispering, "It not go off. We are safe?"

"Yeah. We should be okay now. But we better make sure," Rory gently turned the detonator to see how the lid was held on. There were a couple of bent over metal tabs holding it secure. Rory pried each one up with his fingers. Slowly taking the lid off, he looked inside the metal box. Three AAA batteries sat in the cradle at the bottom. Pulling the batteries out one by one, he handed them to Jaypee. With the third, he finally released his breath.

Jaypee held the batteries in his hand and looked at them in relief - the Caribbean StarLiner swung violently to the left and the batteries fell from his hand to the deck and rolled away.

THE BRIDGE

Captain Amundson and his crew cranked the controls hard back and forth in an attempt to gain control of the cruise ship and steer away from the two Presidential yachts dead ahead.

Karlsson banged with his fist on the controls, yelling and swearing at the top of his voice.

Control suddenly returned to the bridge just as Amundson pushed the thrusters to the extreme left.

The massive Caribbean StarLiner carved a sharp turn in the sea, throwing everyone hard to the floor.

Skye Steele was thrown backward and began sliding across the bridge on her back, helpless to stop herself.

Karlsson's arms windmilled frantically to maintain his balance - his frantic backward steps were stopped violently by the collision with the side wall of the bridge - he slumped to the deck, knocked unconscious.

Breckenridge felt his feet go out from under him as the deck tilted – his forehead struck the back of a chair and he fell to the deck unconscious - his body slid like a rag doll to the side wall of the bridge.

An enormous wall of water was thrust from the side of the massive cruise ship, smashing against the two Presidential yachts and pushing them violently to the side. They were torn away from their anchors and pushed up and over the pier not far behind them. Inside, the two presidents and their entourage were thrown around like rag dolls as the yachts slid over the concrete pier and stopped just short of a large block building.

Skye Steele caught the pedestal of a bridge chair and stopped her slide across the deck.

Captain Amundson was sliding past her when Skye reached out to grab his arm.

Amundson grunted as his arm extended but his momentum stopped.

Skye strained to hold the man in place as he scrambled to get his feet under him on the tilted deck.

Finally rising, Amundson struggled to the controls and began to work to get the cruise ship back under his command.

Skye pulled herself around and struggled to her feet as well. She moved up behind the Captain to help him stay in place at the controls.

More gunfire erupted from the remaining two speedboats.

"Stop shooting at us!" the Captain yelled in frustration.

The Caribbean StarLiner slowly straightened out – but was still running at full speed.

"Captain!" Skye yelled as she pointed dead ahead of the cruise ship.

Directly ahead was Dredgers Key island.

Captain Amundson threw the ship in reverse and yelled, "Brace for impact."

The Caribbean StarLiner plowed into the low spit of land. The 230,000-ton weight knocked over a small stand of trees and gouged its way inland, carving a groove through the sand before coming to a stop beside Maine road.

People sitting outside their trailers on the other side of the street sat there dumbfounded, beers in hand, gazing up at the immense cruise ship that now stood across the street like a brand-new condominium high rise added to the neighborhood.

Chapter 66

RORY MACK STEELE AND SKYE stood at the railing on Deck 3, watching as the passengers began exiting the jerry-rigged gangplank extending from the side of the massive cruise ship.

"Why can't you just take a normal vacation like other people?" Skye asked him.

"Hey! You're the one who set me up on this thing," Rory complained.

"Oh, so it's my fault, is it?"

"No, I'm not saying that. But–"

"There you are!"

Rory turned his head.

Jaimee Morrissette threw her arms around his neck and then gave him a great big kiss on the lips.

Skye raised an eyebrow as she looked at the blonde with the beautiful, deep blue eyes who was kissing her brother with a great deal of passion.

Jaimee broke off the kiss, "The Captain explained everything about my brother and how you solved everything. I just wanted to thank you."

"Well, you've done that," Rory said with a smile.

Jaimee slipped something into the right pocket of his jeans, "No, I mean thank you properly. Call me when you get a chance." With that said, she turned and was gone.

Rory turned back to lean on the rail and realized his sister was staring at him. "What?"

"I'm not saying anything," Skye said. A smirk caressed her lips as she leaned with her hands against the railing.

Below them, on the sand of Dredgers Key island, an entourage of paparazzi and news reporters began to jostle each other for position as a frenzy of picture taking began.

Loretta Black set foot off the gangplank. The platinum-blonde beauty played the photo opportunity to the hilt, like an addicted celebrity, posing and drinking up the attention.

Skye cocked her head, "Isn't that...?"

"Yeah."

"Wow. Imagine a real television star like that being on board," Skye whispered.

"If you like that sort of thing," Rory mumbled.

After a few minutes of posing, Loretta Black turned and looked up directly at Rory. She grinned and waved at him - puckered up theatrically and blew him a kiss.

Rory returned a small, half-hearted wave.

Black gave him a flirty shrug of her shoulders, turned and headed for her stretch limo, drinking in the attention of the paparazzi and news reporters.

Skye stood up, crossed her arms and looked at her brother, "Really? A blonde television star as well? And here I was feeling sorry for you because your vacation was ruined."

"I wouldn't be surprised if you set the whole vacation-on-a ship-thing up so you could use that stupid flying suit of yours."

Skye rubbed her hands together gleefully, "Now that I think about it, it did work out perfectly didn't it? You know what? I'm going to set you up on a vacation to exotic Tibet."

"Tibet?"

"Yeah, you have a tendency to get in trouble. And I always wanted to fly from the top of Mount Everest."